Better Angel

TWO LOVES HAVE I OF COMFORT AND DESPAIR,
WHICH LIKE TWO SPIRITS DO SUGGEST ME STILL;
MY BETTER ANGEL IS A MAN RIGHT FAIR—

Better Angel

by

Forman Brown

Writing as Richard Meeker

alyson books
los angeles | new york

MANUFACTURED IN THE UNITED STATES OF AMERICA.

THIS TRADE PAPERBACK IS PUBLISHED BY ALYSON PUBLICATIONS,
P.O. BOX 4371, LOS ANGELES, CALIFORNIA 90078-4371.
DISTRIBUTION IN THE UNITED KINGDOM BY
TURNAROUND PUBLISHER SERVICES LTD.
UNIT 3 OLYMPIA TRADING ESTATE, COBURG ROAD, WOOD GREEN,
LONDON N22 6TZ ENGLAND.

FIRST PUBLISHED IN 1933 BY GREENBERG: PUBLISHER INC.
FIRST ALYSON EDITION, WITH INTRODUCTION BY HUBERT KENNEDY: JULY 1987
SECOND ALYSON EDITION, WITH EPILOGUE BY FORMAN BROWN: MARCH 1990
THIRD ALYSON EDITION, WITH PHOTOGRAPHS, REVISED INTRODUCTION, AND
          NEW EPILOGUE: JUNE 1995
FOURTH ALYSON EDITION: JULY 2000

00 01 02 03 04 a 10 9 8 7 6 5 4 3 2 1

ISBN 1-55583-573-2
(PREVIOUSLY PUBLISHED WITH ISBN 1-55583-116-8)

LIBRARY OF CONGRESS CATALOGING-IN-PUBLICATION DATA
  MEEKER, RICHARD.
    BETTER ANGEL / BY FORMAN BROWN WRITING AS RICHARD MEEKER—
4TH ALYSON ED.
    ISBN 1-55583-573-2
    1. GAY MEN—NEW YORK (STATE)—NEW YORK—FICTION. 2. GAY
YOUTH—MICHIGAN—FICTION. 3. NEW YORK (N.Y.)—FICTION.
4. MICHIGAN—FICTION. I. TITLE.
PS3503.R812 B48 2000
813'.52—DC21   99-088591

CREDITS
COVER PHOTOGRAPH COURTESY OF FORMAN BROWN.
COVER DESIGN BY B. ZINDA.

INTRODUCTION

When Sasha Alyson asked me in 1986 to recommend older gay novels that deserved new editions, I immediately lent him my copy of *Better Angel*. After reading it, he agreed with my recommendation and kindly asked me to write an introduction for it. Little did I suspect that seven years later the very copy I lent Sasha would be autographed "Forman Brown aka Richard Meeker" and I would meet its gracious, charming, and witty author. For, to everyone's delight, after the publication of the novel by Alyson, Forman Brown identified himself as the author, writing under the name Richard Meeker. The success of that new edition has prompted Alyson to publish the present edition, identifying Forman Brown more closely with the novel — and giving me a welcome opportunity to update my earlier introduction.

Better Angel is probably the first novel published in America to show male homosexuality in a positive light — it even provides its gay hero with an apparently happy ending. In this it also contrasts with many later novels, but it must have especially surprised early readers, who just a couple of years before its appearance in 1933 had only the tortured experiences of *Twilight Men* and the tortuous search for explanations of this "sickness" in *Strange Brother* — novels whose titles tell all. Here, instead, is "love's coming of age" in a story that no doubt shocked some and delighted others, and perhaps did both at the same time.

The 1933 edition is a rarity today, as is the paperback reprint that appeared in the 1950s with the title *Torment*. This later edition was reviewed in 1957 in the early gay journal *Mattachine Review* by Richard Meyer, who noted that its hero, Kurt Gray, was "perhaps the healthiest homosexual in print." James Levin, in his more recent sociological study of gay literature, *The Gay Novel: The*

Male Homosexual Image in America (1983), comments: "Perhaps it is this very wholesomeness which caused it to be seen as less than realistic in a period when few gays thought well of themselves." And indeed, after noting the novel's happy ending, Meyer had added in 1957 that "I wouldn't bet that they lived happily ever after." His review concludes: "Perhaps Richard Meeker, who wrote this pioneer and still highly readable novel 24 years ago, could tell us what became of Kurt — and of himself. For the promise of this obviously youthful work ought to be fulfilled in a sequel." But there was no sequel, for the author was busy with other projects and — Meyer would have lost his bet — was busily living "happily ever after."

Much in the novel is obviously autobiographical. The picture of childhood in small-town Barton, Michigan, in the early decades of this century is especially convincing. Roger Austen, in his *Playing the Game: The Homosexual Novel in America* (1977), even found "a touch of Dreiser realism in the town revival service where they sing 'Just As I Am' and where Kurt goes forward to be 'saved.'" Readers who have shared this agonizing experience will find this episode utterly authentic — and poignant. Equally authentic for the period is Kurt's very real fear of the physical dangers of masturbation. Also in Michigan, it may be noted, is the town of Battle Creek, from which the baleful influence of Dr. Kellogg ("The physician rarely meets more forlorn objects than the victims of prolonged self-abuse") lasted well into the twentieth century.

By the time Kurt leaves Barton for Ann Arbor to enroll in the University of Michigan, he has overcome these fears. By the time he graduates, his religious scruples, too, have faded as his faith turns to the power of love to justify his sexual activity — no longer a solitary vice. Kurt in the meantime has read much on homosexuality, including Edward Carpenter's *Love's Coming of Age,* with its high-minded, Whitmanesque ideal of same-sex love. In literature, he rejects the "decadence" of Oscar Wilde, while giving Frank Wedekind special mention. (Brown probably had in mind here not the question of Lulu's "father": "Do you still practice French?" but rather the happy homosexual scene, with its pledges of love, in *Spring's Awakening.)*

Kurt's musical studies at the university lead in an untroubled fashion to a successful career as teacher and composer. James Levin complains, gently, that "Emphasis on artistic, sensitive, gay male personalities perpetuates an invalid stereotype." But not all the relatively small cast of characters in this story fit the type, and in Kurt's case Brown's obvious knowledge of contemporary trends in musical composition allows an added touch of realism.

Since the major part of the novel is set around 1930 (two characters are seen at a silent movie, while a year later another plans to make a "talkie"), it is certainly realistic that no call is made to "come out" publicly. Yet Brown allows his indignation at the treatment of gay people to show in Kurt's outburst over Frank Harris's autobiography:

What I objected to all through the book was Harris's opacity, his inability to see how little difference there really is between his sort of dallying — and ours...

The only difference — the only damned difference is that for us there's no way of getting social sanction — so we go around the world like a lot of sorry ghosts, being forever ashamed of a thing we've no reason to be ashamed of.

Brown's outrage also shows in the brief episode describing police entrapment. For the most part, however, the conflicts in the novel are the interior ones of coming to terms with one's own sexuality, personality, and temperament — of reconciling our animal and spiritual nature, sex and love, for in his own way Kurt comes close to Plato's idea of love as "the desire and pursuit of the whole."

That love is the theme of this charming novel is indicated already in the three-line epigraph (the beginning of Shakespeare's "Sonnet 144"), from which the novel's title is taken. But Brown apparently felt that his was a pioneering treatment of this perennial theme, and he must have felt the need for it. He has one of his characters planning to write a book "about us," one that is "to be a sort of vindication of our kind of loving," adding: "Nobody's ever done it, really." And his hero, Kurt Gray, reflects earlier in the novel: "Someone will be brave enough to write such a thing someday, to be believed, and to escape unscathed. Not now." Fortunately for us, Forman Brown was brave enough to write it. Happily, he also escaped unscathed and has enjoyed the satisfaction of knowing that he helped many others growing up gay to accept their kind of love as genuine and good.

HUBERT KENNEDY

PART ONE

For it is impossible to conceive any impulse in a human heart which cannot be transformed into Truth or into Beauty or into Love.
—Havelock Ellis, "Impressions and Comments"

I

K URT GRAY was thirteen years old, but as he sat in the broad chair pulled close to the square front window, he seemed still a little boy. Partly it was the light; partly it was the way in which one thin leg was tucked under him, and his chin dug into his fist. Folded together over his book he seemed smaller than he was. It was early March. Patches of graying snow thatched the earth outside; and a gray sky, tarnished with gold from a sun gone down behind the grove of oaks opposite, gave to the light a pale, cold, honey-colored translucence that was thin and clear and yet liquid and winey. The room was in deep shadow, and the boy, his head bent almost to the pages of the book, strained his eyes over it with such a silent intentness that he seemed grown to the heavy chair and to the dim and aqueous atmosphere of the room. The faint sounds of rattling dishes and his mother's step in the kitchen could not break through into his consciousness.

"Now Herakles," he read, "though his warriors were ready and urging him to be off on the long-awaited quest for the fleece, refused to set sail until Hylas was found. For Hylas, famed among all the youths of the country for his beauty, was the hero's favorite. In spite of the impatient grumblings of the princes and of the warriors, Herakles sought his young friend. Through field and woodland he went, calling aloud 'Hylas! Hylas!' but Hylas was nowhere to be found."

"Kurt!" It was his mother. He started as she entered the room behind him, thrusting the book between his thigh and the oaken arm of the chair in a vain attempt at concealment.

"Reading again! And in this light! Don't you know you'll ruin your eyes? If you must read, do put on the light!"

"I was just—" he began, justifying himself. "I was just—"

11

"Oh, it's all right. Run now and get me a pail of water, like a good boy. Your dad will be home for supper before we know it. Hike!" She gave him a good-natured shove as he shuffled through the door, rubbing his eyes.

Kurt Gray had reached the age of thirteen in a state of unusual seriousness, unusual loneliness, and unusual innocence. He had no brothers or sisters, and his parents were already in middle age. They worshiped him, yet he escaped, somehow, being the proverbial spoiled child. A certain pliability which made him popular with the older people he was thrown with — a pliability which was partially a lack of self-assertiveness and partially a shrinking from disagreement — was in reality his greatest fault. This pliability came from his father, a mild, good-humored man who had set out to be a lawyer; and who, because of this same gentleness which prevented his pushing and elbowing his way through the rough-and-tumble competition of the nineties, had ended by becoming a furniture dealer in Barton, Michigan — a town only a few miles from the farm on which he was born. Kurt liked his father, and Elmer Gray had for his son the sort of devotion that borders on the religious, since it contains an admixture of fear. Not that he was afraid of Kurt — it was not that. But there was, even when the boy was very young, an unaccountable feeling on the part of the father that in this small body and brain there was a latent superiority, a tenuous spirituality of some sort which he could never have analyzed, or understood, but which, when the two were alone together, as they were so infrequently, made the man slightly reticent; slightly and inexplicably fearful that he would not please the boy, that his son would be ashamed of him. It was a feeling Kurt certainly did not share, consciously at least, but it created between them a wall not to be penetrated.

From his mother Kurt got, in multiplied measure, the love of beauty and the sensitiveness that set him apart from his companions — so apart that sometimes he wished himself violently otherwise. Mrs. Gray loved her son better than anything else in life. She had been married ten years when he was born. He came at a time when life in the little town was beginning to set her on edge. She had never fitted in very well. There was something of the aristocrat in her that made the women of the town regard her enviously as a snob, or deferentially as a truly superior being. She had come to Barton with her husband after two years of married life. She had been something of a beauty — slender, with blue eyes, pale brown hair, soft and fine, and a clear cool skin. She had never had much of an education, but her mind was alert and objective — the sort of mind that was quick to see the shallowness and dullness of the life about her, and, although it had never known anything much brighter or deeper, to be contemptuous of it. She had hid her dreams. As a girl her passion for color and the feel of things, coupled with a modest talent, had led her to drawing. She had sketched, she had done a few promising watercolors, she had longed vaguely to improve herself, and not known how. The people in the town where she lived thought her talented, and flighty; flighty particularly when she had proposed going off, alone, to Boston to study art. Her father was not rich — a harness maker with his own shop and three other daughters to support. So she had not gone. She had put away her dreams with her brushes.

She had married Elmer Gray because she loved him. She had seen that he was good and kind. She was now seeing that he was ineffectual, and she was beginning to envision herself doomed to the drab life that her neighbors lived; she saw life stretching ahead of her like a gray and barren prairie, with a rebelliousness that, kept so rigorously in check, made her unhappy and discontent. Her unquestioned leadership in the meager social life of Barton appeared to her a petty and unsatisfactory compromise.

Then Kurt had come, and she knew that in him, if ever, her dreams must flower and bear fruit. So she had been glad that he was nice-looking. She had been glad that his eyes were brown, like Elmer's, that his hair was soft like her own, that his skin was smooth and white, that he was straight and without blemish. She had nursed him jealously through illnesses when her lips constricted with fright for the fragility of his little life. She had seen to it that he was well mannered and clean, that he knew his letters and his Bible stories, that he went to school as soon as he was old enough. And how proud she had been when he did the work of two grades in one year, and when he brought home his monthly report cards with the high grades that seemed to give him so little trouble.

She was not unequivocally pleased with him, however. As he grew older, as he started going to school, she noticed in him more and more the pliability that she felt was her husband's greatest stumbling block. It frightened her. Was her dream, that promised so richly, to be frustrated by this softness that Kurt displayed? It frightened her because she did not know how to combat it. She had never known how, in Elmer's case. To him she had talked until she realized it did no good, urging him to be less lenient, to be more belligerent in his business dealings, to stand up for his rights. She had wheedled, she had scolded, she had even at times dared to be flamingly contemptuous — and had invariably regretted it when she saw how it hurt him.

So, when Kurt would come home, as he too often did, white-faced and trembling, to stand silently by the big front window looking off to the river and the ragged line of oaks over which the stacks of the paper mills rose — when she would put her arms around his narrow shoulders — when she would kiss his cheek and he would shake her off, ashamed that she should see his racking bitterness — when, at last, hesitantly, perhaps in a flood of tears, he would admit that the boys at school had teased him about his fair skin: "Where'd ya buy yer paint, sissy? Sissy! Sissy!" — when, with body shaking and hands clenched, eyes strangely dark in his white face, he would sob, "Why — Mom — why, why, why? Why can't they leave me alone?" — when she would see him starting nervously to school a full half hour early to avoid the boys congregating around the door — she was worried and frightened. She and Elmer talked it over together. They tried in every way they knew to interest him in things other boys of his age liked. They bought him a cowboy suit, a football, baseball mitts, boxing gloves. He was always grateful, but never enthusiastic. He would start bravely out with his new possession, becoming, for a splendid moment, the hero of the neighborhood boys because his football or his catcher's mitt would be the best that Elmer Gray could buy. He would play for a while, a little clumsily, always, it seemed to his mother, a little afraid that some awkwardness of his would bring down upon him the terrible barbaric scorn of his playmates. And soon he would be out of the game, his ball flying goldenly up and down the playground, and he, more than likely, headed for the big chair in the front window with a storybook. It always ended so. The closet of his bedroom became a storehouse of little-used sporting things which would lie there until his parents sadly agreed that "Kurt doesn't seem to care much for it," and the ball or the gloves or the racket would be given away.

Kurt's father never attempted to talk to the boy about it. He gave ballbats and skates unquestioningly, eagerly even, as gifts which at Kurt's age would have delighted him beyond measure, and he was puzzled and hurt when they had to be given to other boys. Why should his son be different? Why, he was like a girl. But his contempt, if it ever deserved so strong a name, never found expression. When his wife would appeal to him to talk to Kurt he would always put her off. "Oh, I can't talk to him, Abbie. You can do it better. He's more like you, somehow." And Abbie Gray knew that he was right. But she knew too that he was like Elmer in the very particular that most endangered the fulfillment of her dream. In the boy it was taking different form, that was all.

So she had talked.

"Why didn't you stand up to him?" she asked one winter day when he had come home pale and silent, trying vainly to hide the fact that he had been running.

Kurt was silent for a time, ashamed, but at last came the familiar details.

"Why didn't you stand up to him?" she asked. "You're nearly as big as he is. He's just a bully and a coward. If you'd show him, just once, that you weren't afraid of him, he'd leave you alone." And to herself she thought, "What little animals boys can be!"

"I — I — you mean I ought to've fought him?" Kurt's tone was incredulous.

"Yes, Kurt, even that, if you have to, to stand up for your rights!"

And he had walked away, pressed his nose against the pane of the window, and stood until the steam of his breath against the cold pallor of the winter afternoon made a halo around his brown head. And she sighed, knowing she had not succeeded.

She tried that particular method of procedure times innumerable, realizing painfully on each occasion its inadequacy, its utter uselessness. Her urging had no effect. Then, gradually, almost without her realizing it, a new note was heard in these little conferences, a note that was to become more and more insistent until it dominated her son in a way which was quite beyond her comprehension and which, could she have foreseen it, she would have feared as much and shunned as fiercely as the existing softness she sought to destroy. It was the anarchic note of pride in difference. Perhaps she felt in her quickly sympathetic way that, it being impossible to change him, to make him more like his fellows (a thing she desired only for his own happiness, only to the extent that life might be for him less painful), she might at least instill in him a sense of superiority to his persecutors. Most of all she wanted to comfort him, for she knew that he suffered, suffered bravely; for his silence in her presence at these crucial times was the silence of shame that she, his mother, should see his weakness. How many times his concealment was successful she could not know.

"Why do you mind so, Kurt?" she asked him one day. "Those boys are—" and she shrugged her slim shoulders in a way Kurt adored. "What do they amount to, anyway? You can do lots of things they can't; you're smarter, you're" — how should she say it? — "you're — different. Be different. Be a leader! If they see that you don't care, they'll quit bothering you. Laugh at 'em! I'd fix 'em!" And with dancing eyes she strutted across the room like a triumphant bantam. He had to laugh then. "Oh, Mom!" was all he said, but she thought she saw in his eyes a look she had not seen before, and the look gave her courage. She hoped she had found the means of combating what she feared.

There was no instantaneous change, she soon found. Kurt still continued to spend miserable minutes with his schoolmates and miserable hours of mental anguish when he was alone — the stark and secret suffering of children, stark because the fund of experience and knowledge to combat it, to buoy them up, and finally to console them is so scant; and secret because shame has poisoned them too soon. The unintentional cruelty of adult laughter, with which parents so often intensify the child's suffering, Kurt did not have to endure. Though he still suffered passionately, this new idea, the idea of pride in difference, seemed to offer him some consolation, however slight, and his mother played upon it at every opportunity.

There was in his life one other overpowering fear — the fear of the dark. It was quite as terrible as the other, but since it came less frequently, and since, when he was very young, he had learned that his father was scornfully intolerant of it, he managed to keep it almost entirely to himself. The fear took a peculiar form. It was not a fear of the unseen, of ghosts, of possible hidden presences in the dark; it was fear of blindness. When he was perhaps eight years old he had read a story in a collection of mystery tales his father had got from the library that grooved itself into his mind. It was the story of a surgeon who revenged himself on an enemy by pretending to blind him during an operation, and for a day and a night, by keeping his victim's chamber in utter darkness, had kept up the deceit with diabolical cleverness. The agony of the victim, the horror of the deed, the atmosphere of terror that sheathed it, had insinuated themselves into Kurt's brain more thoroughly than he knew.

His bedroom was ordinarily fairly light at night. The Grays' house, a large frame affair which they had proudly built in the late nineties when Elmer first came to Barton, stood next but one to the corner; and Kurt's room, which projected out over the circular front porch, had two large windows facing on the street, so the arc light from the corner came flickering, pale violet, through the curtains, patterning the wall at the foot of his bed with luminous traceries. In the winter, when the trees were bare and snow covered the ground and the projecting rim of the porch roof, his room was flooded with a dim purpled grayness. As the buds on the soft maple at the corner began to swell and burst in the spring, and as the thick leaves came forth, the room grew darker. But even in mid-July the leafy twinklings, though less diffused, still made a welcome light before his eyes. And so long as there was the slightest gleam of light for his eyes to fasten on, he was not afraid.

But nights would come, now and again, when the light on the corner would be out. It was a nightly courtesy of Kurt's, as soon as supper was over, to run to the front porch and bring in the evening paper for his father. If he saw that night had fallen and the light was out, his whole evening would be clouded by nervous dread. His parents would read the papers, his father would drowse in his chair, his mother would take up a basket of mending, while he, trying to absorb himself in a book, would punctuate his reading with restless trips to the front window to see whether the light might have come on. He would try, on such occasions, to postpone bedtime by a game of checkers with his father, or by coaxing his mother to read a story. When the time inevitably came, he would linger over his good-nights and at last crawl reluctantly into bed while darkness rolled in upon him in terrifying waves. Wide-eyed, he would stare at the opaqueness that should be the window, and not until he could detect some faint glow of star, or some doubtful suggestion of a darkness not quite complete, would he dare to shut his eyes. Even then he would open them again and again to make sure that the teasing half-dark was still visible, until the intervals became longer and at last he would fall asleep. His greatest fear was that sometime he would awaken and find only impenetrable blackness.

When he was nine years old, soon after the closing of school in June, he was invited with his parents to spend a weekend at the cottage which some friends had bought at a nearby lake. It was on the first night of this visit that the thing he had always dreaded and yet expected happened. The grown-ups occupied the two bedrooms upstairs, and Kurt, to his delight, was settled in the living room on the sofa. Although the night was quite warm, there had been a fire in the grate, and as the shuffling feet upstairs were silenced and as the yellow oblong of light where the wooden stairs went slanting through the ceiling flashed once or twice and disappeared, it was very pleasant to lie there on his side watching the fire ribbons dance and waver and send long shadows seeking, finding, receding, across the painted floor and up the red log walls. There were such things to be seen in a fire. Glowing cones of orange-red, with licking tongues of lavender and brass running greedily about them. He fell asleep while the fire danced and the shadows chased across his bed.

He awoke, suddenly, dazedly, into such a blackness as he had never imagined. It seemed to have density and weight, to be pressing in upon him. He sat up, stifling a frightened cry. Rigid, he remained there, held in the vise of his fright, staring into it and confronted by — nothing. Not a gleam, not a spark. The fire had gone out, leaving no ember. The window — where was the window? He leaned over, peering, his arms stretching towards it, his fingers clutching, his whole body yearning towards the light that was not there. He could not see the window, though he felt the pane beneath his fingers. Outside there was the faint hushing murmur of pine branches and the soft slap of water against the wooden rowboat drawn up on the shore — but no light. Nervously he threw back the covers and felt his way around the foot of the couch. He pressed his face once more against the cold pane, but he could see nothing. Was he really blind? Was all light swallowed up forever? He felt along the wall slowly, slowly, until, quite by chance, his groping fingers came upon the button of the electric light. He turned it with happy expectancy. There was the familiar click, but the room remained as dark as before. He moaned a little then. Was he really blind? Was light there, yellow in that small bulb somewhere in the midst of this void, and he unable to see it? The idea sent him, frozen with fear, stumbling back to his bed. It seemed a long way. It was as if some sinister thing had pushed the walls of the room away to an infinite distance and had poured into the space all the darkness of the world. How long he sat there, shivering and afraid, he did not know. But finally, hours and hours later, it seemed, the window square began to gleam faintly, almost imperceptibly. It became more and more clearly visible, and soon he could see the sweeping branch of the dark cypress outside. He was not blind. Something must have happened to the lights. He was cold and tired. When he next awoke, his mother was pinching his ear, and sunshine was warm upon his face.

Later in the same summer he spent a month at a popular resort on Lake Michigan with his mother and an aunt from Chicago who had taken a cottage there for the season. His worry about sleeping in a strange place where the frightening experience of June might be repeated was soon dissipated, for his room at the beach was as light as the one at home. The days he reveled in. The dunes rose steeply at the back of the cottage with their endless waves of white sand; the paths twisted and climbed through the stunted sprawling pines, half-buried in sand — pines that could be climbed, and that gave view far out over the glittering blue lake, and that, if you sort of squinted your eyes, became very like the crow's nest of a sailing ship such as the one Jim Hawkins had sailed on. He could imagine his tormentors, in gay pirate costumes (but none so gay as his), toppling one after the other into the sea after some particularly deadly encounter with his trusty blade. By himself he was contented all day. If they would only leave him alone, it could be the same at home. How he hated going back there and entering a new grade in school, with new boys to leer at him, to press him into corners, to finger him with dirty, boy-smelling hands, and to taunt him with his "powder-face" and his inoffensiveness.

He had acquired at the beach several brown middy blouses such as city children were wearing, and they became him exceedingly. He liked them, as he instinctively liked nice things. But when, on the return to Barton, his mother demanded that they be worn to school, he protested stormily.

"Aw, nobody wears 'em! Girls wear white ones, but none of the boys wear 'em. They'll laugh at me. I won't do it!"

"Oh, yes, you will, dear. They are very nice. You know you like them yourself. Why, I couldn't get you to wear anything else at the Haven. And what else matters? Be different! Be a leader! If you wear them the other boys will all want them — see if they don't! Start a style!"

Kurt knew they wouldn't, but he could do nothing but yield, foreboding in his heart, to this absurd adult logic. And the result was quite as he expected. But Mrs. Gray this time would not give in, and the middies were worn and the shame endured.

It was the same again and again. His mother constantly combated Kurt's fear of doing anything that would bring down upon him the ridicule of the schoolboys with her newly acquired and somewhat roughly formulated philosophy of individuality.

"Why do you want to be like other boys, Kurt?" she would ask. "Everybody who amounts to anything is different. What about all these generals and great men you read about in school? Were they just like everyone else? You don't like the boys that tease you, do you, so why should you want to be like them? Would you want to be like Red O'Dell?" Red O'Dell, a beastly little bully some two years Kurt's senior, had, she knew, taken a particularly inquisitorial delight in leading and directing his persecution.

Kurt wished she wouldn't harp on it so, but he answered as she expected him to. Red had said things and done things that he would tell no one — things which, aside from the shame they inflicted, he felt to be nasty and repulsive. "Those men — were they — were they different — like me — when they were little, too?"

The question surprised her. She was ignorant of Shelley's painful years of public school life, and of other parallels which a wider knowledge might have rallied to support her thesis, but she fabricated cheerfully. "Why, yes, I suppose they were. If they hadn't been, how could they be so fine after they grew up? If a man didn't have something fine and great in him when he was small how could he have it when he got big, Kurt? It has to be there, you see. Don't you think you'd have liked David when he was a boy, or — or King Arthur — or Lincoln — better than Red O'Dell? Don't you think I would have liked them better for my boys than Red — just as I like you better? You will be a big man too, someday!"

Kurt was quite sure he would have liked anyone better than Red, but he wasn't so certain that he'd have liked Lincoln or King Arthur or David so very much. There was only one boy, anyway, that he really liked — the boy who lived next door. He was a few months older than Kurt, and one grade further advanced in school — a slow, thoughtful boy with a passion for making things, and a tolerant disposition. He alone never laughed at Kurt. Often, indeed, he silenced the taunts of Kurt's tormentors with a blunt "Aw, shut up, you! Leave him alone! He don't hurt you, does he? Whyn't you pick on somebody your size!" Nob (where he had acquired the nickname, no one seemed to know; his real name was Arthur, Arthur Bronson) never wanted thanks. He simply and quietly, when it seemed necessary, assumed a sort of guardianship over Kurt, which Kurt appreciated — and his mother as well, for she soon noticed that when Nob was about, Kurt was seldom molested.

Playmates of his own age, besides Nob, were very few. There were a number of younger children in the neighborhood, all of whom adored Kurt. He was always willing to play with them, since they never laughed at him. With them he was always happy. His imagination was keen. He had read all the books he could find to read, particularly if they had in them an element of the miraculous. His copy of Grimm's fairy tales was so worn that it became at last a thick, unsightly bundle of dog-eared pages, but Kurt didn't mind, for if the story was broken off by a missing page or a torn corner he knew how it ended anyway. His greatest delight, when he had a few of the younger children about him, was to enact a play — something he had read or something of his own invention. The plays were always romantic, as fairy tales are romantic, for Kurt loved to pretend being a prince, or, still better, a princess; for as prince or princess he could exercise, in an imaginative way, the suave and silken superiority that was so completely submerged in the everyday routine of life.

The performances usually took place in the large upper floor of the barn behind the Bronson house. The barn was of the sort that preceded the garage in small towns throughout the Middle West — a fairly large rectangular building with a sliding door in front which gave access to a room large enough to house a buggy and a small spring wagon. Behind this was the stable, and overhead, in the loft, a storage place for hay and bedding for the horse. Mr. Bronson, who was foreman of Barton's small furniture factory, though not a well-to-do man, was led by his absorbing bent for things mechanical to purchase the first automobile that was owned in Barton. The buggy, the old horse, the feed, the harness — all that pertained to the outmoded locomotion of the Bronson family — were sold. The stables were turned into a workshop, always redolent of fresh shavings and turpentine (for Bronson was eternally making something or helping his son to learn the tools), and the large loft was left empty, save for a few discarded pieces of furniture and boxes of cast-off clothes. There was a stained, cobweb-festooned window at the south end, and at the north — the front of the barn — a large square door, through which the hay was formerly hoisted. The place made, so Kurt thought, an ideal theater, and no one seemed to mind. Nob took slight interest in it as a theater, though as a fortress he had punctured the sides at intervals with a series of loopholes, and had converted the hay chute into a secret passage with a trapdoor at the top nonchalantly concealed by a much-frayed chenille rug. But, fortress or theater, the two seldom conflicted, and if the circumstance ever arose that an invading army attacked Fort Bronson (as Nob modestly named it), they might remain in complete ignorance of the fact that they were interrupting a performance of that distinguished romantic actor, Kurt Gray, in the title role of Cinderella. For Kurt Gray and his entire company could be quickly, if not very quietly, spirited down the secret passage known only to them and to the intrepid General Bronson, and out through Schey's backyard to the side street. This arrangement pleased Kurt tremendously, for it permitted a shudderingly dramatic exit even when the play was ruined, and it pleased the General because his reputation as a man of sturdy and unwomanish tastes, a perfect Miles Standish of a man, remained uncontaminated.

For the most part, however, Kurt's time when he was not in school was spent with a book, at the piano picking out tunes and pieces his teacher knew nothing about, or with make-believe games in which toy towns and cutout dolls — always with voluminous wardrobes — and miniature theaters held prominent places. His parents read little save the daily papers and the few magazines that were always on the living room table. Their library was small and nondescript — a few padded volumes of Tennyson and Longfellow and Will Carleton, a set of Marie Corelli, and odds and ends from no one knew where. They were glad to see that Kurt enjoyed books, and books they bought. But their buying was indiscriminate. Boys' books galore there were, for Mr. Gray favored these especially as being in some measure a substitute for the boy-life his son evaded so carefully; fairy stories, which Kurt liked best, and such fantasies as the Oz books which found their way at Christmastime to the village drugstore. Kurt read them all, and read them again, and could not be persuaded to part with them. Baseball bats and boxing gloves he saw pass into the possession of other boys with complete indifference, but his books he treasured with a zeal that was almost miserly. He had all the Alger books that were procurable, and liked them, but his favorites among the cheaply printed, gloomily bound

boys' books in his strange library were those in which the element
of the unusual entered most strongly: trips to the moon, balloon
flights over uncharted seas, explorations up unknown rivers,
searches for hidden treasure and lost glories. These and the fairy
tales, which he never forsook, held the greatest fascination for him.

Occasionally, when the members of the theatrical troupe of
Fort Bronson were kept indoors by unsympathetic mothers, or
scattered afield with shocking indifference to the demands of their
art, when books palled a bit, and when playing the piano had
become, by necessity, a boring matter of scales and finger exercises,
Kurt took refuge in his father's store. Often after school he would
hurry home to leave his books and from there hasten down the
wide maple-shaded street past squat wooden houses with low
narrow porches and spacious green yards to Main Street, which
was even wider, and was bordered on either side for two blocks by
two- and three-story buildings of brick or cement blocks, with here
and there a low frame building of an earlier date.

Kurt's father owned the store next to the central corner. It was
of red brick and two stories high. Through the display windows at
the front with their slick gold letters — "ELMER GRAY, FURNI-
TURE" — the store, which was rather narrow, could be seen stretching back for a considerable distance. The entrance door was in the
center, and from it a linoleum-covered aisle led back to a small
latticed office between a heterogeneous assortment of golden oak
furniture — squatty buffets with shining narrow mirrors, round
dining tables with heavy pedestals, mission library tables, uncomfortable fat-looking chairs covered with stiff brown leather, and a
glittering display of brass beds at the very end.

At one side a narrow stairway led up to the second floor, skirting
a high wall. Its brown oatmeal paper was nearly concealed beneath
framed pictures: brown prints of the Angelus, Hope, Sir Galahad,
and the Age of Innocence; with here and there a hard flash of color
in a varnished sunset, an ink-frozen waterfall, or a dish of waxy and
unpalatable-looking fruit. Upstairs there was a long room overlooking the street where rugs and linoleum were displayed. Some
rugs were on the floor in a thick telescopic pile with edges of blue
and red and green and brown. Others, the nicer ones, hung from

great sticks which could be swung, fanlike, to display their colors
and texture. Most of the chairs were upstairs too, and many
wooden beds. In one of the dim corners at the back, where the light
came uncertainly in through cracked and faded green window
shades tacked over the two dust-covered windows, were piled the
mattresses.

It was here Kurt loved to go. Few customers came in, and
upstairs he was nearly always alone. Splendid games of house and
theater could be played. The swinging rugs made scenery enough,
and a disused portière made a very satisfactory costume. Then, after
a play, or a romping pantomime on the cushiony pile of rugs, it was
pleasantest of all to climb to the top of the pile of mattresses, to
creep far back into the corner, and to pretend at hiding in an
inaccessible cave, or just to lie still and not pretend at all.

Sometimes the basement would attract him. Here, in front of
two small dirty windows which pierced through to the sidewalk
above, was the long bench where Jeff, the man who helped his
father in the store, did his picture framing and made price tags and
signs. The little pots of colored ink, the brushes, the small drawers
full of slender silver nails, the tools, the miter box, the rack of
picture-frame molding, bending in its rack at either end with its
own golden weight, furnished him with many hours of amusement.

His life became more and more a life lived alone, a life which
was turned in upon itself for sustenance and solace. Mrs. Gray was
regretful, but she could see no remedy, and so it went on. His
schoolwork, except arithmetic, which he despised, was easy for
him. And with his father's help even the problems of seventh- and
eighth-grade arithmetic — those ridiculous metaphysical specula-
tions so concerned with improbable objects in improbable combi-
nations — were satisfactorily solved. He liked the schoolroom,
because there he was free from the fear of taunts. He could expand,
for there his superiority was unquestioned. He never seemed to
spend much time on his lessons, yet his recitations were always
satisfactory. His teachers liked him because he caused them so little
trouble and because there was in his attitude a hint of respect,
natural and unconscious on his part, and gratifying to them. He
ordinarily liked his teachers — he had no reason to dislike them.

The difficulty of the playground was by no means solved. It seemed less grave to his parents, not because it was in reality so, but because as he grew older Kurt became more proficient in concealing from them the ignominious position he occupied in the eyes of the boys. He would not fight them. The only alternative was to be as stoical as he could — always for him a difficult task — and to hide as well as he was able the bitterness and shame he felt. His mother's counsel he had adopted as fully as he knew how. There was no use in bothering her now. She had done, he felt, all she could do. There was always the danger that she might go to the teacher, to the superintendent, or to some neighbor for satisfaction of some sort, and that would be intolerable. No, it was better to endure the taunts — though every one of them made him cringe — and make believe it didn't matter. He hated Red O'Dell with a cold malignancy that would have amazed any of those who knew him as a quiet, studious, and well-mannered boy. When a scourge of diphtheria killed Red during the winter of Kurt's last year in grammar school, he was glad. He knew it was wrong. His mother would have said so. Norton, his Sunday school teacher, would have said so, and would have talked about forgiving one's enemies, but he couldn't help it. He was glad, but no one knew. His life — the life that really mattered in his growth and development — became a secret one, and although at times he uncomfortably felt that this secrecy was untruthful and wicked, it was inevitable.

II

AND SO Kurt Gray reached the age of thirteen, one of the most difficult of his life, in a state of unusual loneliness, unusual seriousness, and unusual innocence. The seriousness and the loneliness were the natural results of his own peculiar temperament. The innocence was the natural result of the other two in combination. He had wondered about life as all boys do; but being cut off to such an extent from other boys by temperamental barriers not to be surmounted, his wonderings went for the most part unanswered. Babies — where did they come from, anyway? They were deposited in houses in some supernatural way, to be sure, but the whole problem was tantalizing. Girls. What were they like? Boys. His own body was a queer thing.

He had discovered when he was very young and very full of uncertainty that there was a strange intoxicating pleasure to be won from his body. Alone. It was a simple animal joy, probably wrong, but unutterably enticing. It was so wonderful, so lullingly pleasant to lie in the warm bathwater, with the house sounds muffled and far away, and to yield to this newly discovered, this wantonly exotic ravishment of the senses. It was a warm indolent delight that seemed to flood his body with a curious and subtle languor which increased and lulled, and increased, singing in all his veins, until pleasure became almost pain unbearably sweet — and then, suddenly, it would end, leaving him incredibly tired and listless. He felt, though he had never been told, that what he did was wrong. It couldn't be right, such perfection of pleasure, and he never let himself succumb too frequently — the reaction was too enervating, too frightening.

He was somewhat reassured when he learned that other boys knew the same delight. There had been a boy, Barry Van Cleet, two years younger than himself, who sometimes came over to join the players in the Bronson barn. Kurt liked him, and between them for a while a queer clandestine friendship sprang up. They had gone, one afternoon, on their bicycles out the main road leading through the town into the country. After some two miles of pedaling, they turned off into an inviting byroad, sandy and deserted, hid their bikes behind a straggling rail fence where a great billowing elderberry bush quite concealed them, and walked down a narrow grass-choked lane to a cemetery on the riverbank — a cemetery long disused. Here and there, out of the tangle of glossy green myrtle and wild verbena, rose staggering white stones — weathered and stark, their inscriptions almost effaced — and beside one of them Kurt added to his store of knowledge. It began by dares, both eager, both hesitant. It ended in both of them, trembling with excitement, slipping with furtive bravado out of their clothes. They stood there in the warm sunshine like two green figurines come suddenly to life in a place of forgetfulness and silence. There was animal joy then, sheer pleasure in the joy of nakedness, of the touch of flesh, of sun and wind on uncovered bodies. The sudden clatter of a cultivator in a nearby field, and the shout of the farmer as he turned his horses at the end of the furrow, sent them scuttling back into their clothes, a little fearful, a little ashamed, and back to their bicycles.

There had been other experiences, two or three. Barry had moved away to Chicago soon after this, but Kurt had seen enough to know that boy bodies were patterned like his own. Girls were more difficult. He had asked his parents, one evening when they were looking at the paper after supper was over. The question had come, it seemed to them, apropos of nothing.

"I don't believe girls are any different from boys," he said seriously, "only for their clothes."

His father and mother had looked at each other and laughed. He had been ashamed — so ashamed that he determined never to ask again — anything. They *were* different, then. Their laughter had given them away. He wondered about it, and tried to find out from the smaller boys he played with — those who had sisters. He even offered little Jane Damon, whom he liked, a dime if she would — but she had been unaccountably angry and had run home, leaving him in terror lest she might tell what he had done.

Later he had been ashamed, for a similar thing had happened to him, and he had not liked it. One sultry July night, he and Nob and a half-dozen smaller children had congregated on Nob's front porch to examine the most recent product of his ingenuity — a long-handled butterfly net. They had gone forth in a straggling, leaping band to the corner, and spent many frantic and noisy minutes in a vain endeavor to snare a bat that was swerving erratically about the streetlight — sliding swiftly into the dark, and then as swiftly dipping back into the central pool of light, but always just evading the net.

They had grown tired at last, and while they were lying on the cool grass in the gloom cast by the maple tree on the corner, wondering volubly about bats and stars and June bugs and moths and the click and flicker of the carbon lamp, Beany Gorton had appeared and begun organizing a game of hide-and-seek. Bounds were to be half the block, and Beany magnanimously offered to be "It." He was not much bigger than Kurt, and in the same grade in school, although he was two years older. He had narrow blue eyes, and his hair, which was light, was clipped close to his head. Large ears protruded from a rather small head which melted into his blue jersey by way of a soft-looking chin indented by a deep dimple. He was to count to a thousand by tens.

He planted himself against the tree trunk and began counting. There were scamperings and whispered warnings, and in a moment Beany was alone in the shadow of the great tree. Kurt had run between his house and Bronsons', scuttled around the paling fence that separated the backyards from the gardens, run silently along the side of the barn — and, seeing the door to Nob's workshop invitingly ajar, slipped inside. Clinging to the door casing, he listened to the faint "—eight hundred — nine hundred — one thousand! Comin'!" from the corner. Then came the padding of rapid feet, a shriek, and Beany's voice: "One two three for Is'belle!" Another silence, a mysterious rustle of leaves, Isabelle's shrill voice calling, "Cucumber, cucumber!" another tattoo of swift feet, and a boy's cry of "Free!" A moment later there was another, and then a third — Nob's. That meant that Beany was far from goal. A scraping sound by the side of the barn sent Kurt shrinking into the darkness. Stealthy footfalls came closer, and suddenly, black against the stars, Beany's head and shoulders appeared. Kurt crouched motionless, holding his breath, while the blood in his wrists thumped and pounded. The head turned, and a hand came thrusting through the door. When it was just about to touch him, Kurt exploded in a nervous giggle. Beany sprang inside and seized him. "Kurt! It's Kurt," he half shouted, and then, as Kurt struggled to free himself, loosened his hold and whispered, "Shh! Le's have some fun — wait here awhile and fool 'em." Kurt was surprised.

"Hey," he said, "aren't you gonna race me to goal?"

Beany hesitated.

"Naw. Let 'em come in free if they want. Le's stay here."

The night air was soft and warm. Beany's hands were fumbling with Kurt's clothing. It was strange. He didn't like it, and he twisted himself away. Beany's voice was wheedling: "Aw, come on, lemme feel. I won't hurt you any!"

"No. I don't want to. Let me out—" and he ducked for the open door. He found himself stopped by Beany's left arm braced against the sill, while the right went seeking, fumbling in the darkness. Kurt wrenched himself free and started to cry out, "Lemme go, I tell you—" but was interrupted by another voice at the door. It was Nob's.

"Hey, what's biting you, Beany? Everybody's run in free. You'll have to be 'It' again." And he let forth into the night a long wailing "All-y-all-y out's in free-ee!"

"Guess I'd better go home," said Beany sullenly, and as he squeezed against Kurt in going through the narrow door, he whispered, "Don't tell your ma, Kurt."

And then a horrible thing occurred. One Saturday afternoon when the house was dim and quiet and his mother had gone to town he had taken advantage of her absence to look in the encyclopedia for things he was continually curious about. He had learned that such things could be found there. The difficulty was that he understood so little of it. It was like a tantalizing game. One word would lead to another, and that to a third, until he would have a half-dozen of the heavy volumes piled on the floor around him. It was disturbing, and not very satisfactory — whetting his curiosity rather than appeasing it. Then he had turned to the Bible, the large one on the shelf beneath the library table, and read, as he had surreptitiously done before, parts that suggested hidden knowledge: Leviticus, the story of Onan, the affairs of David, of Sodom, of Lot, the Song of Solomon. And the result was as usual. He found himself drawn, willing and yet reluctant, up the stairs to his mother's room, darkened against the afternoon sun. He slipped off his clothes nervously, and in the oval mirror of the dresser admired the reflection of his slim white body against the dim wall. His mother's green beads lay on the dresser. He put them over his head, and shivered as they slid like a cool lithe serpent over his shoulders and down his back. The feel of hands on flesh. Naked bodies —

boy bodies — white, palpitant. Arched feet beating, arms wreath-
ing, flesh quivering, swimming, swimming, patterning white in the
dusk. Gone. Again. His own body, fusing, melting, wavering,
sinking. The joy! The joy! The warm luxuriousness. The pain —
the writhing. And then it happened. What was it? What had he
done to himself — his body? What did it mean? He was frozen
with fear. What should he do? He dared tell no one. He — oh,
Jesus! He sank to the floor like a stricken faun and prayed, hysterically, wildly, until, realizing that he was naked, and cold, he dressed
and waited nervously for his mother's return.

The fear held him, tightened on his throat like cold metal,
but his mother, busy with supper preparations, noticed nothing
strange. The next few days were frightful. The fear that haunted
him now was of something unknown and untellable. That he was
being punished he had no doubt. What he had done had brought
upon him this thing, this disease. Yet how was he to know? It was
unjust. He hated himself, and vowed that never again should it
occur. A week went by and his mind was more at ease, though it
was still, when he thought of it, a mad riot of imaginings and
worryings and uncertainties. Perhaps it was still not too late.
Perhaps the damage he had done himself was not irreparable.
Perhaps whatever had happened would never happen again. How
could it, if he behaved himself? And he knew that he would behave
himself. The fear of the consequences if he failed was deterrent
enough.

And then one night the terror came back upon him like the
Djinn from the bottle, a thousand times magnified. He was, in his
sleep, half-conscious of being seized by an irresistible desire to
indulge in the pleasure he had forbidden himself. He must not —
must not. But it was as if he had no control over himself. The thing
was happening and he was without power to stop it. He was
yielding, and he must not. The fatal sweetness swept over him like
incense-heavy air — sweet, sweet — the delirium of it, the dulling
richness of it, the swelling pulsing joy of it. And then, in one
spasmodic burning moment, it was over. He awoke with a stifled
cry. For an instant he did not know what had happened. He sat
upright in the dark, tense, rigid, terror screaming in his throat

which only his knuckles pressed into his mouth retained. It had happened again. It would happen again and again until some terrible, unimaginable thing came to pass. What should he — what could he do? The shame of it! The fear of it! He could not tell his parents, and yet maybe a doctor — maybe he could be cured. But even as the hope came to him he knew it was vain, for he could never bring himself to tell the family doctor, or any doctor in the town. He dared not. All night he sat upright in his bed, chin propped in hands, fingertips pressing against his teeth, until the streetlight flickered out and the gray morning came thinly in through the window. Despairing and afraid, he dropped to sleep.

During the days that followed he went through his routine of school and lessons and meals automatically, a dull worry constantly oppressing him. Quite by chance he discovered in the sample copy of a cheap magazine which had been left at the door an advertisement which seemed to have bearing on his case. It frightened him and yet at the same time consoled him, for it made certainty where there had been only doubt. It read:

> YOUNG MEN! Are you losing your Manly Vigor? Through bad habits formed in youth are you becoming old before your time? Why be a physical wreck? Write NOW before it is too late to the Krass Medical Bureau, Box 411, Cincinnati, Ohio. Ask for Booklet 7C which will be sent to you in a plain wrapper.

When the little pamphlet came he put it quickly into his pocket, and, at the first opportunity, went up to his own room and opened it. It all sounded fully as serious as he had feared. Much of it he could not understand, but it was easy enough to see that he had been guilty of an unpardonable sin towards his own body. The "secret vice" was responsible, he learned to his horror, for insanity, feeblemindedness, loss of memory, and all sorts of diseases he had never heard of, but which, the booklet said, were "wasting and devastating in their insidious and debilitating effects." He read the cheaply printed pages as a criminal might read his bill of charges — eagerly, fearfully — and when the last accusing sentence was done, he realized that his only hope on earth lay in Rejuvo Elixir. It could be procured at two dollars per bottle from the Krass

Bureau, which was most highly recommended by the Chemico Health Society, also of Cincinnati. He had, it happened, four dollars saved from his weekly allowance of fifty cents, that he had planned to put into the bank soon, but still he thought there were excuses he might make — he could plead the necessity of buying a birthday present for his mother — something — something.

III

Wᴴᴵᴸᴱ ᴴᴱ ᵂᴬˢ ᵂᴬᴵᵀᴵᴺᴳ for the arrival of the medicine, making furtive trips to the post office twice each day to forestall the possibility of embarrassing questions at home, other things were happening which gave his thoughts a slightly different turn. His father came home one night from a meeting of the church board, of which he was chairman, and announced that they had voted to hold revival meetings. His mother sighed, for she knew it meant two weeks of unusual effort, with nightly pilgrimages to the church, prayer meetings in her front room, and the added responsibility that would be hers because of her prominence in the affairs of the church.

Kurt was a little sorry too. Not that he minded the meetings. He was used to churchgoing — it was something to be as little questioned as eating, or going to school. As long as he could remember, he had been to church two and often three times every Sunday. He had gone with his parents in the morning, and sat quietly between them during the hymn and sermon, drowsing sometimes, sometimes amusing himself by fitting together incongruous titles in the hymn books to make ridiculous, half-intelligible sentences. After church he had always stayed for Sunday school, being promoted from one class to another as he grew older — now with a woman as teacher, now with a man; sometimes in a class with girls and boys, sometimes with boys only. He had never liked Sunday school particularly. But some of the stories had been worth hearing, and the puzzles and riddles and jokes in the papers he brought home were fun. Occasionally, too, the classes were amusing; very few studied their lessons, since there was no compulsion to do so. The result was often a rambling discussion which, beginning with Moses in the bulrushes, or Elisha and the she-bears, was very likely to conclude with Ty Cobb or the reason for the greenness of leaves. The teacher he liked best was a young man named Sprigh.

Mr. Sprigh had an amazing fund of inexact information on all sorts of subjects, and a talent for digression; so while the lessons usually suffered, the forty minutes sped — and that, to Kurt, seemed more important.

Revivals were different, though. From former experience he knew that there would be embarrassing moments — moments when he would feel the intense self-consciousness that was so painful to him.

The medicine was slow in coming. For two weeks Kurt waited, almost ashamed, at last, to inquire of the postmaster for the expected package. In the meantime the meetings had begun, and the Thing had happened again. And the two events were not entirely unrelated.

The meetings had started on Tuesday. Kurt had gone Tuesday night with his father and mother; curious, as everyone was, indeed, to learn what the evangelist was like, and what the coming two weeks were likely to bring. The Methodist church to which the Grays belonged was some five blocks from their house, so they had started soon after seven in order to be on hand when the meeting began.

The main auditorium, when the Grays entered, was brightly lit by three chandeliers, whose glaring bulbs always hurt Kurt's eyes and made him sleepy. The heavy golden oak benches, many of them, were already occupied by the people they knew, talking and laughing in low voices over the backs of the pews with their neighbors.

By the time the last bell rang its three clanging notes, the church was fairly well filled; and when the door leading into the wing opened, there was an expectant stillness. Four people appeared and took their places on the rostrum, a fourth chair being hurriedly lowered over the green curtain by the minister, Mr. Benson, who then stood behind the pulpit looking a little worried at the responsibilities he was assuming. He was a tall, spare man with a face that was heavy and long; black hair, thin at the top; and enormous hands.

In the deep hollow voice that Kurt always thought sounded exactly like the sounds he had laughed at when he was scrubbing out the cistern for his mother, the minister began:

"Brothers and sisters: As you know, we are inaugurating tonight a two weeks' evangelistic campaign. There are many things I might say to you as we inaugurate these meetings, but I prefer to let the good brother here who is to be your spiritual guide for the next two weeks say them. I know, all pulling together, great things will be accomplished for the Kingdom of Christ in Barton during the next two weeks. I am very glad to present to you your new guide and friend, Brother Jerome Schantz, whose long career as a gospel worker after his miraculous conversion speaks for itself. I will let Brother Schantz talk to you now, and introduce his party."

The Reverend Mr. Benson bowed awkwardly to a round little man behind him, and stepped down from the rostrum to the front pew where he sat alone during the rest of the service, his great arm stretching along the back of the seat. Mr. Schantz was on his feet immediately — his red face gleaming in the light, the thick lenses of his spectacles shining like the headlights of an automobile. Indeed, he rather suggested a steam engine of some sort. His arms, when he stood up, seemed ridiculously short and fat, and they moved with a pistonlike regularity as he talked. Even his voice was steamy, as if it were being forced up out of his mouth by spasmodic explosions deep down in the round body.

"Welcome, folks!" he began. "I'm glad to see so many of you out tonight. As your pastor has said, we're to work together for the next two weeks, and I want each and every one of you" — here he pointed a fat forefinger at four or five people in different parts of the church — "I want each and every one of you to feel that you are my friends, and that I'm yours. We are going to do great things here, as Brother Benson has said, but we'll all have to help. And now I'll make you acquainted with my helpers, who will want to know you too. This" — and he pointed to the young woman, blonde, pretty in a conventional sort of way — "is my wife, Mrs. Schantz. She will take charge of the women's groups and play the organ, to say nothing of running me."

He looked delighted when the anticipated stir of laughter came to him. Mary Schantz rose and smiled and seated herself again.

"And this" — here he pointed to a sallow young man with oily black hair and an obtrusively checked suit — "is Mr. Brill, Mr. Dan Brill, who will direct the singing and work with the boys. He is a regular fellow, and you'll all like him. And now, as singing is an important part of any meeting in any church, 'Make a joyful noise unto the Lord,' as it says in the Bible. The more noise you make, the better the Lord will like it. Let's sing."

Dan Brill took charge. He talked rapidly, like an actor, Kurt thought. He presented for the approval of the congregation his own pamphlet of songs, price only thirty-five cents, which he wished to use during the services. A number were sold at once, and the money collected by two small boys, delighted at this unexpected opportunity of managing the long-handled collection boxes that looked like wooden corn-poppers. With Mrs. Schantz at the organ, its stops wide open, they sang "an old one to begin with — 'Let a Little Sunshine In.'" Brill didn't like the way they did it. He made them sing it again, and yet again, shouting constantly between breaths, "Louder, get into it, sing, now all together!" and whacking the book against his hand in time to the music until finally everyone in the church was either singing or pretending to. Brill's eye would pick out the silent ones, and after a shouted "Come on, you! Sing! Open your mouth! If you can't sing, make a noise!" and Brill's finger pointed directly at them, they would grin sheepishly and start in.

> *Let a little sunshine in—*

("Shine in," Brill would echo in a booming voice)

> *Let a little sunshine in!*
> *Open wide the portal, open wide the door,*
> *Let a little sunshine in!*

Kurt was not too sure of his voice, but he sang nevertheless. There was something senseless and jolly about the tune, like a merry-go-round. The church hymns in the thick green book, like "Old Hundred" and "How Firm a Foundation," were solemn, and when he had been to Detroit once and heard them in a big church with a great organ booming, they had been thrilling. They made your spine tingle. But these were just a jolly racket.

They sang several songs until Mr. Brill, with drops of perspiration rolling down his pale face, said, "Well, that'll do for now, folks. You've done pretty well. Before these meetings are over I'll have you raising the roof off of this old church every night!" and sat down. Nothing exciting happened. The evangelist outlined his plan for a campaign — a plan which called for nightly meetings, daily "cottage prayer meetings" in various homes throughout the town, and a number of special sessions for various groups. He urged everyone to come to all meetings, to bring neighbors, to pray for success; and, after another song, dismissed them. Kurt went, then, to the front of the church, and remained as close to the wall as he could while his parents were being presented to the campaigners with the effusiveness their position as church leaders demanded. Kurt didn't want to shake hands, but he couldn't escape. "And this," he heard his mother saying, "is our son Kurt." Kurt came to them, dropping his cap as he came, and extended his hand, his eyes fixed on the worn green carpet. Mr. Schantz's clasp was warm, and so strong it made his fingers tingle. Mrs. Schantz didn't offer her hand, and he silently thanked her for it. Her smile, he saw when he stole a look, was nice. Brill's fingers were damp and clammy.

The next night much the same sort of thing occurred, except that there was a choir composed mostly of girls — with old Aeneas Trench, who was always in the choir, and who always sang loudly and off-key, and two young fellows who came, Mrs. Gray whispered to her husband, because their girls were singing. They sang many songs — "Brighten the Corner Where You Are," "Will There Be Any Stars in My Crown," "Throw Out the Life Line," and a new one, "What Am I Willing to Pay." Mr. Brill had them sing this one many times, first all the women, then all the men, then both together. A song to think about, he called it. Then, after a very long prayer by Mr. Benson, a prayer in which no one, it seemed, was overlooked, Mr. Schantz talked. He didn't preach, like Mr. Benson; he just talked. And Kurt thought it much more interesting. He told first about his being at one time a railroad engineer. He spoke with pride of the great locomotive and of the responsibility his job involved. Then he told about losing his job, and being in Milwaukee alone, without friends, about going into the City Rescue Mission where he was given hot coffee, and where he found Christ.

Everyone was interested. In spite of his almost ludicrous appearance — his build, his flailing arms, his flashing spectacles, and his shining head — there was something about the man that made the congregation listen. Kurt saw that even Mame Seligman, in the choir, had stopped giggling behind her songbook. He spoke of the great joy that had come to him then, and of the happiness that was surely in store for all those who would accept Christ for their Saviour. "Are you right with Jesus?" he asked. "Are you giving Jesus a square deal?" He stopped then. There was another song and the announcement that on the following Sunday, at three o'clock, there would be a special meeting for men and boys only.

That night Kurt lay awake for much longer than was his custom. He was impressed by Mr. Schantz, and puzzled. What did he mean, exactly, by "finding Christ"? Kurt had heard the expression so many times, in church and Epworth League meetings, that it had become a label to him of a sort; but of what sort, when he came to ask himself, he did not know. Indeed, he had never thought much about it. Never before had the question come to him so directly; and he wondered, if it should come to him and him alone, as demanding an answer, how he could reply. He had always taken it for granted, when the preacher spoke of "finding Jesus," of "being saved," of "being a Christian," that he was on the right side. And the preacher had, too, apparently, for he had never talked to him about it. But he wasn't sure. Still, he thought, now that he had stopped the terrible sweet indulgence, he was perhaps as good as many of the older people who professed to have been "saved" and whom he had heard testifying and praying lengthily. And yet with him there had been no "experience" such as Mr. Schantz hinted at, and seemed to think so necessary. What was it like, anyway, this experience? "A great happiness flooded over me," Mr. Schantz had said. "The gates of my soul were opened to the sunshine of Jesus's grace and love." Nothing like that had ever happened to Kurt, and he fell asleep wondering about it.

Saturday they had supper earlier than on other evenings, for Mr. Gray had to relieve Jeff at the store, which was always kept open until nine o'clock on Saturdays. So Kurt had a chance to get to the post office once more before it closed to ask about his package. To his joy, it had come. It was not large, disappointingly small, indeed, considering that it had cost him a half of all his savings. He put it under his coat where he could press it close against his ribs, and hurried home and up to his room. The medicine, when he opened the carton, looked like slightly greenish water, and the directions were disappointing. No result was promised for two or possibly three months. But the patient was urged not to give up hope, but to take a spoonful each night before retiring and await results.

There was no meeting at the church on Saturday night, and the Sunday-morning service was just like that of any other Sunday morning, except that there were more people there and the choir was larger. In the afternoon, after dinner, when his father suggested that the two of them go to the men's meeting, Kurt reluctantly agreed. He was half-afraid of what he might hear there to confirm his fears about himself; and yet the possibility that he might acquire some new knowledge, knowledge of which he felt the need so urgently, drew him and he went.

He had seen provocative cards about the town. Several had been left on the buffet-tops in his father's store.

Mr. Schantz's beaming picture appeared prominently in one corner, and across the top the caption: "Five Hot Cakes for Men Only — Bring Your Own Syrup." It didn't sound very religious to Kurt, but it worked, apparently, for when they came into the church it was already well filled with men and boys, boys of Kurt's age and older, some of whom he was sure had never been in the church before. He wondered if they, too, could be curious, just as he was.

There was no one to play the organ, so Mr. Brill started off with "We're Marching to Zion," and soon everyone was singing. They weren't all on the key, but they made a great deal of noise, and the leader seemed pleased. After the inevitable "prayer by the pastor," Mr. Schantz came to the front of the rostrum and began talking. He spoke first of the evils of swearing, then about gambling, and then drinking. Nothing new, Kurt thought, but he waited patiently. What he had hoped for and dreaded came at last.

"And now, boys, a few words to you. Just because you are young doesn't mean that you are without sin. No, indeed. One of the blackest sins in the world is a sin some of you boys are guilty of."

Kurt sat very still, his hands gripping the seat at his sides. He tried to look unconcerned, but he felt that he was pale. The old fear climbed up numbingly through his body like chilling poison. What the red-faced man on the platform had to say was exactly what the medical leaflet had told him — only this, coming forth in the explosive and steamy utterance of a man, filling a whole room with its echoing, was doubly impressive. Mr. Schantz, too, gave some illustrations of horrible things that had happened to boys who had let "this insidious vice get hold of them." Not only was it fatal to the body and mind, but it was a grievous sin, one that could be wiped out only by the sincerest repentance. He went on then to talk to the older men, considering the sins of adultery and fornication — things which Kurt did not understand very well, and indeed could not listen to very attentively because of the thoughts that swirled and pounded in his head. He felt slightly sick, and when it was over and they were free to go home he was glad. His father only said:

"Pay attention to what he says, Kurt. Playing with yourself is bad business. I'm glad you're a clean boy."

Kurt almost choked then. Why couldn't his father have told him years ago, if he knew, and saved him this misery he was enduring now — saved his life, maybe. The fear of what he had done now took on a moral and religious significance that he had not previously considered, and it mingled in his mind with a bitterness towards his father that he could not subdue.

The meetings went on, and every night Kurt was there, sitting between his father and mother, but always a little closer to Mrs.

Gray. As they progressed, Mr. Schantz's talks became more positive and more fervid. Sin, the world, the devices of the devil which
lurked, unsuspected, all about — in dancing, in cardplaying, in the
theater — all these he denounced hotly, and with a sincerity no one
could doubt. His appeals, too, became more frequent, and more
searching. He began to take note of those in the congregation who
came regularly, but who, it was apparent from their manner, were
not church members. There was always a little fringe of these
outsiders, and the fringe grew nightly as word of the evangelist's
oratorical powers went abroad. They came in, usually, after the
meeting had begun, sat in the back seats, and after the benediction
hurried out before anyone had a chance to speak to them. Some of
these people Kurt knew by sight — old Dan Buck, a fat white-
bearded farmer who did truck gardening on the edge of town; Bert
Crandall, a puffy-faced young man whom Kurt disliked instinctively and about whom he had heard older boys at school whisper
mysterious things; and Mabel — Mabel, whom he didn't know.
She was a pretty woman with very white hair who ran a little
popcorn wagon on the main corner near his father's store. His
mother, he knew, never spoke to her; and whenever she was
mentioned, his father and mother would exchange wise glances
and laugh, a little disdainfully. Everyone knew Mabel; she was a
bad one. The others Kurt didn't know, but there they were, night
after night, and Mr. Schantz more and more directed his steamy
thunderings at this outer fringe.

At last, one night, after an unusually impassioned picture of the
dangers of a life of sin and the contrasting joys and compensations
of those who were saved, he invited all repentant ones to come
forward and surrender themselves to Christ while the choir sang
"Just As I Am." It was a tense moment. The wavering, slow-sad
tune seemed to palpitate in the walls of the church, to fill it like
damp air, almost to drip from the rafters and window-peaks. Kurt
felt something moving and stirring within him as he had never
been moved before.

> *Just as I am, without one plea*
> *Save that Thy blood was shed for me*

And that Thou bidd'st me come to Thee,
O Lamb of God, I come, I come!

Was this thing the experience he had been wondering about? There was no response from the fringe of sinners, and Mr. Schantz talked again. There was almost a sob in his voice.

"Will all those who already know the joy of being safe in Jesus' arms, stand?"

There was a creaking of seats. What should he do? His mother rose slowly, and then his father, and, ashamed, he too got quickly to his feet, although something told him over and over, sneeringly told him: "You're a coward, a coward, a coward. What are you getting up for? You're a sinner. You've not repented. You're afraid!" Mrs. Schantz had come down into the congregation and was talking in a low voice to some woman a row or so behind. He could hear only snatches of what she was saying through the reiterated verse of the song: "—repentance — Jesus saves — loves us all — sister — you are tired — evil ways — come now—" and a moment later there was a loud sobbing, and the woman, a tall, slender woman who lived alone on the street in back of the Grays, and who often did sewing for his mother, leaned heavily on the arm of Mrs. Schantz and started to the front of the church.

"Amen! Amen! God be praised! Who else is brave enough to take this great step? O brothers, O sisters, if you only knew the joy and peace it would bring you — the peace that passeth understanding! Won't you do it? Won't you do it now — tonight? Don't turn your back on Jesus! He's calling you — calling so tenderly. Won't you come, folks, won't you come?" Another verse of the song — "*O Lamb of God, I come, I come*" — two more stumbling penitents at the altar. Something was pulling at Kurt. His throat ached; his eyes burned with desire to step out and go too — cleansing himself of sin. But something stronger held him back — and the meeting closed.

So it was each night during the week until the next to the last meeting — Sunday. Each night Kurt had been roused to a pitch of excitement that was unlike anything he knew — an intense desire mingled with an intense shame. The excitement of a book was different. The excitement of the terror he had put so resolutely behind him was different, yet less different, for there, too, was a mingling of shame in the sinning which made the indulgence sweeter. Two forces pulling, pulling, in opposite directions, and the boy in the center bearing all the strain and wondering dumbly which force would finally claim him.

The talk had its usual effect. But in place of the customary song following it, Mr. Schantz announced that Lottie Garber would sing a solo. Lottie was a high school senior, with a round face, soft dark hair, and a very red mouth. She had a clear soprano voice which his mother disliked because it "tremoloed," but which Kurt loved to hear. She had been sitting in the back row of the choir beside Jerry Keller, her beau. They wrote things to each other when no one was looking. Kurt had seen the hymnbook Lottie used, and it was scribbled full of notes. Silly, he thought. Tonight she sang a song that had a melody very much like that of a waltz that had been singing through Kurt's head for days. The words were pretty, but Kurt wondered why Jerry was grinning so foolishly all the while Lottie was singing:

> *I come to the garden alone*
> *While the dew is still on the roses,*
> *And the voice I hear ringing in my ear*
> *The Son of God discloses.*
> *O He walks with me and He talks with me*
> *And He tells me I am His own,*
> *And the joy we share as we tarry there*
> *None other has ever known.*

It was not until weeks later that Kurt discovered, quite by accident, the book she had sung it from. The words "The Son of God" had been marked out, and, in Jerry's handwriting, "Jerry Keller" inserted. No wonder he was grinning. Lottie was singing a love song for the mutual delight of the two of them. But when she sang it that night, Kurt did not know, and it seemed to him sweet and appealing.

She sang the last lingering note, and for a moment the church was silent. Then Mr. Schantz began appealing for converts. He told how God had blessed his efforts in Barton, and how, at this climax of the campaign, he hoped for even greater results. The appeal went forth. Mrs. Schantz and Brill were going through the back of the church, talking to individuals here and there in voices of droning persuasion. Some looked sullen, but most seemed simply ashamed and embarrassed. Kurt could sympathize, for he felt the same struggle going on in himself: the almost irresistible attraction of being for once in his life heroic in an important way, a way that mattered; and the shame that hung, why he could not say, like a weight upon him. Would there be an opportunity for him? He hoped; he feared. And he did not know which emotion was the stronger.

And then it came. "Are there none of you, church members, perhaps," he heard the explosive voice saying, "who have fallen from the great ideal; who feel now a new birth of the spirit, and who want to make a fresh start, a fresh avowal of your faith in Christ as the great Saviour of men? Brothers, sisters, who'll be the first to come? Come on, folks! Are you all satisfied with yourselves? Is there nothing in your lives that you are ashamed of? That you want to be rid of, washed clean of? O you young folks out there, you young men and young women — what about you? Why not confess your evil ways and be forgiven? Though your sins be as scarlet yet shall they be washed whiter than snow. God is love, folks. He will forgive you however great or however small your transgression. Can't you see Him bending down to you, stretching out His beseeching hands to you, pleading with you to come? There is a fountain filled with blood, folks, drawn from Emmanuel's veins, and all who wash beneath that flood lose all their guilty stains."

His voice rose like a chant, filling the room, as the two gleaming spots that were his eyeglasses swayed back and forth.

"Won't you come, folks? Won't you come? Don't do it for me — do it for Jesus. Learn the peace and joy that only this great step can bring into your hearts. Ye must be born again, He said. This is the time, folks, now, tonight. He stands knocking at the doors of your hearts, folks. Take Him in, for He may never pass your way again. Take Jesus into your lives — get acquainted with

Jesus. Come now — now — now — come and shake hands with Jesus!"

The voice seemed to come straight to Kurt. He hardly dared lift up his head. Was Schantz looking at him? The two gleaming lenses in the glare of the light seemed to be peering with a blind yet penetrating insistence into his very heart. He felt his face and ears burning, but his hands were cold. He was shivering. Eyes — eyes everywhere seemed to be focused accusingly on him. Was his mother's arm urging him to go up there? Was she saying inside her, "Be brave, be different! What do you care what people think? If you are doing the thing that you think is right, let the rest think what they please!"? Was she saying that?

Near him a seat creaked and without raising his eyes he could see that Gertrude Bowles, the president of the Epworth League, had arisen. He could hear the rustle of her dress as she moved down the aisle and towards the rostrum. Someone else came from farther back. "Amen! Praise the Lord!" said Mr. Schantz, and he was echoed by two or three old men who sat near the front.

"Will no one else come? Is there no one else brave enough to take this stand for Jesus tonight?"

Almost against his will, and yet with a surge of feeling that swept him like a thundering inundating wave, Kurt suddenly found himself on his feet, moving towards that impelling voice, and standing, red-faced, almost defiant, before the curving oak rail of the rostrum. What happened after that he hardly knew. There was a prayer "for these precious young souls who have dedicated themselves to the service of the Master," everyone sang "Blest Be the Tie That Binds," there was a confused buzzing murmur of voices about him, there were faces swimming in hard shattering light, there was Brill's hand clinging pallidly to his, there was a sharp clap on his shoulder from Mr. Schantz, there was his mother's arm around his shoulders — *Blest be the tie that binds—*"

At last he was out in the night under the cold far stars, walking between his father and mother. They were proud of him, he knew; and he was glad, now, with the great gladness of youth for what he had done, hard as it had been. During the few interminable minutes he had stood before the rostrum he had prayed for forgiveness, prayed as passionately as on that afternoon of realization that he had done something to himself; and there was now a satisfaction, an implanted hope in his mind that, in the sight of God, he was less guilty — that his repentance would surely save him from the consequences of his sin.

IV

KURT WAS in high school now. Being a freshman was not entirely pleasant, as it opened one more gate to his tormentors. They bothered him less and less, however, as time went on and they found that their persecutions had so little effect. As far as the schoolwork itself went, there was very little difference. He had four teachers instead of one, which made things more interesting, and there was the added novelty of moving about from room to room and not being kept the whole day in one square chalk-dusty place.

Barton High School was a small one. It had never had an enrollment proportionate to the size of the town. The factories were the cause of that. Their doors were always open for young muscles, strong bodies, nimble fingers; and the temptation of twelve dollars each week and the attendant independence that such a salary and such a life seemed to involve was a strong one. So as soon as they were sixteen many of them bought overalls and drill aprons and dinner pails and became slaves of the whistle as they had been slaves of the bell. Often when Kurt had occasion to go on the far side of the river, where the paper mills and the shoe factory and the cabinet works were, he would see older boys he had avoided in school — stripped to the waist, their bodies shining with sweat, moving through the weird scene of billowing steam and the acrid smell of disinfectant, pushing trucks of paper or snatching a breath of air at one of the open windows. It was a hot unhealthy place, the paper mill. Beaters were the worst, reeking with steam and bleach, but it was all abnormally humid and odorous. In the sorting rooms, where fingers flew through bags of refuse and rags, or through long grimy windows at the clicking stitching machines of the shoe factory, he would see girls who were not so much older than he. He would hurry past, always, a little ashamed for them all and for himself, somehow.

So the school had never been large. Nor had the teachers been particularly good. They were quite young, most of them, recently graduated from one of the state normal schools or colleges. Some were a little rebellious at the fate that had planted them in so small a town and so poorly equipped a school; others were homesick. All of them were conscientious enough, but very few fulfilled Kurt's ideal for a good teacher — that she be interesting. His criticism, if he found her just, went little farther.

At high school, too, the little clique with which Kurt had been identified all through school solidified and took on something of a social significance. Kurt's "room" in school had contained, from the time Kurt had caught up with it in the fourth grade, a group of what Mrs. Gray termed "unusually nice children." They were the children of storekeepers, mill officials, and professional people; all of whom, coming to Barton at about the same time, when its industries were opened, had settled there comfortably and had children. By a wholly unconscious process of selection the group had reached high school with six boys and six girls, all of about the same age. The group formed, always, the nucleus for any activity of their class, and as time went on and they emerged from the first to the second year of high school, their importance became proportionately greater. Kurt belonged by virtue of his father's position in the town and by virtue of something in him that children were drawn to, even when they teased him. In the circle he was popular enough; and, partly because within it his fear of persecution was allayed, he was troubled hardly at all.

There were frequent parties. The occasion would be a birthday or a holiday of some sort, and invitations would be sent out. Then, arriving one by one or in groups of two or three, they would come, late in the afternoon. There would be a supper with plenty of jam and cake and ice cream, there would be an evening full of games — guessing games, or, sometimes, depending on the hostess, romping

games — and by ten o'clock all would start for home. They would
all go together; the girls in front, screaming and giggling — the
boys behind, trying to tread on their heels, singing popular songs
in cracked, uncertain voices, running ahead to hide behind trees,
where, by jumping out, they could elicit shrieks from the girls. One
by one the girls would be deposited at their homes, and at the last
one, the boys would say good night; there would be shouted jests
and taunts and chaffing as they went off singly or in pairs into the
darkness. And the party would be over.

There came to be a feeling of "belonging." The little group was
known to have the nicest parties. They were always at the head of
things. They were, in the embryonic social life of the school, the
elect. It was an unwritten law that if any one of them gave a party
the rest were automatically invited — and no one else was. That he
"belonged" gave Kurt a deep satisfaction. It pleased something in
him, it gave him a sense of superiority in one field, and a human
one at that, which had been warped and thwarted in others.

His home, with its books and music — increasingly, his music
— the school, "the bunch," the church — these were his life. Home
and school were the staples of it. The "bunch" and the church were
its diversions. He believed in the church fervently, for it meant to
him his hope of salvation. He had gone astray, and only through
this new-old relationship could he expect to retrieve himself. Then
too it gave him some chance of exercising his talents. He joined the
Epworth League. He could play better than any of the girls, so he
was at once elected organist. It was an office he enjoyed. He could
discharge his duty, the simple one of playing three or four Sunday
school songs during the course of the meeting, and reasonably
expect to be exempted from participation in the rest of the service.
Playing he didn't mind, ever. There was the organ; there were his
fingers against cold firm keys; there were his feet pressing the
wheezing pedals — something outside and supporting. He was
always afraid, however, of being called upon for prayer or for
comment of some sort. That was different. Occasionally he was,
and his embarrassment at such times was painful. He found himself, as he walked to the church through the late afternoons, always
formulating a prayer, or a "testimony." He might be called upon,

and he must not make himself conspicuous. He must not disgrace the faith he had publicly accepted.

He could now go to all these meetings at the church with the feeling that, whether he really belonged or not, in the eyes of the church he did. He had declared himself before a crowded church, so when questions came that a year ago he could answer only uncertainly, only with the guilty sense that he was cheating, he could now answer secure in the knowledge that no disbelieving eyes were watching him. Yet, could he? Why was he, without exception, embarrassed so terribly at these times? It was, he knew in his heart almost without daring to let it come to the surface of his consciousness, because there was a doubt in him — a doubt of his experience. Could it be authentic, the Great Religious Experience the preachers talked about so glibly — that exciting, ashamed, nervous feeling that had surged over him and carried him half against his will to the front of the church? There must be something more, must be, and he felt himself a hypocrite. All his life he had been pretending to things he was not, in order to simplify the task of living: pretending to be brave when he was afraid, pretending to things his father and mother wanted for him, pretending to be sure when he was unsure. Not that he reasoned very logically about it — feeling was too urgent in him. The whole situation into which he found himself drifting bothered him, but to accept the masquerade made things easier, unquestionably — and other people too, he supposed, might behave similarly. The difficulty in this particular case was that he could not be sure whether it was masquerade or not. When he looked at himself he thought it was. When he looked at others in the church, in the Epworth League, he was not so sure. He was, he thought, as good, as sincere, as they.

He was not at all sure, either, whether it was really this newly accepted faith that helped him to conquer his evil habit. He liked to think so, but perhaps it was nothing more than fear — his overpowering fear of consequences. The frightening thing happened again and again. The medicine he had long since despaired of. Every night he went to sleep with the fear upon him, and when the tantalizing dreams would come, he was sickeningly reassured of his own guilt. A dozen times he determined to see the doctor.

A dozen times he walked slowly past the doctor's office, determined to enter. But always the shame of admission prevented, and carried him past, sick at his cowardice.

And then in the summer came relief. The Grays and the Bronsons had rented a cottage at the lake for the week of the Fourth of July. They had all been swimming, and on the return from the beach in the heavy flat-bottomed rowboat, while the older folks sought the cottage, he and Nob had gone into the boathouse to dress. It was a dark cool place. The light came in only from below, through the shallow lake water, under the edge of the building between the piles with a strange gold-green color that wavered and trembled on the rafters with a liquid softness. They dressed slowly. Nob sat, dangling his toes in the water. Suddenly he said, in a choked, embarrassed way that was not at all his, "Say, Kurt — this is — a — kinda — funny, but — I mean — do you ever have — funny dreams or anything at night — I mean — you know — kinda funny dreams—?"

Kurt knew. He said so, but little more. Nob, however, the ice broken, made it a confessional. The two of them, side by side, solemnly sat, forgetting to finish the task of dressing. Kurt said nothing except to give assent once in a while when Nob would end a sentence with "Do you too?" or "All boys do when they get to be as old as us, I guess." Nob's experience had been so much like Kurt's own that he could hardly keep from crying for sheer relief. Nob had been more fortunate, though. He had addressed his question to Dr. Brody, who wrote a health column in the Detroit paper, and had received a little book which answered all his questionings. "It just happens when we get so old, and it won't hurt us any. Gee! Wasn't I glad to get that book! You can have it if you want, when we get home."

PART TWO

I

"WHAT does it feel like, Kurt, to graduate from college?"

The voice might be coming from anywhere. All he could see as he lay on his back, fingers interlocking under his head, was blue — no cloud, no bird — nothing but blue. He knew of course that it was Chloe. Although he could not see her, he was conscious of her, sitting in the grass somewhere near his head. If he bent his eyes far enough to the right he could see the splotch of yellow that was her jersey.

"Oh, I don't know." He pulled a long stem of grass and chewed the crisp end lazily, enjoying its sweetness. "I don't know. Sort of — silly, and sort of right."

"You're funny. You never know anything."

"But I got a Phi Beta Kappa key," he said, grinning, as he flopped suddenly onto one elbow and faced her.

A smile rippled the corner of her lip that was towards him. Her hands were clasped about her knees. Her head — "from some once lovely head," he always thought — was tilted back, and against the June sky she was like a cameo done in some strange and disturbing medium. The curved throat, the strong chin, the full expressive lips, the Roman nose, the low forehead, the sleek lacquer of black hair pulled smoothly over her head to a knot low in the neck — she was like the portrait on a Messina coin, or a bas-relief from a Roman theater. He looked at her as impersonally as if she had really been one.

She turned towards him, her eyes veiled against the sun.

"I wish I'd known you when you were a little boy. What were you like, I wonder?"

"Oh — I don't know. Not much like I am now. You wouldn't have liked me. I was always moping around by myself. And then,

53

when I was older, I *know* you wouldn't have liked me. I was an awful little prig. I was even fat!"

He laughed in remembrance, and she laughed too, looking at his slim length on the hilltop.

"I wanted always to believe in something. Then, it was God."

"And now?"

"Well" — he hesitated — "now it's — oh, why does this all seem so very hard to say — it's music, it's poetry, it's — it's all this!" His arms, flung out suddenly above his head, came down on the turf at either side of him. His right hand touched hers. He drew it quickly away and sat up.

"Maybe we ought to go home," he said. "Where's Derry?"

"Derry? Oh, he's off in the woods somewhere, picking things, I expect."

She whistled shrilly, and from across the shallow valley, thin and faint, came the answer.

"Why do you like my brother Derry so much?"

Kurt eyed her sharply. "Why — why do you like him?"

"Because he's my brother. He's not your brother."

"No, he's not my brother."

He unfolded himself and stood on the brink of the hill, hands cupped over eyes, looking towards the point the whistle seemed to have drifted from. He answered slowly.

"He's such a good egg, Chloe. He's not always pleasant, but there's something strong in him — something certain. I wish I were as certain."

He sat down again beside her, and together they watched the hollow where the woods thinned into low shrubs, very green now, and lupin-spattered grass, for Derry to appear.

"Uncertain. I've always been that, I think. Uncertain and alone."

"Have you been so lonely with us?"

"Oh — not that!" he said anxiously. "Not that! Please don't think so! It's been marvelous — you and Derry. When I think how you took me in, that first year — that awful first year — and rescued me from the Demon Landlady of Dover Street" — they both smiled — "well, you saved me, anyway, and now you've made me almost one of the family. That's what four years can do. I know most all of your family secrets, and—"

"And you still like us a little?"

He grinned for reply. "Aren't you ever sorry you played the Good Samaritan?"

"Sorry! Kurt Gray! You've been the Samaritan — peacemaker, consoler, counselor, everything fine. And still you're lonely?"

"You're just pretending not to understand, Chloe. Tell me you are! You must know what it is. It isn't physical loneliness — like being lost in a barren land. It's — it's worse. There are such walls between us, all sorts of walls that won't be broken down; and no matter how many friends we make, we're lonely just the same. Some of us are like that. It's a strange thing inside us that sets us down in a lonely place, walls us up, and leaves us there."

Both were silent. A meadowlark, skimming through the valley, darted up in an arc of unexpected song.

"And now, it's leaving you all, and more loneliness. I wonder sometimes—" His voice stopped and his forefinger twisted in a strand of meadow grass. "What have I done? Written a few sentimental tunes, two or three college songs — pretty bad ones, too — a piano thing that old Scronfeld liked (but what does that mean!) and maybe — only maybe — one or two good songs — songs that you think are great because I wrote 'em. Isn't that true? Oh, let's talk about something else!"

"Let's not. I know that someday you'll do something big — and I'll be most awfully proud — and—"

Her hand stretched out to his. He did not see it, and it drew back and lay for a moment, palm skyward, against her eyes. "I wish it weren't over — wish you weren't going away. Maybe I — maybe we'll be lonely too."

"There's Derry!"

A figure was emerging from among the trees opposite. They sat watching it, smiling at its antics when they were discovered on the hilltop. The figure stooped, and with exaggerated nonchalance, pulled a great stalk of mullein. Waving it in one hand, Derry came tripping across the green of the hollow, a burlesque Pavlova, stumbling over imaginary rocks, and brushing himself free of imaginary burrs and thistles.

They laughed, and Chloe said, "What a monkey he is!"

Derry at last came panting up the hill. He was shorter than Kurt, with stout wrists and ankles, and hair almost as dark as his sister's. That he was her brother was evident. The profile was the same, but about his face there was a looseness that hers lacked, a mobility that could be utilized in a hundred ways. It was the face of a comedian, changeable as a showery day.

He went tripping clumsily around them in circles, tossing stalks of weed over their heads, and singing in a raucous falsetto, *"C-hall me early, Mothaw, for I'm to be Queen of the May."*

Kurt made a dive for the Terpsichorean ankle, and Derry came sprawling to the ground.

"Derry! For heaven's sake, snap out of it!"

"Derry, you fool!"

"Yes, children. What about it? Shall we up and away?" and he started to his feet again, but Kurt, tugging at his shoe, pulled him back.

They were all laughing.

"I expect," said Kurt, "it's time we were going home. Your mother will be worrying about us."

Chloe laughed, a little harshly. Derry smiled. "Yes," he said, "trust Mother to be worried. It's the best thing she does."

"It's too nice to leave; but I suppose we'd better." Chloe rose, sighing and stretching her arms above her bead, aglow with the slanting sun.

They all went, arm in arm, over the hill, Chloe in the middle, Derry trying to sing one of Kurt's college songs, Kurt crying, "Cut it!" and Chloe laughingly being peacemaker.

II

HIS GOING to the state university had been settled upon unexpectedly. That he would go to college was taken for granted, by himself, by his parents, and by the town. He was a "smart boy."

Nob, who had worked a year in the factory with his father after graduation from high school, was going to a small Methodist college upstate. The Grays thought it would be nice for Kurt to go with him, and so it was decided. Then, in July, an old school friend of Elmer's, a successful lawyer in Chicago, driving through Barton to his fishing camp in the north, had stopped off for the night. He liked Kurt's quietness and his deference; and, because this man was friendly, and didn't slap him on the back or pinch his arms to test his muscle, or thump him in the chest, Kurt liked him. The whole evening Elmer and Mr. Hansen talked of their law school days and of half-forgotten friends and dimly remembered episodes which acquired new glamour from their long immurement in memory. Kurt saw his father that night in a new way — saw him for the first and only time as a man who had once been young. Hansen had slight use for the small college and its "piddling professors," and some enthusiasm for his alma mater, and so, before bedtime, it was half decided that Kurt go to the university.

Going away was not easy. The idea of entering the university appealed to him — the independence of it was a gesture, of sorts. But he had never been away from home, to speak of, before, and the hundred-mile journey seemed a great adventure. And it was harder for his parents than for him. They feared for his loneliness, overtly; but, in their hearts, most of all for their own. He was very close to crying when he left, very close to crying all the way to his destination, and very close to crying when he emerged from the train into the dingy station — noisy with shouting students and welcoming friends, meeting "rushes" and making a great stir about it all. The room the taxi took him to was one his mother had arranged for with its proprietress, who had been, years back, the wife of a minister in Barton. That was, of course, sufficient recommendation. But it did not prevent Kurt, when he was safely in, with the door shut tightly behind him, from crying. And then he felt better.

Mrs. Meacham was an austere woman, although her rotundity belied it. She kept his room clean, but took a prying interest in his affairs which annoyed him. They were innocent enough, to be sure. He passed through the bugbear of enrollment, acclimated himself a bit to campus ways, attended freshman mass meetings; joined the Methodist church, went to a social there "to welcome new students" and found its friendliness a little bumptious and embarrassing, its jollity a little alarming; studied conscientiously, and, oftener than a young man should, went to sleep on a pillow wet with tears.

The Graylings were his salvation. Chloe Grayling sat next to him in French class. The instructor arranged the seating alphabetically, and "Mr. Gray, Miss Grayling" soon became to Kurt an oasis amidst the Kleypers and Hjorths and Jezewskis. It seemed a formula for agreeable comradeship. She spoke to him the first day. If he came early to class she was always sitting in a window at the corridor's end, waiting for the preceding class to be dismissed, and they would talk, of lessons, of classmates, and, after a few weeks, of themselves.

Kurt had never had a girl. The gang had been the gang. There were matches and spooners, to be sure, but Mrs. Gray thought it all extremely silly. He had never learned to dance, for dancing, at the age most young people learn it, had been taboo among the Barton Methodists; and anyway he had never wanted to, especially. Nor had he wanted to go with a girl like so many of the other fellows he knew. Kurt walked home with Chloe Grayling one noon. She seemed such a good sort — not "boy-crazy," Mrs. Gray's epithet for the girl type she most deplored. He met Mrs. Grayling, a tall angular woman with gray eyes and heavy iron gray hair that seemed always too loosely fastened. He was invited to lunch.

Derry came in from high school, and all three sat in the small living room a little abashed and uncertain until the piano gave Kurt an unwonted bravado, and the ice was broken. Mrs. Meacham's piano, where he roomed, shone with newness, but she kept it rigorously locked; and when he was aching to play it, she was asleep, or busy, or not to be disturbed, or grudgingly reluctant. And finally, she said, she had mislaid the key. So it had all come about quite simply. With the second semester he had left Mrs. Meacham, not without difficulty, and established himself with the Graylings as Derry's roommate.

He was not certain he would like the arrangement, much as he liked Derry, but anything was preferable to staying on with Mrs. Meacham. His parents had approved the change after much eloquent reasoning on Kurt's part, so that worry was removed. He had never lived so intimately with anyone, however, and at first it was hard to accustom himself to a more social way of life. He had been maidenly in his modesty, using the clothes closet as dressing room. He had debated with himself at length over the spiritual necessity of kneeling at one's bedside at night to make one's prayer efficacious; and, deciding that it must be done, had knelt, with fear in his heart of Derry's probable jesting. But Derry, unpredictable Derry, had been impressed and had said nothing. He too seemed a little afraid of Kurt at times, conscious of a seriousness in him that was beyond his own comprehension.

On the whole the two got along unusually well; and by the end of his freshman year, Kurt had been taken on as an accepted adjunct in all the goings and comings of the Graylings. His presence at Sunday dinner, at the occasional party that Chloe or Derry would give, at family outings and picnics was taken as much for granted as Derry's own. He liked it. In the evenings both Derry and his sister studied, and Mrs. Grayling read, or crocheted interminable yards of edging for pillow slips and towels, her long dark face almost sullenly intent in the glare of the overhead light she always insisted upon using. The friends he made on the campus were accepted by the Graylings as well, and their friends by him. So the change from Barton to Ann Arbor had been, after all, less revolutionary than it had promised to be. The whole environment of his extra-domestic life, to be sure, had changed. But otherwise he had simply substituted a new family for an old one. There was still a home in which he was free to do as he chose, a piano to play when he liked, all the quiet certitude of family that he had always known.

Mrs. Grayling had been difficult at times. Beneath her somewhat masculine exterior, her stoicism, he gradually discovered an emotional intensity that surprised him. She was passionately jealous of the affection of her children, worried over them incessantly, was often querulous and fault-finding and difficult to please, and could, on occasion, lose herself in storms of anger or hurt self-pity which all of them dreaded. Yet normally she was agreeable enough, and to Kurt she took an immediate fancy. In him she confided, embarrassingly sometimes, because in him she felt, young as he was, a balance and a sanity which was her unconscious lack.

The spring of this first new year away from home had brought to Kurt a third frightening experience, yet one mixed with a new and unholy joy. Mrs. Grayling had been unwontedly peevish, and Derry, as usual at such times, had gone into a sulk. He had come into the room where Kurt was reading, thrown himself across the bed with a sigh that seemed to say, "Be sorry for me if you dare!" sullenly refusing to answer Kurt's questioned "What's the matter, Derry?" and had gone promptly to sleep. Mrs. Grayling, weeping volubly, had shut herself in her room, and Chloe, exasperated by her mother's behavior, and her brother's, had gone to the library. Such scenes were disturbing, but Kurt was growing accustomed to them and somewhat reconciled, for he knew that another day would see everything set to rights again.

Derry wakened late in the afternoon and, at Kurt's suggestion, had gone to supper with him at the cafeteria, and then to an early-evening movie. They had come out into a night full of warm moonlight, and walked without talking much after Derry's initial "What do you say we walk a ways?" out of town beyond the last almost-defeated gleam of streetlight, and sat down on a hillside. They had been quiet at first. Then something in the white silence of the May moon had melted down the reticence their eighteen years of living had built up. Talk, slowly undertaken, had drifted little by little to forbidden things, to exchanges of confidences — and, at last, to the thing Kurt had fought so stoutly for the last four years, complicated now because shared with another.

After it had happened, the joy of it turned to fear. Not to bodily fear this time — he knew better now — but to religious fear, a fear for his soul's damnation. It was enormous, his guilt, and its enormity grew upon him through the walk home and through the endless sleepless hours of the night. Unprecedented, this act, and unmentionable. No one, he was sure, had ever been guilty of so heinous a sin. He seemed, as he thought confusedly about it, to stand alone, beyond possibility of forgiveness, blackened eternally, and he envied and marveled at Derry for the matter-of-fact way in which he took it. He should hate Derry, he knew; yet he knew, too, that he did not. When a few nights later it happened again between them, he knew, although he stubbornly refused to accept the fact of his knowledge, that he was caught in a new snare, inextricably — a snare which he did not understand and for the explanation of which he had no slightest intimation of where to go.

He went home in June. His pleasure in being there, in seeing in the *Barton Observer* the item *"Kurt Gray, the son of Mr. and Mrs. Elmer Gray, valedictorian of his class in the local High School last year, returned Tuesday from Ann Arbor, where he is at present Barton's only representative at the University"* was shadowed by his consciousness of guilt, of his hypocrisy, and by his longing for Derry. At home it was so, and at church, where he was welcomed as a valuable addition to its somewhat anemic life. He played the organ, he talked at the Epworth League about the status of religion among university students, with all the time the consciousness of his unfitness upon him and the realization that it all seemed much less important to him than it had a year past. Upon him too was the consciousness that his religious faith was much less sure than when he had left. Freshman biology had taught him things about the origins of life against which he at first rebelled, but which in the end he was too clearheaded not to accept as true, or at least as more credible than anything he had hitherto learned. He wanted desperately, as he told Chloe so much later, to believe in something, always to believe in something. His attempt to adjust his knowledge to his faith, his mind to his heart, his thought to what he wanted to think, was in him a real and bitter struggle and one from which he emerged slowly — clinging stubbornly, tenaciously, to the last tatters and remnants of a faith he knew was inadequate, because, as yet, he had found nothing to replace it.

He had gone back to the university in the fall, back to the Graylings' and to Derry, fearing that Derry might have forgotten, that Derry would not remember, for their relations had been unmentioned during their correspondence of the summer. They were both shy when they met, but both knew instinctively that the new relationship was to continue. It was implicit in their eyes, in the clasp of their hands. So the years that followed had been years of joy unprecedented, and of shame and remorse and promised reformations, of miserable doubts surpassing all those that had made up so large a part of his previous life.

With Derry it was different. He was, to use Chloe's favorite and apt description, unpredictable. The moral question bothered him not at all. Too, there was in him an adventurousness that Kurt lacked. He accepted the strange liaison, as novel to him as to Kurt, as a thing physically delightful, nothing more. His feeling for Kurt changed little. He regarded him sometimes with envy, as one whose lessons were learned with little effort and who had some sort of natural distinction that set him apart; but for the most part he was simply an easily persuaded partner in whatever Kurt wanted to do. His was a strangely objective mind, willful, capable in the ordering of objects and the manipulation of things, but utterly incapable of abstract thought. Kurt would try, sometimes, to read to him a poem he had especially liked, or to discuss with him some idea from his philosophy classes. But Derry would not understand, and seemed indeed to take a willful delight in not understanding. Swinburne had come to Kurt, at nineteen, as a revelation. The sonorous lines of Atalanta, that to him were of a beauty unguessed, shimmering, wonderful, were to Derry only tiresome and incomprehensible.

In Kurt there was growing a feeling for Derry that he did not for a long time try to analyze or understand. He only knew that this mercurial person could cause him more delight and more misery than anyone he had ever known. Derry's state of feeling became almost an index of his own. Derry's unaccountable spells when he would retire into himself behind walls as high and impregnable as those of a medieval town, and be sullen and silent, meant untold dismay for Kurt. Days when his timid advances were met with scornful silence, or indifference, tortured him. Rebuffed, he felt all the shame a woman feels when her lover is unyielding; yet the idea that he was in love with Derry never occurred to him. It was so utterly beyond the range of all his experience, real or vicarious. A fellow fell in love with a girl. That was love, and all of love. His situation was, he never doubted, absolutely unique. Shame covered him like the invisible cloak of his old fairy tales.

So the years of college passed. Because of Derry and the Gray-lings, Kurt always remained, as a collegian, something of an outsider. He became known on the campus as a shy and talented young man. His interest in music had become stronger and stronger until it became the dominating one of his life. His college patriotism found expression in composing a few college songs, which won him some attention and respect, even from the athletic set. Because he was so quiet, his reputation as a scholar exceeded his actual accomplishments. As he grew older he still retained in multiplied measure the undefined quality of superiority. In his manner, unassuming as it was, people with whom he came in contact felt the aristocrat. It was his mother in him. He became conscious of it, gradually, and fostered it, half-consciously, as a protective device. Into the small group of "intellectuals" the university could boast among its student body — those who wrote for the *Daily* or for the college magazines — he never fitted, but was always respected. His music reviews for the *Daily* were written clearly, and showed a sharp appreciation of the right things. But he never mingled much with the crowd that stayed around the editorial offices, so many of whom had less right to than he. He was an interesting fellow, it was agreed in the office, but not very social. To strangers they would say, "That's Kurt Gray," as he went by the window, his slim body held stiffly as though for an expected shock; his hair, brown, and soft as his mother's, always a little too long, not from choice or for effect, but simply because he dreaded barbershops so much.

And now it was over. There would be only commencement, a summer at home, which his parents demanded, and then east for a new plunge into music — another experience desired and dreaded. The last days would, he was sure, never be forgotten, so pleasant were they. Examinations were finished. A part of life was finished. There was nothing to do but steep oneself in the June weather; its mellowness seemed almost symbolic of the attachments he had made, of the peace he was now feeling — a peace pregnant with unguessed possibilities. It was an unsure peace, and in it he reveled while he might. Why was it that he, so happy in his life with the Graylings, must tear himself out of their lives like an uprooted tree? At times he was ready to throw everything over for it. His career, whose call he knew in his heart could not be denied, he was almost willing to surrender.

His last night in Ann Arbor brought him a surprise. Late in the evening he and Chloe were sitting together in the swing on the porch. It was a stifling summer night. Mrs. Grayling was dozing inside. Derry had gone off somewhere in the car. They had said little. It seemed all to have been said the other afternoon on the hilltop, and with that conversation in both their minds, both were reluctant to begin again.

"I've something I must tell you before I go, Kurt," said Chloe at last.

"Yes?"

"You'll be surprised, I think. Or maybe not. Maybe you'll have guessed it."

"You know what a good guesser I am, Chloe."

She laughed, thinking of the game they had been playing not long before.

"I'm going to be married soon — in August, I think."

Kurt was too surprised to answer, for a moment. It would be Roy Carsten, of course. He had wondered if it mightn't end that way. Yet his principal feeling, for the moment, was one of pique. He had never thought of Chloe, or of any girl, as other than a comrade, but this unexpected news was a shock to his indifference. It brought home to him, this brief statement of hers, and the minute of silence that followed it, her peculiar value as a friend. She supplied in some measure what Derry failed to supply. But that was foolish. She would marry, of course, and Roy wasn't a bad sort.

"You *are* surprised." Her voice cut into his confusion.

"Yes, I am, Chloe. I didn't know. Should have, I suppose."

"I'd like to tell you about it, if you don't mind." Her inflection asked his permission.

"Do!" he said.

"It's strange." She spoke slowly. "It's strange, I'm not sure I love Roy. But he loves me, I think, and, Kurt — I'd do anything to get away. Roy's got a job in Detroit — advertising — and it will get me away from Mother. You're shocked at that?"

"I think I know, Chloe."

In swift parade marched pictures of the past few months: Chloe obviously interested in Roy Carsten; Mrs. Grayling opposing her, querulously disliking Roy, saying cutting things about him on all occasions; Chloe rebellious at her mother's domination; Mrs. Grayling making melodrama of her rebellion. It was a case between the two women of temperaments too similar in some respects, too different in others, ever to understand. Chloe's calm insistence on her right to love and marry whom she chose exasperated Mrs. Grayling, and she revenged herself by being consistently unpleasant when Roy or his affairs came up for discussion.

"Am I wrong, Kurt, to do it?"

"Gee, Chloe, I don't know. Your mother *has* been unreasonable about Roy, and he's a good chap. You — oughtn't you—" He was embarrassed and stopped awkwardly. Then he plunged ahead. "Oughtn't you to be sure you love him, or am I just old-fashioned?"

She laughed a bit, softly. "Funny boy! You're right, of course, and I suppose I do — but — oh — more than anything else, it's a chance to get away — and I must get away, must."

"I hope you'll be awfully happy, Chloe. You know that, I guess." Then he added, because he couldn't help doing so, "And I hope being married and all won't keep you from writing to me once in a while. I guess I've been counting on that. You've been so sympathetic — always — with me; the real me, inside, that does the things you think may mean something someday. Derry likes me too, but he — well, you know Derry and his letters."

She took his hand again, pressed it, took it suddenly to her lips, and then was gone into the house.

He hardly understood that. He was glad she was going to get away. She was too young, too full of promising things to be so submerged and defeated. Roy didn't seem her type, though, and he was afraid they might be unhappy. It was a little sadly that he sat in the swing waiting for Derry's return.

III

THE GRAYLINGS had driven him home, spent the night, and started back for Ann Arbor the next morning. The night with Derry — he had planned to say so many things, but he said nothing. Derry, tired from driving, and apparently unmoved by the impending separation, slept soundly. Kurt, his arms rigid at his sides, stared at the ceiling with its familiar patternings of lavender shadows, and wished them gone, wished them swallowed up in the blackness he had feared so as a child. His whole lonely life seemed somehow implicit in those shadows. More than anything else he wanted Derry's kiss and Derry's promise to remember. But Derry never awakened until Mrs. Gray called them for breakfast, so their parting was simply a clasp of hands and a few conventional words of farewell in the presence of his parents, of Mrs. Grayling, and of Chloe.

When the car turned the corner and was out of sight, his mind seemed seized with numbness. He turned and went listlessly in at the kitchen door, then lingered uncertainly near the books on the table and the music scattered about the floor near the piano. All day long the numbness held him. He read by snatches, sprawled on the davenport; he wrote two highly unsatisfactory letters; he rummaged through the music cabinet and, coming upon an album of Chopin nocturnes, played them over, from cover to cover, in a slipshod way, passively approving their lulling eroticism.

The meals with his father and mother were silent and uneventful, and the short evening, with a cribbage game between his father and himself, passed in some unaccountable fashion. Bedtime — his father went first, yawning and switching off the overhead lights, and then his mother with her expected and therefore doubly irritating "Better come to bed now!" He made no answer, but sat still until her footsteps reached the upper hall. He put his magazine down. The house was intimate and pleasant with only the one lamp at his elbow lighted. He sat still, dumbly thinking that there must be other days like this, days almost without number, it seemed now, until he could leave in August. He got up from the chair slowly and went to the kitchen.

The back door had been left open, as the night was warm, and the oblong of soft darkness seemed to call him forth. He unhooked the screen door and stepped quietly out into the night. The sky was full of stars, and the air was pervaded with a softness that came to him as a new experience. Stars were usually so distant, so glitteringly, so frighteningly precise and jewel-like. But tonight it was as if a dark veil had been flung across them. They were almost friendly. Now maybe he could think. Think. He needed to do that. There were so many things he did not understand, things that had never seemed so important as now. And they all centered, tangled, about himself and these two who had driven away this morning. Derry and Chloe. Derry and Chloe. And he must understand. It was a duty which he dreaded, and, paradoxically, craved to perform. It was his, individually. Neither of the other two could understand. Or, no, that was not fair. Chloe could understand, he trusted, if she knew. But there were things she did not know, must not know, things it was unthinkable that she should know. And he had not forgotten her kiss on his hand.

How strange and twisted it all was. There was Chloe with her cool gray eyes, her smooth black hair, and her mind which he felt he knew so well — her mind tempered and adjusted to a spiritual sympathy that was constantly amazing him. Chloe, never wholly happy, always questioning, always seeking, reacting to every thought and suggestion — like himself, never quite certain: Chloe with this mental equipment that he had come to know so well and to prize so highly during the past years, and Chloe with her woman's body that he knew not at all.

Then there was her brother, with his eyes gray too, but scornful; his dark hair tangled, his mind alert, objective — as incapable of fine sympathies as of deceit. Derry, with this mental equipment that was as clear and free of subtleties as a lump of polished glass, yet that constantly puzzled and repulsed him by its very concreteness. Derry, with the man-body he knew so well; the cool white skin, the firm chest, the lean belly and strong back, the thick thighs and calves, the wide blunt-fingered hands. There was a loneliness in Kurt, an emptiness, that throbbed and pulsated in the night. It made him think again of the darkness in which he used to cower.

The past few months had seen growing in him a beginning of understanding. He had read for the first time the new psychology — Brill, Jung, Freud, Ellis, Carpenter; he had discovered Wedekind. From them he learned that his sin and Derry's was not the unique sport he had believed it to be. There were others, it seemed (at least in Europe there were) of his sort. Plato he reread with a new interest. The high idealism of the *Phaedrus* and the *Symposium* had captured him and engulfed him as a flood. Now that there was a whole summer of inaction ahead, he could begin to formulate into ideas, maybe, the feeling that had been growing in him.

He was in love with Derry. He belonged to that strange class of humanity, the singularity of whose position appealed to the romantic in him at the same time that it overwhelmed him with its pathos. "I am the love that dare not speak its name," he read. He divided his time between his music and a stumbling search for knowledge. There was in him a yearning for the vicarious companionship of others like himself. Of an actual companionship other than Derry's, he never dreamed. It was as if he had been initiated into some secret fraternity, and, at every discovery of some new communicant in ages past, he felt a thrill of pleasure. There was Plato, beyond a doubt. There were Cellini, and Michelangelo, and Shakespeare. There was, he felt almost certain, Shelley.

Night after night, while his mother lay awake waiting nervously for his return, he fought with himself alone on the quiet streets, under the stars or the hiss of summer rain. A walker by night. The struggle went on wearingly, everlastingly, with small promise of victory on either side. The secrecy of his position maddened him, and yet it was a sweet madness. "I am the love that dare not speak its name — shame — name — shame—" The words were an insinuating counterpoint to his feet. The exaltation of his love sent him running, sometimes, along the grass-grown roads at the edge of the village, his arms raised to the sky, his face thirsting for the stars.

Nothing so rich, so filling, so troubling, so goading, could be evil. The world might say what it chose. "He is my lover! He is my lover!" He longed to shout it from the rooftops — "Behold, world, my lover!" He wept in the grass by the roadside for the blindness, the unfeeling stupidity, the unfairness of the world. He bated them all, the scoffers, the leaden-eyed. He throbbed with the music of rebellion and youth. He clutched his fingers in the cool dark sod and exhausted himself with weeping.

And then, always, his feet took him back through other dark streets to his own house, his own familiar room. What could he do — "I a stranger, and afraid, in a world I never made." Someday, he swore to himself, he would be brave. Now he could not. He would go wearily to bed, angry at the cough his mother gave to inform him that she had not yet slept — that he had kept her awake with worry. What he knew: what she knew. The chasm appalled him. Could it ever be bridged, he wondered?

His philosophy developed slowly, too slowly, and he was only too conscious of the great gaps in his new creed. It came to be, as days and weeks went by, a new religion. The old, by now, was an outgrown shell. Here was a love which the world, had it known, would have denounced as shame; a love whose altar fires must always burn in secret; whose priesthood walked alone, discovering only now and again, and then by chance, some other follower of the faith. He knew that he felt it to be beautiful and worthy of praise, but he knew too that he must endure always the martyrdom of silence. No boasting of his love — his first love — no word of it dared he breathe. Always, always, it seemed to him, life demanded secrecy and silence.

He had longed for Derry to know, as he knew. Derry must know, and yet he felt certain that Derry could never be made to understand. They hardly spoke the same language, he now realized. There was no way of making him see so high and perfect an ideal. Derry's letters through the summer had been brief things, full of laughing episodes of their summer life in Ann Arbor, of Chloe's approaching marriage, of a new friend, David Perrier; with a casual "Wish you were here" which Kurt fastened on avidly, cherishing and remembering. The new friend caused him some uneasiness.

He was afraid he detected in the letters some hint that David was taking his place.

He knew David as a clever student in architecture, whose hair, fellows said, was marcelled, and whose nails were always too gleamingly manicured, and whose eyes he had always found disturbing. He was not the sort you would ever call "Dave." He was David. That Derry should allow this outsider a place was unthinkable, and yet he feared it might be so. He tried as best he could to fit David into this new scheme of things.

He too, perhaps, was of the fellowship. Yet something in him rebelled at the idea. The ideal was too fine, too high. David, he felt, was too satisfied, too shallow to deserve this new and awesome calling. There was no niche for him.

The thought that Derry, incomprehensible Derry, had taken him in was sickening. He wrote a letter to Derry, and never mailed it. What he secretly feared was that this newcomer, this interloper, would say, "I love you," before he, Kurt, had said it in the way he felt he could now say it. Love to him was so indubitably the love of one for another ... there could be only two. For him, he knew there could be only Derry. That for Derry there might be David, or others, seemed incredible, frightful, yet he was increasingly certain that it was so.

He did send a letter at last. It was a halting thing, he felt, but his fear that Derry would not understand made the formulation of his faith nervous and worried. He waited anxiously for a reply. It failed to come. A week passed. His mind ran in circles in a lonely place, coming always back to the point from which it started. At last, only a week before Chloe's wedding, he wrote again:

Dear Derry,

The You I am writing to, I'm afraid, doesn't exist. I may be wrong in thinking so, and in that hope I write. There has been no reply to my letter of a week ago. You would accuse me of being fantastic, possibly even sentimental, when I say that the silence of these days has hurt me deeply. You are busy, I know, but there are always minutes when a few words can be written, even during the busiest days. Neither have I heard from Chloe, but that does not trouble me. Why?

Because I like you better, for one reason, and still more because I am less sure of your feeling for me — and it is that constant uncertainty that makes me so unhappy.

You are a strangely objective person, intolerant of emotion, yet full of it; and incapable, I have sometimes thought, of real sympathetic feeling. In addition you are more masculine than I. I am in many ways your exact opposite. My richest life comes always from the realm of thought and feeling rather than from that of things outside (color, sound, motion — the theatrical in life). There is a great deal of the feminine in me. If you will consider our friendship in its full course, from the time I first met you, you will realize that. It has been I always who have been the submissive one, you the aggressive. I have not once, that I can remember, failed to submit to your will and desire, and I can recall a great many times when you have received my rather timid overtures coldly.

As the years have gone on, the tie between us, so far as I am concerned, has grown stronger and stronger. I have come to hope and almost believe, sometimes, that there was between us a friendship based not solely on physical attraction, but on the spiritual thing men call love. I love you, then. That is to put it most simply. It is the fact that this simple statement, meaning so much to me, would make you uncomfortable that troubles me. Are you so conventionally minded? Can your objective mind not see the beauty of such a relationship? I keep hoping that you feel as I do, and I am continually disappointed.

An instance? The night of your brief visit here in June, there was on your part a withdrawal into yourself that was almost sullen. It was the last time we would be together for months. If you had put your hand in mine or your head against my shoulder I should have been content and happy. But you did not sense my need. You failed. It has been so, so many times. To you — what does our relation mean? I have tried to understand. What do you really feel towards me? You admire me, you think me good-looking and clever, perhaps; you like me a great deal. But if I should cease to exist, would it matter so much to you? Would there not be others? For me, there could be none. I am waiting now, waiting for our meeting next week. Do not fail me then. It would be harder than you can imagine for me to go away, so far away this time, if you should.

My love,

Kurt.

He read his letter over. It seemed a little dramatic, a little oratorical, yet it must be sent. He dropped it into the slot at the post office and returned home to busy himself with sorting books and music and a dozen going-away details. "Marking time," he thought. The fact that Chloe too must be left behind was almost forgotten in the fear that he would lose his place in Derry's life.

IV

KURT CAME BACK to Ann Arbor the day before the wedding. Derry met him at the station, pinched his arm, said, "Hello, kid! I guess you were worried some!" and laughed slyly. Kurt laughed too. In the light of Derry's smile all histrionics seemed silly and unimportant. The car took them up the hill and around the campus. "Home," thought Kurt. It was really another home, a place it meant something to return to.

The day was too full for thinking. There were flowers to gather and arrange, the caterer to see, Mrs. Grayling to console and pacify and wish at heart a thousand miles away, and a dozen details that no one seemed to have thought of. Derry was perfect; all he could desire. Talk and explanation seemed superfluous. The letter, thought Kurt exultantly, had had its effect. But before they slept, Derry said casually, "David wanted to come over tonight, but I thought he'd better not. You can see him tomorrow. You'll like him, I think. I know he'll like you — he does already. He's seen you on the campus, and he's begged your picture from me. He's crazy to meet you."

Kurt's satisfaction thawed and disappeared. He did not want to meet David. He knew, he felt, what he would be like, and he tried vainly to pierce Derry's mind, to understand certainly just what place David might hold in it. He had slight success. Not that Derry was subtle or secretive. He took, as a matter of fact, a torturing delight in talking to Kurt of David, in hinting at a relationship he would not freely admit. Kurt, choking down his questionings, said nothing. Was this jealousy, this weak, sick feeling that was upon him? Derry had failed to understand. Was there nobody, nobody in this whole world of patterned people who could understand? His misanthropy grew with his growing loneliness. Alone even lying here, beside the one he loved, alone.

The wedding came and was over. No one, Kurt was positive, was so nervous as he — not Chloe, not Roy, not even Mrs. Grayling, who, at the last moment — through one of those sudden changes that made her, like Derry, an enigma to everyone — had become tractable and even pleasant. He laughed at himself as soon as the ceremony was over. "You'd have thought I was the groom," he said to Roy, and then to several others, not knowing what to say.

One reason for his nervousness was the presence at the wedding of David Perrier. He had arrived only a few minutes before the ceremony. He had come, with Derry, into the bedroom where Kurt was finishing dressing. His eyes were troubling. There was in them, Kurt still felt, an intent to convey something without saying it.

"I'm very glad for this chance," he said, smiling. He clasped Kurt's hand longer than strangers usually do. "I've heard so much about you, from Derry, and on all sides."

Kurt smiled, and inwardly wished to the devil all such clichés and those who uttered them.

That was all. After the wedding, Chloe changed to a straight black dress which she had never worn before, and which subtly set her apart, he felt. "Something's changed in her," he thought, and tried to read her eyes as she shook hands. He did not offer to kiss her, and when she said good-bye at the station and offered her lips, he blushed and hesitated. She kissed him swiftly on the cheek, and was lost in a crowd of relatives. Fool! Fool! Why couldn't he have kissed her! He felt David's eyes, cruelly curious, upon him. No. No one was laughing. The train pulled away from the platform. With the rest he waved, and turned. David was beside him, and together they rode back to the house, saying little.

There, all was confusion. Folding chairs were strewn about, and voluble relatives were everywhere, chattering and munching the remnants of the cakes and sandwiches. "O Lord!" breathed Kurt as he came up the walk with David.

"Yes, isn't it a mess! Wouldn't you like to come over to my place for a bit, until things clear up here?"

Kurt looked at him curiously. "What's become of Derry?" he asked.

He was answered by Derry himself, clattering down the stairs with a flower basket.

"I've asked Kurt to come over to my rooms awhile, Derry, until you get rid of some of this turmoil."

"Grand idea. Go 'long, Kurt. I'll have to stick around awhile, I suppose, to keep the mob in check — and Lord knows how long they'll stay! Don't hurry back — and be good children!"

He blessed them paternally and gave them a shove down the steps. They walked slowly, talking of the school, of Chloe and Roy, of David's drawing, of Kurt's music. "I want to be alone — alone — alone" ran like an insistent pedal point through Kurt's mind.

"Here we are," said David.

They were turning in at an old house on a narrow street.

"I like it here because there's no one else in the house except the deaf landlady. She lets me do pretty much as I please, though I'm afraid she doesn't always approve."

The room he took Kurt into was surprising. Kurt had read of such places; he had never seen one, never supposed they existed so close at hand. It was, in its perverse way, perfect. Yet there was something in it, as in some of the Beardsley drawings, that revolted him. The walls were hung entirely in black cloth. There was a fireplace of vivid blue and orange tiles, and opposite, a low couch piled with cushions of a dozen shades. There was a coffee table, there was a Buddha, there were brass bowls and lacquered boxes, there was a lovely white statuette of a Greek Antinous that by the intensity of its whiteness and its cleanness of line made the rest of the room seem more artificial.

"It's — it's charming," said Kurt.

"Look around a bit. Help yourself to cigarettes. I'm going to make myself more comfortable. Back in no time."

He disappeared through a curtained door. There were no chairs; only cushions and low stools. The couch seemed most inviting, so he propped himself on pillows and lay still, too weary with the day to care, very much, about the room or about David, or about anything. He smoked idly, and closed his eyes. There was a step in the room. It was David. He had opened his collar and put on a Chinese coat of black silk, with a scarlet lining.

"Comfortable?" he asked, smiling.

"Very!" said Kurt. He waved his hand about him as David sat beside him on the edge of the couch. "You're not very collegiate, are you?"

"God forbid! Don't tell me you mind!"

"Of course not. I'll admit, though, this rather takes my breath away. I hadn't supposed there was anything quite so — so exotic in this he-man's university."

"No?" David fingered the sleeve of his dressing gown. Was he amused, Kurt wondered? He must talk, he supposed. One couldn't just lie there and blow smoke rings.

"No," he went on, "and you know it quite well. I don't run about much, but when I do I'm always confronted by pennants and golf sticks and traffic signs and covers from *College Humor* and *Photoplay*."

"I know. Stupid, isn't it?"

"I wonder. We all of us have a way of being so sure of our rightness. I suppose those pennants are much more right for them than all this would be, say. I can't quite picture an All-American halfback rhapsodizing over this."

They both laughed.

"You're apparently a tolerant soul, Kurt."

There was a silence. What was he to say to this fellow whose eyes were always upon him so disturbingly, carrying on, as it were, even while he talked, a second conversation with his eyes — a conversation in a language Kurt did not understand?

"You've a Victrola, I see. Can't we have some music?" What would he choose? He seemed to have a great many records. Kurt closed his eyes and waited. *L'Après-Midi d'un Faune.*

"Good! Good!" he murmured.

"I bought it after your review in the *Daily* last winter," said David, and lapsed into silence. Kurt opened his eyes only once, but closed them quickly when he felt those of David always upon him. He was almost afraid he understood their meaning.

There was the raucous noise outside of a Ford stopping, the scrape of the horn dying with the motor in a buzzing wail.

"It's Derry," said Kurt.

Feet pounded up the stair, and Derry came in.

"David," he said, "can Kurt stay here with you tonight? Some of the aunts have decided to stay over. I can sleep on the davenport, but that leaves you out, Kurt. I'm sorry it's happened like this, but you'll have a good time here."

"Of course you may stay. You will, won't you?" His voice was eager.

More politeness. More formulas. He was afraid to stay, and furious at Derry for not arranging in some way that this, his last night before going east, they might have spent together. He might have managed somehow, if he had wanted to badly enough. Derry seldom wanted the right thing at the right time. He felt a wounded self-pity. "I give everything to Derry," he thought, "and he casually turns me over to someone else. I wanted him tonight. He should have known that. He should have known."

"You'll stay, Kurt?" asked David's voice again. "Do! Do!" pleaded his eyes.

"It's decent of you to take me in" was all Kurt said.

"I brought your bag over, and now I'll have to go back," Derry said. "Come over in the morning, Kurt. I'll not be so rushed tomorrow."

Derry left, banging the door behind him. It was hurt which Kurt felt most. People shouldn't be able to hurt other people so. Derry was, sometimes, like a Frankenstein, incapable of understanding. He must not let David see how he was feeling. David had, in the meantime, put another record on the Victrola, and to the music of it he seemed terribly and starkly alone — hungry with his love and sick with disappointment. What he craved was understanding. And what he despaired of ever finding was understanding. The nostalgic sweetness of being young, of having a secret from an antagonistic world, swept over him with the music, and had he been alone he would have cried out, and paced the floor. The irony of the impulse curled his lip. Why not cry out? He was alone — really alone — always alone. These eyes that promised so disturbingly could not intrude on his aloneness. He would be as much alone in a crowded street as in the woods on an autumnal noon. Always, everywhere alone. David's voice was piercing through:

"Shall we have some more music?"

Music was too disturbing.

"Could we walk a bit?" he suggested.

"Good idea. It's nearly dinnertime, anyway."

As they walked it was an effort to make conversation. Kurt wanted only to be alone, in mind and body. He yearned for it, and played, with a sad sort of satisfaction, with the idea that had formulated itself in his mind with the flow of the music in David's room. It made him seem a romantic figure, romantic because of his difference, because of this invisible yet impenetrable wall which was building, building, building between him and the world. How big did one have to be, he wondered, to live so always, feeding always on oneself, and, spiderlike, spinning such beauty as one might out of one's own being? The thought of the years ahead, old age, sent his mind huddling and shivering back to a present when loneliness could have, being young, a sad and acrid beauty.

They dined in a tearoom Kurt had seldom been able to afford. The dinner was good. They talked again of books, of music, of things both enjoyed. Kurt felt in David — perhaps because of his exterior, his monogrammed cigarettes, his nails that were too perfectly polished, his clothes that were just too correctly fitted — that his mind too must be a thing of surface glitter, of right opinion; right, by the sophisticated standards of the young wits and clever-minded scoffers. He kept conversation pretty much on that level, but once, twice, an enthusiasm flamed through the languor of this elegant young man. Kurt suddenly wondered how much this exterior, that both attracted and repelled him, concealed — how just his judgment had been. Was this too, perhaps, but another wall, but another means of protection? The thought intrigued him, and he forgot himself, playing with it through this casual talk of people and things at dinner, and, later, back in David's room. He found himself consciously prying into this mind, consciously trying to fathom it. Was it possible that here too was a soul sensitive and afraid, masking its fear and its solitude behind a cynical and sophisticated exterior? He forgot his own loneliness in conjecture. Walls, walls again. Why was it that people sat eternally repeating platitudes when they wanted to thrust through to the pulsing realities? And he perhaps too, this one I have disliked, is wanting to break the wall and dissolve the barrier.

The fire died down at last. The room seemed to grow as the light flickered and faded. Its black walls dimmed and receded. The white statuette of the Greek boy stood alone, white with an almost phosphorescent whiteness in the gathering darkness, glowing against and through it. They had been for a long time silent. David rose, then, from the cushion where he had been sitting cross-legged by the fire. He stood for a moment before the hearth, his head thrown back. Kurt could not see his hands, but he knew from the rigidness of his position that they were clenched before him. It was a pose he recognized. He was almost sure now. If he were only brave enough—

And then David turned. Kurt could not see his face, but his voice was one he did not know. Its languorous correctness was gone. It was half-stifled, as if by fright. He came to the couch where Kurt lay and was silhouetted against the uncertain flicker that filled the room. Then he dropped down beside him, and his hand, touching Kurt's, closed over it. Something in Kurt went rigid with resistance. He would draw his hand away. All the malice he had felt rising towards David during the past few weeks surged up in him coldly. But strangely he did not stir.

"Kurt Gray — Kurt Gray—" The voice came huskily. "I'm afraid as hell. I must say this, or I'll die. I — oh — I've wanted to so long, thought it over and over and over, known just what I would say and how I'd say it — and now, now that you're really here as I've pictured you so often — it won't come. You see — Kurt — after I've said it, you may hate me always — but I must say it — I must, I must. I — I love you, Kurt — oh God, how I love you!"

Kurt's throat constricted. A coldness pressed like metal against the back of his neck. What was this — what was this—

"Oh, Kurt, don't hate me, please. I've waited so long, fearing you wouldn't understand, trying to find out the words to make you understand, trying to learn from Derry if you would, and I couldn't be sure — I've had to take this chance at last."

Kurt could feel his tenseness like a leaping spark through the darkness.

"Will you tell me one thing — Kurt? Do you love Derry?"

His secret. His secret — yet now he could not lie.

"I love him," he whispered.

"I thought so, Kurt — I thought so. Now I know at least that you will understand what I'm feeling. Now I can say everything. There is always such fearful danger in this — this breaking down of walls."

His own words!

"Breaking walls. Yes. There was a chance, you see, such a great chance, that you weren't like that — that you weren't — 'queer'" — he laughed in derision at the word — "and then — and then you see — you'd have left me and I'd have lost you. Now there's maybe a chance that I can make you like me—"

Kurt said nothing. His head swirled with uncertainty. This was a thing he had not foreseen. Was it possible to love two people at the same time? What was he to say? Derry's indifference—

"I am going to kiss you, Kurt."

The face, the eyes, drew to him out of the shadow. Lips against his own — not Derry's lips. Why did he lie so still? Why was his tongue curled helplessly in his mouth? Why did he allow this? It was mad, mad.

"You understand now?"

He lay still, without answering, his arm across his eyes. He had been false to his ideal — or had he? Nothing was certain.

"What can I say?" There were torturing minutes of silence. "There is so much to understand — you've surprised me so—"

"I know, I know — my dear."

"It — oh, I don't know how to say it to you. I'm not, I guess, a person who gives himself very easily, in any way. Not many people know me. That's my reputation, isn't it? So it's a shock to be so taken by storm. All things with me — things that have mattered really and deeply — seem to have grown so slowly, so very slowly and stumbled so — I can't make this seem—"

"I felt that, Kurt. I can't expect, I know — but it's been slow with me, too. I've wanted to know you so long, so awfully long. I used to meet you on the Diagonal sometimes. Derry seemed the only way — and now you know, and — oh, what's the difference! It's such a damnable constraint that's put on fellows like us, Kurt. If you hadn't been one of us, you see, I'd have lost you, you would have despised me, even laughed at me. And there's nothing so bitter, so utterly cruel on God's earth as the intolerance people have of this sort of thing. Why are they so damned smug! I hate them all. They think we are scum, some sort of decadent perverts. And I know, and you know too, Kurt, that nothing so beautiful, so filling, deserves such hate. It's unreasoning. It's beastly and hellish."

The wall had disintegrated and crumpled like a dream. Here was a wall down, a mask set aside, a something real and vibrant and amazing, a language he understood. Amazement was perhaps Kurt's chief reaction — amazement at himself and at David. Was it possible that this was the suave superior young man with whom he had dined so short a time ago, this eager tense boy? The voice went on in the dark — about dreams, ideals, and he let it go — liking it, wondering at it, yet afraid because it upset him so, because his throat pounded and his scalp tingled with it.

"I love you, Kurt. I've never loved anyone as I love you. You believe me, don't you? Derry was just a wedge, a gate to you. O Kurt, there's only one way I know of to show you how fearfully much I love you — dear, dear boy!"

Darkness. Hands not Derry's. An arm beneath his shoulders, not Derry's. A swift and burning joy — and Derry not sharing it.

A night of restlessness and fitful dreaming. A morning of promises, and, at last, because he knew David wanted it so much, his proffered kiss on David's eager lips.

"I guess I like you a good bit, David."

"You'll learn — I'll teach you — make you learn."

The room by daylight seemed a gloomy place, almost oppressive.

"Your room is made for the night, David."

David smiled at him from the tumbled couch as he went about the room flinging back the heavy drapes and letting in the cold clarity of the day.

"I'd be utterly happy if time were all night — provided you were here. It's so secure and certain. The night you can make what you please. The day seems to run away from you, to be such common property."

Kurt shrugged his shoulders. "It's the room. Daylight wouldn't be so — so ominous, anywhere else. You should get yourself a day room, too, one that's all light as this is all dark."

"No. I'm quite contented with this. I'll just keep the curtains closed."

They breakfasted on toast and jam and strong coffee drunk from Chinese bowls.

"You're really going to New York today?"

"I'm supposed to see Korlov, Monday morning."

"It's all wrong, Kurt, that I should have so little of you when I've been so long waiting for you."

Kurt was silent.

"Maybe I'll be seeing you soon, though."

"No! You're coming to New York, too?"

"I want to. Ozzy wants me to come to Philadelphia, but I want to go to New York. I always have, more or less, and now that you're to be there ... I love it. He'll let me, I think. He's a pretty good sort."

Kurt looked puzzled.

"You don't know Ozzy. He's a — a sort of guardian. He's been — very good to me." He smiled, a little ironically, but said nothing more.

Kurt walked back to the Graylings' alone. In him there was a singular mixture of emotions. There was elation and guilt. He had

been untrue to Derry, and to all the theorizing he had so painfully
built up during the summer months. Something had happened to
his carefully constructed code, or to a part of it; but in the debacle
he had found a lover and a greater understanding. It flattered
something in him. Derry had never given him that satisfaction.
Derry was an uncertain quantity. Always, Kurt suspected, it went
no deeper with him than the physical thing. Derry had never said,
"I love you." He laughed a bit, and found a spinsterly summer-
school student staring at him curiously. It was funny now, almost,
to think of Derry in the role of lover. Yet he had always wanted that
so much — still did. He had let David supply the lack in a moment
of pique and indifference. Was it to go on?

He needed time to think it all out again, and for the moment
his mind rebelled. He tried to forget it all. The heavy luxuriousness
of summer was soothing. The morning sun, mottling through the
elms, was warm on his back and made pleasant patterns on the
walk. Patterns that would change and thin when fall came; from
day to day the change would hardly be noticed, and then, at last,
there would be only the skeleton shadow of bare branches. A
potpourri — from the opera *Martha*. His mind veered back to the
ten-cent edition he had bought at the piano store in Barton,
unknown to his teacher, and worked at much more sedulously than
at his scales — a bit of this air, a bit of that, clumsily bound together
with arpeggios and obvious modulations. Then, at thirteen, its
disjointedness had seemed beautiful. Now the similar disjointedness of his thinking seemed, if not beautiful, narcotic and inoffen-
sive. He was reluctant to bring it to order. Let it go for now.
Tonight, in the sleeper en route to New York, he would settle it all.

But it would not settle itself. He left after supper, a pickup affair
with bits of this and that left from the wedding refreshments. He
stood on the steps of the Pullman watching until the darkness and
a hiss of steam drowned them all. He went into the brightly lighted
car with the picture still in his mind: Mrs. Grayling waving gloomily, Derry racing along the track shouting unintelligible lunacies,
David behind him, waving not at all, alarmingly correct — but with
eyes that bothered him more now, he thought, that David was not
there, than the night before when he had been so close.

There were too many threads, and they were too tangled. What was to come, what was left behind? He lay awake for hours, it seemed, with thoughts as inchoate as the dulled thunder of the train, the occasional flashes of light as he was swept through little stations, the muffled *crescendo* and *diminuendo* of crossing signals, like cleverly played glockenspiels. The potpourri again, with a new accompaniment. David — Derry — David — Derry — love — love — David — David.

V

KURT FOUND HIMSELF plunged so deeply into his work that he had little time to formulate his reactions to the city. He had gone to a Times Square hotel which David had recommended as being reasonable and accessible. He had spent the evening after his arrival threading his way through the crowds on Broadway and Seventh Avenue. The cheapness and glitter of it sent his mind shrinking into itself. But the river of stars above his head, turned to a luminous orchid with the reflected and softened glow of the street signs, was strange and thrilling. He walked until he was tired, until his head buzzed with the mingled clangor of voices, of feet shuffling on cement, the grating of taxis, the rumble and screech of streetcars, the sullen subterranean thunder of the subway. It was crushing. And somewhere in this confusion he must find himself a place of quietness and aloneness. The light from a tower nearby flashed intermittent bars of lilac and vermilion on the coverlet of his hotel bed, and it made him think, suddenly, of that other lilac through that other window of his old room at home. "As the moor hen builds her a nest in the watery sod, behold I will build me a nest in the greatness of God."

A city can do strange things to people. To Kurt it did little, spiritually. It broadened him, as all new knowledge must. It taught him things about people in crowds. It taught him by observation many things he had known before only through his books. But it wedged itself, its buzzing, kaleidoscopic, uproarious self, almost not at all into him. It was as if his aloofness, his aloneness, was a round and polished surface on which the wedge could never find entry, but was deflected and sent, tangential, touching but never intruding, on its blind way. For he was still very much alone; and learning, he sometimes feared, to cherish his aloneness with a miserly satisfaction — to gloat a bit over the smoothness of his life. He gave it small thought for the most part. He was too busy. But sometimes he felt, without being willing to admit that he felt, his own life's oppression, and yearned for the prick of the wedge.

He worked at his music as he had worked in college — without questioning the rightness of his endeavor. His study here was the part of music he liked least — the drudgery of mechanics in composition. But he knew its necessity and labored at it with no feeling of martyrdom. An acoustical mathematics, it was, as necessary to him as conventional mathematics to an architect. He could always reassure himself and at the same time divert himself with a concert or with the perfectly realized scores the public library afforded him.

He found himself a room far uptown. David had suggested the Village; but the Village, as he walked through it the second morning after his arrival, seemed to him even more oppressive than the Forties. The drab brick fronts, the littered streets, the garbage in the gutters repelled him. The occasional blue door or gay window or fretted gateway denoting an interior utterly belying the squalor without, interested him; but, he knew, could not make him content. If he were like David, it might. David could live inside, but something in him demanded an outside too.

So his third morning of searching took him up Riverside Drive, where the sweep of the river, with its fringing trees, was something he could look at and maybe love a little. The room he got at last was small, but it was high in a gable, and it had a window looking out across the Hudson, and he knew it would do. Here he spent most of his time. Classes and practice over, he would hurry back to it. There was usually something waiting for him there — a letter from home, from Derry, from Chloe, from David. The old ties, save David — one new one. He laughed sometimes to think how little difference place seemed to make. His whole emotional life was still bound up with these same personalities, not present now to laugh and talk with, but nonetheless, though rather unsatisfactorily, present.

From his father and mother and from Derry, letters were transparent enough — the doings of the passing days at home, facetious comments on people he and Derry had known in college. The letters from David and from Chloe were more disturbing. David's were full of promises and protestations and threats to descend suddenly upon him and carry him off to some distant and exotic rendezvous. They were eager and hungry and rebellious (Ozzy apparently objecting to the New York idea) at the fate that kept him for an additional year in Ann Arbor. Were they a bit too facile? At any rate they were letters such as a fictional heroine might thrill to receive, and they pleased something in him.

He could, at this distance, detach himself almost completely, and regard the scene — David and himself — as an interlude on the stage; two lovers in a world apart, a fictionized world. It influenced his replies; for his letters to David, while much less exotic and unrestrained, were almost equally literary. He thought them sincere. They were sincere, but they were cast in a literary style. "The rain is cold tonight. It runs like silver down my small window. The flame under the kettle is blue in the dusk. Why aren't you here for tea, David?" Or, "I'm lonely. I shall walk along the river. The lights will waver in it, and on the benches under the almost naked trees there will still be, here and there, two, or one; two alone, or one alone; and I too will be lonely."

With Chloe it was much the same. Had he been wiser in the ways of women with men, and men with women, he would have been more circumspect. For Chloe's letters, as the year grew older, became more and more personal. Though she never said so, openly, in her letters, Kurt could overhear in them a growing dissatisfaction with her life. He had feared it would be so. Chloe was so much a creature of moods, so elfin at times, so jealous of the beauty of life, so different from Roy. She had been for a long time almost his only audience, and certainly his chief encouragement. His songs had been sung first, or only, to her. Her sympathy he

could rely on. She had urged him to continue. Her marriage, she
had assured him, should make no difference. So he had continued
to write to her of his work as he had previously told her of it, to
scribble off the themes of his new compositions for her.

They were having a hard time of it, Chloe and Roy. Roy was
not well. He was listless and took little interest in his job. He was
irritable, and Chloe had to work, herself — first in the art department of a Detroit department store, later in the office of a private
school.

"I'm just home from work," she wrote. "A snowy cold day.
There was no letter in the box from you, as I had hoped there
might be. I want so much to talk to you again. I could almost
jump a freight such afternoons as this and come straight to New
York."

And Kurt would reply in the same vein. Night after night he
would sit in the small shadowy room writing carefully phrased
letters to the other inhabitants of his small world.

"I'm becoming a man of letters," he wrote to David. "It's not
right; psychologically I'm being repressed and God knows what, I
suppose. I should go on a social spree occasionally, to be psychologically sound and normal and safe from the analysts. But I don't.
Don't want to. I simply sit here and write to you, and to Derry and
Chloe, because you're not here to talk to. Other people don't
interest me much. Should they? Am I *Le Misanthrope* in modern
dress?"

It was to him a world removed from reality, yet perfectly real
and vital to him. It was almost like the old days in Barton, playing
theater in Nob's barn. Only now he was essaying the more difficult
histrionic feat of playing all the roles himself. To Derry, and to
Derry's family and his own, he was most matter-of-fact. He should
have liked to carry his small drama over into his letters with Derry,
but Derry would not play up. To David he was the absent beloved,
to Chloe the romantic young artist relying upon her for encouragement and understanding. He was, without being aware of it,
dramatizing himself, and doing an admirable job of it.

He went home for the holidays and stopped off for a day and a
night at the Graylings'. Derry was there, bursting with delight to

have him back, punning and playing the fool as he had always done. David had been called to Philadelphia. Chloe had come home too, alone. She had little to say, but Kurt could feel her watching him, and he dreaded seeing her alone, carrying over into actuality the situation their letters had created. When Mrs. Grayling had gone to bed, however, he sent Derry away. "I want to talk to Chloe for a bit, kid. Go to bed — but don't dare go to sleep, for after I'm through with her I shall want to talk to you the rest of the night."

Derry, grumbling and complaining, and signaling behind his sister's back, did as he was told.

"You want to talk to me, Kurt?"

"Isn't that what we've been promising ourselves all these weeks?"

The fire was burning dully in the grate. Kurt lay on the davenport. Chloe took a cushion and sat beside him on the floor. Her eyes were fixed on the dying fire.

"Someone ought to paint you that way, Chloe."

She started. "How — what—"

"In silhouette, against a wall all flecked with fire colors."

"Oh — no." She stretched her arms over her head, brought them down rigidly behind her, and lay back on their support.

"It's — oh, I can't tell you what it is to be here with you again, Kurt dear."

She shouldn't. He was afraid of what she might tell him.

"You're happy, aren't you, with Roy?"

She only looked at him, and then immediately back into the fire, not answering.

"Kurt, why is life so strange, so wrong?"

"Is it so wrong, Chloe?"

She was silent then for a long time. He fancied she was crying. Suddenly her hand brushed her eyes, and seeking gropingly for his own hand, fastened over it.

"I've missed you so," she whispered, "so terribly."

He drew his hand away quickly and sat up.

"Chloe, please! You mustn't, you mustn't."

He got up brusquely and walked to the fire. He felt himself trembling. What was this? Did she love him? He didn't love her, he knew. He liked her, he had perhaps even tried to persuade himself, when he was writing those beastly letters, that he loved her. What had they said, those letters? He must be more careful. She should never have said that. He felt her standing behind him, and stiffened.

"I must, Kurt." Her voice was breathless, and the words seemed forced out of her lips against her will. "I must — I must. Why pretend that I'm happy! I'm not — I'm hating it all. Roy's a boor. He laughs at what I say and read and think. I can't talk with him. We don't speak the same tongue. Oh, it's been such a rotten mistake, this business!"

He did not turn, but he knew she was behind him, rigid and tense, her mind crowded with resentments against Roy which pushed her unresisting towards him.

"Please, Chloe. I'm sorry." There seemed nothing else to say. He faced her and put his hands on her shoulders. He felt her relax and sway towards him, but held her tautly away. "Here, let's sit down now and talk about it." If it were solely that, it was unfortunate but not utterly serious. People were finding all the time that they were mismated. He had been afraid of it. This thing did not touch him, save as a friend. If only she did not love him, or fancy so—

"Tell me about it, if you care to."

"It's just that I don't love him, Kurt. I wonder if I ever did. I've tried, honestly I have. Oh, it's as much my fault as his, maybe. I wouldn't have married him, I guess, if Mother hadn't been so eager that I shouldn't. I did want to get away — still do. I can't stand home any better now than then, for long. But the marriage is wrong, Kurt, all wrong and twisted. We've nothing in common. Roy hates what he calls my 'highbrow manner.' We're the Kennicotts all over again. Maybe I'm wrong, but I can't see that it's right or moral to go on living with him, feeling as we both do."

"What are you going to do about it, Chloe?"

"I — I've done it already, Kurt. I saw a lawyer this afternoon. He said I could get a divorce pretty easily and without much fuss. I'll have to claim non-support."

"Non-support? Does that seem quite square to Roy?"

She looked at him questioningly before she replied. "Does it seem unfair to you? He's not supported me, you know, and since this imagined illness of his we've had a pretty wretched time of it."

"You mean he's not ill really?"

"Of course he's not ill. He looks perfectly well and eats and sleeps well. You don't know his family. I didn't either. They are all that way — always fancying something's the matter with them. The doctor calls it a nervous condition, very peculiar — but he has to call it something, I suppose, to collect his fees. They are enough, God knows!"

"You think you can't try it just a bit longer, to make sure—?"

"Sure! My God, Kurt! I *am* sure! If marriage can't make two people happy it's as wrong and as immoral as — as the things they put people in jail for. There is no other way out. If there were any other way at all of freeing myself, don't you suppose I'd do it? But there isn't, and I must be free. O Kurt—" She laid her head back, the curve of her throat like marble in the half-light, and cried silently, her fingers clutching the chair arms. What could he do or say? He walked behind her, and with his hands stroked her forehead and the sleek blackness of her hair.

"Don't cry — don't cry — there's such a lot in the world for you, Chloe," and he went quietly upstairs. Derry was asleep, and he undressed in the dark and crept into bed without rousing him. The scene in the room below had upset him. He was not sleepy. He tried to reassure himself. "I've had no part in this. It's not my doing, not at all my doing." Yet back in his mind, like a festering splinter, was the thought that perhaps, all innocently, he had.

VI

CHRISTMAS ... It was not a white Christmas, and Kurt's parents bewailed the fact. It was cold, but the heavy clouds held no promise of snow. An unusual season, everyone agreed. Inside the

Grays' house, everything possible had been done to make up for the unaccommodating weather. Mrs. Gray had hung wreaths of holly in the windows, and paper bells on the chandeliers. In the front bay window, just as when he was a little boy, was a Christmas tree shining with tinsel and paper stars. On Christmas Eve they all went to church for the "big tree." Kurt saw the familiar barrenness of the place with an amused smile. He received the greetings of the people who knew him pleasantly. They were good people; such badness as they were guilty of was unwitting. Stupidity was their greatest sin. And if you looked at the church simply as a club of some sort, stripping it of its spiritual pretenses, it was no more and no less baneful than the Odd Fellows or the Eastern Star.

Spirituality ... what was it? He was conscious of it in himself, without conceit, and conscious of a lack of it in most of these dull-eyed faces around him. Yet they were religious and he was not. Goethe's "Who has Art has also Religion; who has not Art, let him have Religion" flashed through his mind and made him smile at the hopelessness of ever making these people understand so simple and obvious a truth. It made him seem a conceited snob, but he knew it to be true. *"Il est un homme spirituel,"* he had heard Korlov say one time of a Polish poet of his acquaintance. That was the thing, *"spirituel."* The English never had created so exact a word for it; though many of them, he suspected, possessed the quality to a higher degree than the French. But it had taken the French to name it.

A group of towheaded children, dressed in starchy white and proudly conscious of their new shoes and ties and ribbons, were singing a whining little song about sheep and a star and a baby.

He thought of Schantz — Schantz of the shining glasses and the steamy voice — and of his own youth, and the stormy emotions of those days. He looked curiously about him, and in the choir and here and there in the congregation he could pick out boys and girls as old now as he had been then.

"It's they. They are the ones! What are they thinking and feeling? If I were brave enough I would know them all. Their armor isn't riveted yet. They could be saved." Saved. The words of

Schantz and the words of his own mind mingled strangely. "Come to Jesus, come to Beauty and Understanding. Let Beauty come into your hearts — you boys — you girls — your young sweet souls — white bodies — who'll come — who'll come? All young, all beautiful, come to Jesus, come to Beauty and be saved." No, there was not enough courage in him. "But I will not lose this," he promised himself, "I will not ever lose this."

Christmas and his brief vacation passed quickly enough. There was much to talk about for a time, much he could tell his father and mother of New York, where they had never been. Then the time began to drag a bit, and he became eager to return to his work. He had a letter from David, full of regret that they had been unable to meet during the holidays. From Chloe he heard nothing. Then, three days after Christmas, and four before his departure for the East, a letter came from Detroit in a hand he did not recognize. He opened it and the signature "Roy" confronted him. His heart skipped a beat, and he put the letter hurriedly into his pocket; and, at the first opportunity, went to his room. He read it, his fingers trembling. It told him briefly that Chloe had filed suit for divorce; but it told him further that, when pressed for a reason, she had said, "Because I love Kurt." Roy wanted a meeting the following day in Grand Rapids.

What did it mean? Why should she admit to Roy what she would not avow to him? He wished he knew Roy better. Would there be a scene? He felt singularly incompetent and weak. There was nothing for it, of course, but to meet him as he suggested, and yet it would be difficult to manage. His mother would think it strange if he were to go away for even one day of his vacation when his stay at home was so brief. He foresaw lies and explanations and evasions and just now he was too nervous to concoct a likely story. He hated the whole mess.

He finally went downstairs.

"Oh, Mother! I've a letter here from a chap — a music publisher I met once in New York. He is in Grand Rapids and wants me to see him. I think, if you don't mind too much, I'd better run up the first thing in the morning. I can be back by noon, and it might mean something for me."

She looked her disappointment, and he hated the necessity for this untruth. But she only said, "Of course, dear. I hate to have you away even for a minute, you're here for such a dinky little while anyway, but you know best, and maybe as you say you ought to see him. And you can still have some of that pork pie I was planning for your dinner tomorrow."

Next day the rain that had been threatening came down in cold sheets, lashing against the panes and freezing as it fell. His mother awakened him. "It's a terrible day, Kurt. You'd better give up your trip to the city. I'm afraid you'll catch cold."

He sat up, awake at once. "No, I'll go. The weather won't hurt me."

"But it's so cold and nasty out, dear, and you mustn't go back to New York with a cold or a sore throat."

Still the worrying mother. He laughed off her remonstrances. "You treat me like a little boy, Mum!" he said, feeling as he said it very much like one. Putting on his slicker over his topcoat, he set out for the station.

He arrived early in Grand Rapids and sat on a station bench waiting for Roy. He was overdue, but the trains were late, due to the weather. Kurt was cold and miserable. He hated Roy, he hated Chloe, he hated himself for allowing this thing to happen. The wedge. The wedge. Was this to be it at last? Was the calm progression of his life to be upset in this utterly common way? Tabloid headlines jumping out blackly from pink paper amid the tumult of Times Square flashed like shots from an erratic motion picture through his mind: "Young Musician in Love Tangle; Composer Blamed for Breach" — oh, it was sickening, incredible that this should happen to him.

A train came pounding to a stop under the streaming iron roof. Kurt got up and watched the cars anxiously. There. There he was. He swung off the last coach, which had come to a stop outside the shelter. He was without a hat, and wore knickers. He arrived before Kurt breathless, shaking the rain from his coat, and turning down his collar.

"Hello! Gee, what a day! It was sunny in Detroit early this morning — not at all like Christmas — so I came as I was."

Kurt managed to say the expected things.

"It was damn cold on the car. Can't we get a cup of coffee somewhere, and talk as we eat? I'm froze." His teeth were chattering.

He was more nervous than cold, Kurt knew, and that gave him some encouragement. They went to the station restaurant and drank in silence.

"You're looking well, Roy."

"Yeah? Say, where can we talk?"

There was nothing for it but the waiting room. It was a sorry place, an unsympathetic place, but the rain was coming down harder than ever; and the walks, the poles, the wires, were glazed with ice. They took a bench in the far corner of the room, near a pounding radiator, facing the wall, yellow and gray above the streaked wainscot.

Neither spoke for a moment. "Let him start," thought Kurt. "He must start. What will it be? What will he have to say?"

"Well—" Roy was hesitant. His fingers played nervously with the buttons on his coat. "Gosh, I'm still cold. Well — there's just one question I've got to ask, I guess. You know what's happened between me and Clo — about her wanting a divorce, I mean. If she were free would you marry her?"

"No. No, Roy — I've never thought of such a thing."

Liar, liar. He had. Of course he had. But never seriously. Only in this world of make-believe, this fictional world of his letters and Chloe's; in which they were paper men and paper women, manipulated at will, thinking in a fictionally right way, behaving always with the logic of the world of romance. But perhaps Chloe had been serious? If he could only explain all this to Roy, if he could only say, "See here, can't you understand it's Derry I love — Derry and David?"

"I thought not. You see, I was just about floored when I got wind of all this. I knew we hadn't been hitting it off very well, of course, but I thought she loved me. And I love her, Kurt, I really do, and if she goes through with this it will finish me. I haven't got much of a reputation in my field yet, but it won't help what I have got any if it gets around that I'm being sued for non-support. It's that that hurts. I've not been well. I'm not, now. You can see how nervous I am, and she — oh, hell!"

Kurt listened without comment. Let him say it all.

"Well, I went out to Ann Arbor to see her right away. Mrs. Grayling met me like a thundercloud and sailed out of the room. I'll bet she listened in, too, damn her. I wasn't mean, but I guess I was a little excited. I asked her if she thought she was giving me a square deal, asked her what I'd done that she didn't like. She wouldn't say anything, and wouldn't sit down, or ask me to. Just stood there, white and so damned superior, while I kept on talking and asking her what was the big idea. Finally she sort of wilted and went right down on the floor in a heap. 'If you must know,' she said, 'it's because I love Kurt.' Gosh! You could 'a knocked me over with a feather! I guess I stammered a little. She went on then, sort of crying — said you were someone she could admire, someone who understood her — that I had never been, that she had always loved you, and you would marry her as soon as you could. Well, I just walked out after a while. Couldn't do anything else. I was pretty sure she was wrong."

He seemed anxious to keep Kurt from embarrassment, and Kurt was grateful.

"You've written her, I know—"

"Yes, of course. We've been friends a long while."

"I know. But I know your sort and Chloe's, better than she'll admit. You're what they call the 'artist type.' Women fall for you. To my kind you'll always seem just a little nutty (you'll excuse me for saying this right out). It always seemed to me a little phoney, a little put-on, all this highbrow stuff, and I thought I could laugh Clo out of it and bring her down to earth. I couldn't. The more I kidded her, the worse she got. She thinks you're worth admiring and I'm not. That's all. I sell advertising in Detroit, and you write music in New York. So you're an artist, and I'm a Babbitt. That's what she's cracked over."

Kurt started to interrupt.

"No — I know — you are, of course. Oh, maybe she's not been happy; maybe I've not been pleasant all the time, but when she gets on that damned superior manner of hers it makes me sore, and I suppose I rub it in. It seems to me like such a lot of hooey. But I do love her, Gray."

They could never hit it off, thought Kurt.

Roy continued. "I don't know what to do. I've thought about it all the way over here this morning. If I'm right, and I'm pretty sure I am, you're the only one who can patch this thing up."

"You know I'll do anything I can, Roy."

"Well, I figure it this way. See if I'm not right. She's hipped on the idea of your being an artist, with ideals and everything. All right. If we could jolt her out of that, it might fix things. I mean, couldn't you write her and tell her that what you're doing is just a lot of hokum? That you're just in it to fool the world into giving you a big graft? Oh, it's not true, of course it's not true," he added hastily, sensing Kurt's instinctive shrinking at the idea, "but couldn't you do it?"

He thinks it *is* true. I can understand Chloe now, and Roy too. How dare he ask me that? Why doesn't he look somewhere else? Can't he see that this is as important to me as his happiness is to him? It would be sacrilege, an unspeakable betrayal.

And yet he was sorry for Roy in a way. He knew in his heart that he should do this thing, and yet he knew at the same time that it would never work out as Roy planned. He knew Chloe too well, and she him.

"It won't work, Roy."

"I think it will. She won't know I've seen you, see? That's part of the scheme. Let her think this all comes on your own — you've been thinking it over, see? And decided—"

It seemed an impossible request. It was smashing such an important part of his world. Yet there was a chance that it might work. Any outsider would say so, he felt. Would it? Wasn't there something deeper? If there were, could he destroy it so cold-blood-edly? Wasn't it possible that, with love or without it, Chloe's faith in him meant more to her than any relation she might have with Roy? It seemed a preposterously conceited thought, yet wasn't it possible? Still he was sorry for them both. Should he do it?

"I don't think it will work, Roy. I can't explain, for you wouldn't understand — which probably sounds exactly like what you're used to hearing from Chloe. But it's true. If you want me to write the letter, though, I'll do it. I don't know how good an actor I am." And in his own mind he added, "When it comes to abasing myself."

"Good boy, Kurt. I do think it will work. If it won't, it's all up with us, and you're a good scout to do it for me, whatever happens."

"Oh, forget it. I'm not going to help you much, I'm afraid. I *am* sorry for all this, Roy."

He felt a traitor to his own cause. How could Roy calmly ask such a thing of him? It would be cruel and untrue. He was glad, when the announcer shouted: "Hastings! Charlotte! Lansing! Detroit! *B-o-a-r-d!*" and Roy disappeared on the train. He paced the platform for a half-hour waiting for his own train and wondering why he had been such a fool as to promise that absurd letter. He tried to phrase it, but it seemed, however he worded it, glaringly false and insincere. What will come of this? What will come of this? He was hazy about divorces and trials and the law, but he knew they sometimes involved scandal and ugliness. It would kill his mother.

His head whirled with fear of what might happen, with remorse for all his innocent literary philandering, with regret at his promise, with what he should tell his father and mother of his trip to the city. Nothing was clear. He only knew that he was desperately sad and sick and leaden with unhappiness.

Dinner, a little late to accommodate his train, was a torturing half hour. What he said about his "interview" with the nonexistent publisher he never knew. It was an effort to eat, to talk, to look at his mother. "What's wrong, son? You're not eating much. You ought to be hungry after a jaunt in weather like his." She said it in a half-dozen different ways. He praised the pork pie and tried to reassure her, knowing all the time that he was not succeeding.

When his father had gone back to the store, he went to his room, shut the door, and opened his desk. Even the paper looked accusing. He chewed the end of his pen. At last he wrote:

Dear Chloe,

I've been thinking of what you told me the other night, and wondering if we all aren't fooling ourselves. What is there to all our vaunted idealism *(sounds like a Fourth of July oration)*, our Art with a big "A"? I look at myself and wonder how genuine it is and how much of it is just a veneer. A lot, I guess. It's the money I'm after. *(Don't think, don't dare think what you are writing.)* The rest doesn't matter. The bluff's the thing, and so it turns out that I'm no better than the most bumptious Rotarian — not so good, in fact, for he at least is no pretender—

He crumpled it and flung it across the room. He tried again, and again, each time with the same result. If she had a scrap of intuition she would see through any one of them as easily as through a clear window. It was no good. They didn't sound like him; they weren't him. Oh, what the hell! He took another piece of paper and wrote:

Dear Roy,

I can't do it. If my failure to write the letter I promised to write puts me utterly in the wrong, from your point of view, I shall have to accept it. Chloe would never in the world believe the letters I have been trying to write. They were jokes, and pretty poor ones at that. They would only cause her, and ultimately you, more unhappiness. I'm sorry.
Kurt.

He slammed the desk shut. As he did so he heard his mother's voice below. "Kurt! Kurt dear!" He couldn't go. And yet he opened his door and went quietly down, the letter in his hand. She was on the davenport, her lap full of mending.

"See here, boy, what's wrong? What happened in Grand Rapids this morning?"

"Nothing. Nothing."

"Yes, Kurt. You've not been yourself at all since you got back. Come — sit down here." She pointed to the space beside her, moving her sewing basket.

"Oh, please, Mother—"

Why not? It surged in him to be told. He felt, sitting beside her, curiously like a little boy again, her little boy who had come home breathless and silent and afraid.

"I went to Grand Rapids really, Mother, to see Roy."

Mrs. Gray's hand fluttered to her throat. She was white.

"Roy — Roy—? Chloe's husband?"

"Yes. What's the matter, Mother?" She looked ill.

"My heart. Just a moment. You — you startled me so. What — tell me all about it, dear, please—"

"Chloe's going to get a divorce — you knew that. Roy says she's — she thinks she's in love with me."

His heart hammered, and suddenly his head went to her lap and he sobbed, terribly. All the uncertainty and fear came flooding out. And he didn't care and was not ashamed. Her arms covered him protectingly, and she crooned, consolingly, little-boy words until he was quieter. He told her all of it, then, lying with his head against the softness of her.

When he had finished, she was silent for a long time, stroking his hair.

"It will all be all right, Kurt," she said at last. "Chloe shouldn't have said that, under any consideration, even if it were true. I can't forgive that. But people do uncalled-for things sometimes. Once" — she hesitated — "I've never told anyone this, Kurt, not even your father, but one time, about a year after we were married, someone knocked at the door. This very house, it was. I was sewing, as I am now, in this room. It was one of our best friends. He came in — why shouldn't he? — and before I knew what was happening, fell on his knees — asked me to run away with him — said he couldn't live without me. I felt very much as you do now, Kurt. I got him away, somehow, told him he was being very foolish, and never to think of such a thing again. It all seems silly now, for he's still a good friend of your father's, and getting bald and fat. But such things do happen. You're good-looking, Kurt. Women are bound to like you, maybe even to run after you — so it pays to be careful, always."

How strange. His mother. He tried to accept it, but it was hard to see her, in this room, puzzled as he was now, and, he reflected, much more certain of the rightness of what she did. But she was in love, and was loved, and unquestioning of either. For him the problem was distorted in ways she could never understand. Chloe loving him, if she really did; and he loving her brother; and Derry loving only his mercurial self. A strange triangle, this. Was ever there such a situation before? Someone will be brave enough to write such a thing someday, to be believed, and to escape unscathed. Not now.

He kissed his mother, and went out to mail the letter. That night he wrote:

Dear Chloe,

I've been thinking about you, you and what you told me the other night. I'm sorry it is so, but the decision is yours, irrevocably, isn't it? And I'm confident you'll do the right thing. Unless I hear from you to the contrary I shall know that you are going ahead. If you do, I'd suggest that you do not write to me again until everything is settled. It may spare you some unpleasantness, for people talk so easily. It's too bad that it is so, but it is. Doesn't this seem wise? It may be hard to be wise or prudent at such a time, and possibly my letters might bring you some cheer during these trying days. But you can forego them, and I will forego yours, and then, someday, they can start all over.

Love.

Kurt.

Nothing more came from Chloe. From Roy, the day before his return to New York, came a brief note:

Dear Gray,

I knew when you told me you hadn't written that it was all up. I don't blame you. I guess there was no help for it. I hate like hell to sit idle under a charge of non-support, but it seems to be the best way out now. I won't contest.

Roy.

When he got to his room again in New York, there was a small pile of mail awaiting him, and on top a telegram. It was from Chloe, and said only:

YOU ARE RIGHT NO LETTERS UNTIL MARCH.

VII

THE NEW YEAR brought slight change to Kurt. Study was the important thing. Korlov, the crabbed old teacher of composition, to his great surprise, presented his name for a foreign scholarship. He was doing well. His quiet zeal was winning him attention, rather tardily, but surely, just as it had in college. The bleak days of January and February went by uneventfully. March brought with it a hint of spring. Without warning there came a day that *was* spring, spring unmistakably, even in this armored city. The air had in it a vague and teasing softness. People dreamed along the Drive as he came home, and sat absently on the long disused and sooty benches.

Work was a burden. He had left early for home, and caught an uptown bus. He let three pass, for he wanted one with an open top. He climbed the narrow iron spiral and swayed to the front seat. He took off his hat and stretched himself to a new receptivity. Work — everything — seemed, of a sudden, unsatisfactory and of little consequence. He was lonely. There was no one else on the bus top, and he wanted someone, anyone, to be there. He wanted Derry, he wanted David. He wondered why Chloe hadn't written, and what she would write. He swung off the bus at a convenient stop, crossed the roadway, and sauntered along the path.

"Got a match?"

The chap was young and good-looking. He looked as if he would like to walk along with him. Kurt gave him a light and walked on. He wished, suddenly, inexplicably, that he had waited and walked with the boy. Maybe he was lonely too. The river, under a miraculously blue sky, was like blued metal. The melody of a Mozart sonata went like a silver chain through his head, looping and relooping its fragile loveliness through him. It carried him to his door. But the door, today, seemed not so much a door as a barrier that would shut him out from this new yet perennial softness that was in the air. He hated his winter clothes. He'd change them and come out again. Let the lesson go hang for once. There wasn't much light left.

On the table was a letter. It was from Chloe. He had been expecting it. If all had gone well, she was free. What would she say? He ran up the stairs, got into a sweater and corduroy jacket, and, with the letter still unopened in his pocket, ran out to the street. He found a park bench and, with the promised spring all about him, opened the letter. It was a quiet letter, and he was glad. There was nothing ecstatic about it. He read:

I am Chloe Grayling once more. They gave me back my old name. These two months have been hard ones, as you can guess. Mother has been surprisingly decent about it all, but Roy's family hasn't. They made themselves a little ridiculous at first. Later they were openly nasty. But I didn't care much.

Oh — what do I feel? As if I had waked up from a bad dream. I want more than anything else, I think, a city, a big city to lose myself in. I've a little money — not much. I didn't ask for alimony. Could I, do you think, find a job in New York somewhere? Anything, I don't care what. I need a change badly. Mother, of course, can see no reason for my leaving. I've had an offer of work in the secretary's office at the university. But you know, and she does, if she would admit it, that it's impossible. We simply don't get on well enough together, whoever's the fault may be.

There was more. Nothing about the two of them save the satisfaction of being once more able to write. He swung his arms over the back of the bench and looked out across the river. A use for churches, he thought; they do improve the horizon. He grinned at the wickedness of his idea, his mind flashing back to Barton and the Epworth League meetings of years ago. To have Chloe in New York. Someone he could see in the evenings, or have dinner with. The idea was enticing. His mother would object, he knew, and the hint of responsibility for him that Chloe's letter contained bothered him. He tried to read it again, but it was too dark. If she does come, and can't find work, and goes broke, what then? What is she hoping for? She knows I can't help her, with money. All the unanswerable questions of Christmastime came trooping back upon him. Prudent. Prudent. You're just an old maid. She's simply a good friend, maybe your best friend, and you're afraid she's going to claim more of you than you are willing to give. Forget the practical details, this time — to the deuce with 'em.

But nevertheless his letter to her that night was not too enthusiastic. Work would be hard to find, he feared, and living dear. But he would be glad to help if he could. And it would be nice to have her there.

The spring was undoubtedly early. April was saturated with it. Tunes as silver and as lilting, as gay and as sweetly sad as a troubadour's chased and patterned through his head incessantly. And he had not the will to catch them and freeze them into black notes and bars. His prodigality amused him. April brought him the scholarship — and his joy in it was very great. A year in Europe, with scholastic requirements not too strenuous, a new land, freedom such as he had never known — a beauty, he hoped, that he had longed for and dreamed of from boyhood. He would go in June. The summer in Fontainebleau and Paris, a month or so of loafing wherever he chose; then Rome, perhaps, and Munich. His head was so full of these provocative names that the present, in spite of the glamorous weather that softened and remade the whole city, seemed hardly worth noticing.

And then Chloe came. She arrived almost unheralded. When he came in one afternoon, full of dreams of Fontainebleau and June, the yellow envelope was awaiting him, a swift reminder that this was America, and April.

"MEET ME GRAND CENTRAL TOMORROW MORNING NINE SEVENTEEN CHLOE." He was a little angry, a little afraid. He hoped she'd have money. He was a little low, himself. He'd have to find a room for her at once. What would she want, he wondered? Would she be satisfied with a place such as his? What would these two months be like? It was not yet dark and he went out, scanning the stone fronts of houses on the crosstown streets for "Rooms to Let" signs, trying to imagine from the noncommittal brick or stone or grated doorways what the inside might be like, and always rejecting the house as for some reason unsuitable. Finally he gave up. It would be as well to wait until she arrived.

She looked not much different. She was pathetically glad to see him. They stood together in the concourse, oblivious of the milling people all about. She held up her face and looked at him, saying over and over again, "O Kurt, it's so good to see you again! So good!" And it was good. He was glad to see her, and he despised himself for his timidity and his worryings. She was here, and he was glad. That was enough. He squeezed her arm, and, laughing, hurried her through the crush of incoming commuters and into the subway. "We'll go to my room," he shouted in her ear. As the crowd thinned they found a seat and shouted inanities at each other, happy as two children. An old man across the aisle smiled at them and nodded his head benevolently. They came out into a world bright with April sunshine.

"The nicest part of a subway ride is the coming out, isn't it, Kurt?"

"You're learning fast!"

"Oh — I like this!" she said as they swung over the shallow ridge of hill and the river spread before them. The trees were faintly green, and the wind blew a colored Sunday supplement crazily, hesitantly, down the street and against their feet. They both laughed at its antics as they kicked themselves loose from it.

Once in Kurt's room, Chloe took off her hat, arranged her hair, and sat down on the bed. It was strange having someone here in this room. No one had entered save himself and the cleaning woman since he took it in the fall. He felt that this was something unprecedented, dangerous.

They talked for a long time, of Derry and her mother and the feeling and reactions of the past two months. And then he told her of his scholarship, watching her closely.

"In June, Kurt, you'll be going?"

"Yes, in June. Won't it be great?"

"Oh — it will, it will!" She sighed her pleasure. "I'm so proud of you, Kurt, and so happy for you. It's what you've wanted, isn't it? And you do deserve it."

It seemed genuine. His imagining had been all askew. If it were true, as Roy said, that she had said she loved me, he probably hounded her and drove her to it. He could hear Roy's monotonous voice drilling, accusing, torturing, until she might say almost anything to silence it.

She had some money, he found; not much. They had lunch sitting at a counter in a gleaming drugstore, and started hunting a room. She was not fussy. Price was the important consideration. They found one that suited not far from Kurt's own.

"If it's too far from whatever work you find to do, you can move after your month is up."

Life changed, unbelievably. The loneliness, the monastic concentration on a single end was gone. There was the coming year to plan for, there was Chloe to talk to. Evenings were no longer blank expanses between dinner and sleep, to be filled in with minute and worrying manipulation of notes and rests and signatures. Chloe, furthermore, was in luck. She got work almost immediately in the registrar's office at Columbia.

"Won't Mother rave!" she said to Kurt. "'You could have done exactly the same work and got more money for it right here at home, and had no expense, and here you go trailing off to New York—' and so on ad infinitum. But it's so marvelous to be away, Kurt, to be really free. I never have been, you know. It was Mother, first, and then Roy. Most people make the break when they go away to college — they leave their families behind — but we never went away, you see, Derry and I. We just stayed. And there was no change. That's been all the trouble, I think: Mother shrinking and hardening inside, and we growing and expanding, and the two of us getting farther and farther apart; Mother fighting all the time the widening of the breach, fighting, fighting, never seeing its necessity and never giving in."

Evenings now were something to look forward to. They would meet for dinner somewhere. Sometimes they would go to a movie and sit restfully in the dark, the flicker and shift of reflected light playing over them and their quiet neighbors while the organ trembled melting sentimentalities. Then a stroll along the river, and, on the steps of Chloe's house, a laughing good-night and a promise for the next evening. Sometimes she would meet him at Korlov's studio in the Fifties, and on a Fifth Avenue bus top they would go to Washington Square through the glitter of a New York dusk for supper in some pseudobohemian restaurant, where other people from other towns not New York were trying to look as though they had been born to the bohemian purple. They knew it to be fake, but found in the dim lights, the candles, the gay china, the air marbled with smoke, something desirable.

Then there would be a symphony concert to hear, and an exit, into the din of the city when it was over, with a new armor to withstand that din — a shining armor woven of sound against the age, an armor in which one could walk the whole night splendidly and forgetfully. Again they would dine hurriedly near the square and walk through the squirming life of the East Side, down Allen Street under the dark thunder of the "El," past windows crowded with pink and blue quilts and shining brass pots and candlesticks for people from uptown to exclaim over. Or, when it rained, they could sit in Kurt's room while the water rushed and pounded on the gable and gurgled down the trough with a soft insistence. Chloe was good company ... his friend. His sweetheart? He fancied so sometimes, though no word of it passed between them — and always at the thought the image of Derry or of David rose, forcing the thought from him, and he knew where his love lay.

She was so like Derry, and yet so different. He fancied in her eyes sometimes a hunger that frightened him and set him to wondering. He was twenty-two, and so far as girls went, ignorant as a child. Something in him told him to experiment and find out for himself. "What if you are all wrong in your fine idealizing?" it said. "You're afraid, that's all." He felt the hunger growing in Chloe. She had been married. Her knowledge frightened him. He had seen the look in the eyes of girls along the Drive in the April twilights, and because it hinted of mysteries into which he was uninitiated, it embarrassed him invariably and sent him hurrying on with lowered eyes. He had seen the same look in David's eyes, but that he now understood and could cope with. He looked about him in the streets and was ashamed. He seemed sometimes to be surrounded by boys younger than himself, who were years older in experience. He almost hated his parents at such times for not letting him dance, for not making him want girls. Or was he, really, incapable of loving a girl? Was he really different, really one of the beings he read about so zealously? He was, of course. It had all been decided and the ground fought over a thousand times. Yet some slight increment of uncertainty made him torture himself still with analysis. He could never tell Chloe, of course. How was he to make her understand?

It was a threatening afternoon. Low clouds, like dark wool, hung almost to the treetops, and the air was oppressive with the promise of rain. They had supper, and were walking towards the river when the rain broke in great spattering drops on the pavement. They ran the last block and arrived in Kurt's room wet and laughing and breathless.

"You'll have to get dry. It'll probably stop soon."

He gave her his dressing gown and a pair of slippers. She spread her clothes on the cold radiator and, propping the pillows behind her, lay back on the bed. His desk lamp sent oblique shadows up the sloping panes and angles of the ceiling, and made a broken half-light in the room.

"I'm glad you let me take care of you once in a while, Chloe. It makes me feel responsible and almost grown-up."

"Grown-up?" She laughed. "You silly boy! You know ever so much more than I, and I believe you're quite aware of it. You're fishing!"

He shrugged his shoulders. "In books, maybe."

"In lots of ways. You sense things. You overhear things. You're bigger than you know."

"You say that because you are a poor deluded creature, Chloe," and he smiled at her. "Your slipper's coming off. You will die insisting that I'm an artist when I'm only a sort of musical poetaster. If I ever have a biography written of my funny life, I shall certainly want you to do it."

"Don't say that, Kurt. You're not a whatever it was you called it. You're the real thing, or will be. Maybe I'm not a very good critic for you, but I won't have you say that!"

"There! You see, illogical lady? In one breath you say I'm wise — in the next you say I don't know myself — and to know oneself, platonically speaking, is the very essence of wisdom. Knowing as I know, however, isn't everything. Experiencing counts too — at least the wise men say it does, and I've experienced very little. I've never even been desperately ill since I was a baby — and that doesn't count because I don't remember it. I've never been hurt except in little annoying ways. I almost wish I could be, sometime."

She was silent, looking at him curiously. Then she said slowly, "And do you think that my marriage has given me an experience you haven't had — perhaps need?"

She had come to the point brutally. He would have preferred not to say it, to play with the idea but not to admit it. How should he answer? He was afraid, again afraid of these direct confessions, these turnings of his feelings and his thoughts inside out, particularly to a woman.

"Perhaps that."

"It wasn't a beautiful experience, Kurt. It should have been, too, since it was my first. But I didn't love Roy ever, I think, though I told myself I did and did my best to pretend."

What was in her eyes? She could teach him if she would, and if he dared. But did he really want to know?

"Come here, Kurt."

He went to the bed and she took his hands in hers and looked up at him searchingly.

"Sit here."

He sat beside her.

"I'm going to do something for you."

She seemed suddenly old and wise and he incredibly young and inexperienced. Her hands clasped behind his head, and she drew him down over her until their lips met. Her breasts were warm and soft against him, and her lips hot and moist. Too hot, too moist. They fastened upon his own, and something in him went cold and rigid. What was this? A kiss? This shame — this burning shame? Would it never end? The world was one red, endless turning. It whirled days and eons away and still the lips held him until it seemed his lips and these other lips were grown obscenely together, and to tear them apart, flesh must be torn from bleeding flesh. When it was over, he walked blindly to the window and pressed his burning face against the pane that streamed with rain. He wanted to cry, he wanted to disappear forever. Yet she had done it for him. This was a part of knowledge. He felt old again, but no happier.

Chloe lay still a moment, then rose, slipped on her dress, pressed his hand in passing, and was gone.

What did she think of him now? He could have possessed her completely, and he had felt only helpless dismay and a shriveling disgust. This was nature, raw and living. He did not want it. He walked to the mirror and stared at his image. "Kurt Gray, Kurt Gray, what are you? What will all this mean to you? Years are going on and on. Derry will marry sometime, you know. David — dare you count on David?" Oh — what does one do when he gets older? Kurt put on his slicker and walked in the rain, aimlessly, steadily, until he was too tired to walk farther. Then he went dully to bed.

There was a reticence between them now. Chloe's hunger was unappeased. His own, or the one he had suspected might lurk in him somewhere, undiscovered, did not exist. They walked and talked as before; but something, like an invisible wall, had come between them. May was going, and on June eighth he was to sail. The news of his scholarship had brought him many letters — congratulatory, sad, envious. His mother and father were proud of him, but not quite reconciled to his going so far away. His mother's letter made him sorry for her, but glad for his independence. They did not feel they could come to New York to see him off, and it was this that hurt his mother most. It hurt him too, but he steeled himself and wrote her pleasant cajoleries and gay expectancies of the summer and the coming year, and promises of the fine things he would bring back to her.

Derry was graduating, and Mrs. Grayling, with an unexpected generosity, had promised him a hundred dollars. He was going to use it to come to New York and see Kurt off and visit his sister and, if all went well, perhaps to stay. David was coming too, to spend the summer in Woodstock, sketching. His letters were still ecstatic; still "counting the hours till I see you" letters.

If it had not been for Chloe his happiness would have been complete. He had failed there, and he could not learn what she thought of his failure. There was no stiffening of the will that could drive him to success there. He felt reproach in her look, in the touch of her fingers on his sleeve, although nothing further was said.

He was to sail Saturday. Derry and David were coming on Friday morning. Thursday he finished the last details of tickets and passport and visa and packing; Friday should be a gala day. Thursday evening it was warm, uncomfortably so. The air was still and humid, and above the city the stars were brilliant in a flannel sky. He took Chloe to dinner in the Village. They smoked and talked and finally took a bus as far as Central Park, where they joined the other loiterers who strolled aimlessly up and down the graveled paths. They found a deserted bench beside a pool that reflected the stars and was recurrently sheened blue and crimson, blue and crimson, blue and crimson, as a great electric sign across the park flashed against the sky. A hundred, a thousand, an endless number of benches, here, in every city in the world, holding each two lovers. We might be any two of these lovers, he thought, as Chloe leaned her cheek against his shoulder; but how strange, how at odds they were with this universal mating. Something in him yearned to mix itself in this democracy of love. Why couldn't he, like that young chap in the white trousers, like the sailor who had just passed, take his girl in his arms and make the old, the universal pledge? Of all young men in this early summer night he alone seemed discordant and perverse.

They said nothing. Slow feet scuffled near them, sometimes, and the pool flashed blue and crimson, blue and crimson. Suddenly her hand was holding his. It was cold, and his own hand fastened over it protectingly.

"Kurt — Kurt dear—" Her voice was tense and frightened. "I'm afraid I love you."

He stood up quickly, his fists clenched. Then he turned and put his hands on her shoulders. He looked into her shadowed eyes.

"Chloe — I was afraid of that too."

"You mean — you don't — love me?"

"No — no — I don't know what I mean. Only you mustn't, Chloe. I'm — I'm not worth it."

"Dear! Dear! Don't ever say that. You're worth all I can ever give you, and more, more than I can give you."

She was longing, he knew, for his embrace, his kiss, his endearments. It was beastly that she should have to play the lover.

He couldn't play up. It wouldn't be fair. He sat down again miserably.

"I can't, Chloe, ever."

She turned, frightened.

"What do you mean?"

"I only mean — oh, Chloe, please don't let's say any more about this."

"Kurt — you're frightening me; you're hurting me! What is it?"

How should he say it? Shame burned through him like acid.

"You read a book of mine not long ago, Chloe. It was called *Love's Coming of Age*. Do you remember?"

"Yes, but—"

"Do you remember a chapter about — about—"

She broke in almost hysterically.

"No — no — no, oh no — not that! You aren't that, Kurt, you aren't that — tell me you aren't!"

She twisted her fingers in his coat.

"I'm afraid I am, dear."

Sobbing, her head dropped to the back of the bench.

He leaned over her, trembling, uncertain.

"Don't, Chloe! Chloe, dear, don't! I like you awfully much. You had to know it sometime. It wouldn't have been fair or kind any other way. Don't cry so, Chloe, please don't!"

He sat, half facing her, and drew her head against his body.

"Listen, dear. You told me once, Chloe, that I was the best friend you had in the world. I'll tell you the same. You're the best friend I have — the best. And such a friendship is worth having, isn't it? Isn't it finer, maybe rarer than the other thing? It's such a strange mix-up, such a queer lopsided triangle, yet the lines are all straight and perfect in their way. I've loved Derry for years. He doesn't love me much, if at all. You love me. Three relations, different, right, wrong, who knows? Don't let it mean unhappiness for you, Chloe. I'm sorry I told you so bluntly. I didn't know how else — if I hadn't liked you and known you so well I would never have dared. But I knew what you were hoping, or thought I did, and I couldn't let you go on hoping so."

Her voice came to him, muffled yet familiar.

"It's all right, Kurt, all right. I don't quite understand yet, but I'll try. It's all right, friend Kurt."

"Let's walk, we'll feel better."

They stood up, and he kissed her forehead tenderly.

"Kurt — oh, Kurt—" Leaning on his arm she seemed suddenly happy, transfigured with happiness. "This may be the thing that's ours exclusively, yours and mine. All these others" — she gestured vaguely in the dark — "all these other twos go on in the old way. We'll go on and on in the new way, and build, oh, who knows what?"

And arm in arm — like two lovers, thought Kurt ironically — they walked home.

His feelings after he was alone, and indeed all next day, even after Derry and David had come, were mingled. He was glad Chloe had taken it so sensibly. It had even given her, it seemed, after the first shock, a deep, almost mystic elation. Here was to be a unique, a spiritual friendship. The ideal was his own, but it failed to make him happy. He had given a part of himself, his secret inviolate self, to another. All the following day David's eyes were on him, David's too-knowing eyes.

It was a day for laughing and foolishness. Arm in arm, four abreast, they had swung down the Avenue, making jokes of everything they saw. They lunched in the Village; they took a subway to Coney Island, and, tiring of the blare, back again; they went to a musical show. At the end of the evening, they left Chloe at her house and returned to the hotel.

Kurt had given up his room the day before, and taken one here adjoining that occupied by Derry and David. They both came in, and all three sprawled crosswise on his bed, quiet and tired. David, after a few minutes, turned out the light, released the shade to the top of the window, and lay down again close beside Kurt. The room was high above the street, and the city-sound came to them muffled and distant, a low cacophonous counterpoint to their thinking. A boat moaned four deep notes, and they all looked up and smiled in the uncertain light.

"Won't be long now," said Derry, giving Kurt a poke in the ribs.

Kurt and David smoked silently, their eyes on the summer sky, luminous through the window squares. David turned at last, took his hand, and spoke slowly. He spoke of many things, and to Kurt he seemed wise and experienced, darkness concealing what he could never help mistrusting, if ever so slightly. He spoke of a cathedral, dim with incense, trembling with music, to which young men such as they came to worship. Some were priests in the temple, others were urchins defiling its beauty. They, these three, David and Derry and Kurt, should be a priestly trinity. What they felt for each other was high and fine and worthy. No one outside the cathedral could understand this. They would sneer and perhaps even persecute, but the faith in the rightness of their strange creed must stand, shining and perfect. He took Derry's hand too, reaching across Kurt, and joined all three on Kurt's breast.

"The three of us, always, priests in the temple. Shall it be so?"

Kurt was strangely elevated. Here was his own ideal, the one he had groped for so long, with such struggle, told him again in a prose poem whose symbolism came like a fine and subtle vindication of his own thinking.

The night, the street sounds, the curious sense it gave him of being set apart in the midst of a multitude — three human beings bound by one desire, by one splendid ideal — swept him on to a fine and rapturous approval too deep for discussion.

"You've said it so beautifully, David" was all he could say, and he kissed him. He would have kissed Derry too, but Derry, somewhat disappointingly, had fallen asleep. Kurt and David lay there then, talking softly of the coming year, making promises for the future — a life together somewhere, the three of them, which should be the ideal realized, the cathedral glorified, the service newly consecrated. It seemed only fair to tell David of Chloe.

"Chloe understands all this, David."

He seemed frightened. "You mean — you told her—?"

"Yes, I told her."

"You — you were very brave."

"Or very foolish."

"Perhaps."

"No, I don't think so. I know her better than you, David; better possibly than anyone else on earth, and I know she can understand."

"No woman, Kurt—" began David.

"But she's different. You must believe me, she is. You *must* believe me. You'll understand how it came about someday."

The towers against the sky were becoming blacker as the sky paled and brightened and then turned to dull ash, to rose, to amber.

"You'll be tired, Kurt, for your trip."

"Oh, what difference?" Kurt laughed softly. "It's all to be a new adventure, David — for you, for Derry, for me, for Chloe too. What better time to start a new adventure? Only please remember, and make Derry remember, that I'm alone. You two will have each other — I will have only the ideal. It's high enough and fine enough to carry me through, if you both will help me. Will you?"

And not long thereafter, as the great boat swung out into the river, amidst the thicket of waving arms on the pier he could see the three of them, standing together, with Chloe's red scarf floating above their heads. A little woman in front of him stood on tiptoe and sang in a strained and excited voice, *"Sailing, sailing, over the bounding main—"* interrupting herself with little exclamations of "There he is! I can still see him! Good-bye! Good-bye!" All this world of departing humans gliding away from the greater world of staying humans with so little effort. His throat was tight, and he waved as frantically as anyone else, perfectly aware that none of the three could see him. The people became puppets, the puppets a blur, with a tiny wavering spot of red that was Chloe's scarf — and under it Derry, joking, probably; Chloe exalted, yet ready to cry; and David, with the disturbing eyes that seemed always to follow him. He felt curiously superior to the waving people on the deck as he pushed through them and sought his stateroom.

PART THREE

I

H<small>E HAD STUMBLED ON</small> Sauvergne and the studio. A week in
Nice, with the usual trips to Cannes and Antibes, to Grasse, to
Monte Carlo over the Grande Corniche; a week of pleasantly
lonely evenings spent in threading the narrow streets of the old
town, of strolling along the Promenade des Anglais while the sea
sucked and thundered in the soft darkness; a week of the Nice of
between-seasons, with its crowds of stolid tweed-clad Germans,
taking advantage of the reduced rates — its shop fronts half-lat-
ticed behind the ladders of painters and window cleaners — its
general air of a busy housewife preparing for important company,
and willing, in the meantime, to be rude to the casual visitor; a
week was quite enough.

On the last day of his stay, with accommodations already
arranged for his departure to Italy, Kurt went wandering again.
Sauvergne, seen from the motor road to Cannes as a steep hill
bristling with lurching tinted houses, had piqued his curiosity
before, but always when he saw it he had been en route to something that seemed more important. Today he took the bus to the
market at its foot, and started climbing its narrow cobbled main
street. The climb was surprisingly arduous. Halfway up he dropped
willingly to a clean-swept doorstep to rest. On up the hill and
around the bend the houses continued, leaning on each other for
support: cubical houses and narrow houses, with walls of cream and
écru, of palest blue and peach and apricot; walls baked to a pastel
harmony by the brilliance of the sun; walls pierced with small
windows and studded doors, and enlivened with pots of geraniums
and washlines gay with scarlets and yellows, hanging like limp
eccentric banners in the heat. An old woman, with black shawl
pulled tightly over her head, and blue skirt making skirls of dust on

117

the cobbles, clattered carefully down the decline in her wooden sabots.

He could have shouted! He continued on up the street, past the *épicerie,* which, with all its divergences, was singularly reminiscent of the general store across the river in Barton. He passed the church with its massive cracked walls, its deeply recessed windows, and its chalk-defaced door. He passed three entrancingly narrow street entrances that beckoned down circuitous narrow ways, arched and buttressed now and again until it seemed the whole small town, like a set of carefully balanced dominoes, might depend for its stability on that of any one of its members. A town of surprising light and shade. He passed two painters, Americans, obviously, at work, the legs of their easels forced into extravagant angles by the sloping of the street, their canvas stools precariously atilt. At last the summit, and the wall of the chateau, ponderous and forbidding, with its battlemented top and the great ramp which led up to its heavy carven doors. Yet from the inner court a pepper tree waved a green denial to all this grim exterior, and a mimosa trailed its grace over the broken wall.

Beyond the triangular place du Chateau, the street seemed to end in a blue door. But as he crossed, he saw a passageway, almost incredibly narrow, angling off to either side down a sharp incline along the two walls of the house with the enviable door. He took the right turn, and gasped at the expanse of blue that rushed up at him — the blue of the Maritime Alps, like a floating cloud, distant and misted; the blue of the glittering Mediterranean; the blue of the whole arching sky — a blue world washed in gold. He turned again, and against the yellowed wall read, *"Studio à louer."* For rent — he seemed to know that this was for him. He turned back and knocked at the blue door. The house echoed emptily, and he was about to turn away when a voice from somewhere beyond the wall shouted, *"La porte du jardin, s'il vous plaît, à gauche—"* and then in English, "Come around to the garden gate — around here to the left."

He was met at the gate by a stocky man with a heavy face and short neck and a head of very black and very curly hair, closely cut.

He was dressed in a flaming orange shirt, smeared with paint, and a tattered pair of canvas trousers.

"Hello! Come in. You saw my sign?"

"Yes. I'm interested."

"Oh." His look was hard to interpret.

The garden they were in was irregularly triangular, sloping sharply down and away from the house with the blue door in a series of terraces, the whole confined by high walls of stucco weathered warmly mellow, running down to the point of the triangle where they were interrupted by a smaller stucco building with a roof of orange tile.

"My name's Rubin. Leo Rubin. You've probably heard of me?"

"I'm afraid not."

"No? I paint, at any rate. That's the studio, there." He pointed to the small building at the base of the garden. "I paint in the house. There's a good north light in the studio, you see, and there are two living rooms underneath that I've no use for. Come along if you'd like to see 'em."

Kurt followed the broad back down a graveled path, six stone steps, through another blue door into a little square room, bright with blue and yellow. The floor was of red tile, the walls plaster, but the crude furniture, the shelves, the dishes, even the tiles of the charcoal oven which jutted out from one corner of the room were blue and yellow, as if some part of the world outside had been distilled in the pigment of their coloring. Two tiny windows with blue shutters, painted crudely with the beads of saints, looked out on the Alps. The other room, yet smaller, held only an iron cot, a wooden chair, and a heavy Provençal chest.

He took possession the next day. His first week in Sauvergne approached perfection, it seemed to Kurt. There was some loneliness, to be sure, but there was a quietness, a rightness about this new and unforeseen life that was deeply gratifying. He brought forth his oldest clothes, and bought a pair of canvas sandals to wear on his bare feet. He learned the names of supplies that had not been in his grammars; he discovered the joy a fire of pinecones may bring of an evening, and the speed with which an omelette may be burnt over a charcoal blaze. The piano he had had sent out from Nice was ornate with licorice-colored wood and brass candleholders, but it was not a bad instrument, and the tunes he played on it were gay ones.

The hills all about were covered with twisting paths. There were no fences, and walking was a joy. There was a gorge, dark with craggy rocks and murmurous with its tiny torrent not far away. There were other towns within the scope of an afternoon's walk, where, when the day began to chill, one could get great bowls of steaming tea, and Provence honey in blue jars, with little toasted buns to spread it on. There were closed gardens where oranges glittered among glossy leaves and walls were more provocative than protective. There were nights when the stars were so bright that the sleeping town glowed dimly in their light. Then his steps would echo alarmingly in the quiet streets, and he would walk quickly, a little guiltily at this unseasonable hour of ten when all good citizens were snoring in the darkness, until he came to the quieter path of clay and pebbles that led through gorse and ground pine to a hilltop where one could see the town — a pale silhouette against the dark sweep of the sea, with the far glow of lights from Nice and, to the right, the smaller constellation that was Antibes, with the ever-repetitive questioning of the lighthouse on the Cap.

What occupied his mind on these golden days he would have been hard put to it to tell. The summer at Fontainebleau, pleasant as it had been in many respects, with its new friendships, its quaint environs, its almost nightly excursions on foot or bicycle through the clean shadows of le Fôret, with suppers of coarse bread and cheese and strawberries and Bordeaux at Barbizon or Courbet — the summer had been tiring, too. The slight but certain feeling of obligation his scholarship imposed on him had made him, perhaps, more industrious and more conscientious than many of his fellow students. And now, with two months of loafing ahead, he was glad simply to live like some young and irresponsible animal in the glory of this new place, to bring himself into a sympathetic kinship with it.

He thought of his work very little. There was in him a quiet consciousness that the source, the spring of his inspiration, was

there, ready to his touch when he should want it. He thought
often of New York and the small triangular world within it that
was his. From Derry and David he heard often. There were only
assurances — these from David — of the continuance of the ideal,
of the sacredness of it, the certainty of its rightness and its
durability. He himself had slight need of such assurance, for the
ideal had dominated him with an ascetic persistence since their
parting in New York. So fervent was it that he hardly thought of
his body at all. Its hungers were fed by a white flame; appeased,
and nourished, and whipped to lethargy, by the stark beauty of the
ideal.

From Chloe he rarely heard, and he regretted her silence. The
shock she had sustained at their parting must have been, he now
realized, greater than he knew, and he wondered at his daring on
that distant night. She had seemed to emerge from it. But as he
remembered those last few hours with her in June, he had
misgivings. She was so strongly a creature of moods; it seemed
scarcely credible that the strange reversal of emotion she had
displayed that night could have deepened and endured to convic-
tion and acceptance.

Then came rain, unprecedented rain. For a week the windows
streamed with it, the garden ran with muddy rivulets, the hills were
obscured behind the sliding thunderous curtain of silver — all day,
all night, the soft thunder of rain. There was nothing to do but sit
inside and wait for it to stop. The fire helped to dispel some of the
dampness, but Kurt's depression it could not dispel. Day after day,
night after night, the downpour continued. It was hard to work,
even, for into the music the insistent and monotonous drum of the
rain would force itself. He wrote a song:

> *I have been prisoned with bars*
> *That keep more rigorously the stars*
> *From shining through my windowpane*
> *Than steel — November's leaden rain—*

It started so, but he gave it up in disgust. And then came a letter
from Chloe. It was surprisingly thin. It read:

Dear Kurt—

I can be quiet no longer. I'm pretty certain you don't know how utterly you are being fooled. Derry, as I don't believe you are aware, is living with David. They have a "studio" in the Village — God knows what for. They seem, or at least David does, to be happy. As to Derry I'm doubtful. David fits into the picture. He is artificial and weak. Derry, as you know, has very little mind of his own when it comes to relationships such as these. He's carried away with the glamour of this one. They are surrounded by "pretty boys" and the whole thing sickens me. As to Derry, I give him up. He's a fool, and he'll get over it in time. But you — Kurt — I like you too well to see you deluded, and I'm pretty sure you are wrong in what you told me the night before you sailed. David has nothing to offer you but a spineless sort if idealism, and you have too much of worth, Kurt, to allow him or anyone like him to dissipate it. I seldom see them, as I won't go down anymore. David has money, from some source. Derry has a job, though how he keeps it I don't know. David is supposed to be taking graduate courses at N.Y.U., but he seems to be neglecting them sadly. Hints that he is writing. You are such an incurable idealist, Kurt, don't let an inferior ideal possess you—

He read the letter again and let it slip to the floor between his knees. Half-thoughts swirled uncertainly in an aching emptiness, and the rain thundered on the tiles and soughed and gurgled in the eaves. He put on his jacket and went out into it, bareheaded. The hills were gone, the sea was gone; there were only the rough cobbled streets streaming with water, and gray walls hedging him in. He walked till he was shivering before he came dumbly back to his own door. His fire was out and he was too miserable to notice his discomfort, too upset to consider how much of what Chloe wrote might be false. He was conscious only that his carefully schemed world, so strange, and yet so simple and perfect and to him transparent, like the fragile creation of some skillful Murano glassblower, had shattered. His faith that had kept him aloof and assured through these lonely months was dissipated. He could have laughed had he not been too choked with despair —

the despair of disillusion. "Fool, fool, fool" beat and echoed emptily in him.

It was then that the unforeseen, the coincidence that makes life often seem so fictional and fiction so living, occurred. The postman brought a telegram. It was from London, and two days overdue. It read: "ARRIVING NICE WEDNESDAY TRAIN BLEU MAY STAY SOME TIME HOW ABOUT SAUVERGNE CAN YOU MEET ME TONY."

Tony McGauran. He looked at the telegram again, and realized with a start that this was the day. His watch told him that he had but half an hour to catch his bus to Nice, and he must meet Tony. He threw on his coat and slipped and clattered down the Rue Piolet. He was just in time for the *char-à-banc*. He hardly knew what he felt. Tony McGauran. He knew he would be glad of Tony's company, but Chloe's letter, above all else, rang in his ears.

Tony he had hardly expected to see again. On the boat coming over he had first seen him — a slender, golden young man with light hair, very wide blue eyes, and a sensitive, thin-lipped mouth whose smile was a delight. On shipboard he was everywhere, knew everyone. And yet he was not too bumptiously self-assertive. He knew everyone — that is, save Kurt, who sat in his deck chair with a book and looked on. Kurt fancied, sometimes, at dinner, on deck, that this young man whose name he did not know and whose very genuine popularity faintly irritated him, was watching him curiously; and his indifference became more noticeable.

The last night out he was on the foredeck. It was a brilliant night, with a great low moon and a smooth sea. In the morning they would be in France, and at noon, in Southampton. The dull vibration of the ship's motors slowed, and a far small light to the left, flashing in yellow deliberation, was England. He stood, bareheaded, for a long time, the soft wind folding in around him, until the strolling couples had all gone and he was alone. Then, of a sudden, he was not alone.

"Hello!"

"Oh — hello."

"Grand night."

"Isn't it?"

"You — I don't think I've met you. I've noticed you so often. You seemed, if you'll pardon my saying so, so well worth knowing. You're Kurt Gray, aren't you? I'm Tony McGauran."

He looked at Kurt, smiling. Kurt regarded him curiously, shyly. He too was bareheaded. Over his dark coat a white scarf was wrapped like a stock about his throat. In the moonlight, the wind whipping his light hair about his bead, he was Byronic, like the pictured hero of some Victorian romance.

He went on.

"You must have thought me an awful ass on this trip — stewing around all day and all night with everyone. You were so quiet, yourself. I wish I knew how you do it. I don't seem able to help myself. I always do the same thing. I know everyone — and have no friends." He laughed ruefully.

And so the conversation began, and at last developed into a mutual recital, as such conversations are likely to do: on Kurt's part, because in this new acquaintance there was a magnetic urgency he found it hard to withstand; on Tony's, because, as he said, he couldn't help it. "I'm a conversational exhibitionist" was his own appraisal.

He was an actor, and he was going to London to appear in a Philip Barry play. He was twenty-one. His father had been Scotch, his mother Milanese. He had been born in Brussels; educated in Edinburgh, and later at an exclusive private school in Connecticut and for a short time at Amherst. He had run away from college in his freshman year and managed to get on the stage in New York, where he had met with some success; and now, here he was, with an aura of adventure about him so different from Kurt's quiet background that there was in Kurt an immediate and perhaps slightly envious sympathy for this quixotic young man. They had leaned against the rail talking until the first pale rays of dawn showed the dove gray hills, and Cherbourg standing against them, dim and aqueous.

Later in the week they had met again in London — this, in the brief stay Kurt allowed himself there before going on to Paris and Fontainebleau. Kurt had seen the play, and found Tony to be a surprisingly capable and attractive actor. They had dined together

once. Since he had been in Sauvergne he had had three highly
dramatic and very brief letters, for life to Tony was a game of
leapfrog from one romantic episode to another. His openness to
life was a constant dare, and things happened to him. Kurt was
always amused, half-incredulous, and invariably surprised, because
his own life was in contrast so smooth and easy to trace. Don Juan
and St. Francis in a single body, thought Kurt. And here, with the
unpredictableness of a summer shower, was Tony, coming to
Sauvergne.

The train, fortunately, was late. He would have missed it
otherwise. The rain had continued to fall, and every occupant of
the bus, in ascending or descending, it seemed, had taken double
the usual amount of time, shaking off the wetness or preparing
to brave it. The sun, when Nice was at last achieved, seemed
almost incredible. An omen? He hoped so as he ran for a taxi.
And then, arrived at the station, he found he must still wait. *"C'est
la pluie, vous comprenez, m'sieu'. Le Train Bleu est Presque toujours
en avant."*

He paced the platform under the dripping glass roof of the car
sheds, now a-glitter in the sun, and at last, with a shrill tooting and
an attending and vaporous cloud of steam, the Train Bleu slid to a
reluctant stop.

It was easy to find Tony. He descended from his carriage in an
aura of correct arriving — the handsome young adventurer doing
Europe. A West End topcoat was flung over his shoulders, and he
was surrounded by a mound of gleaming baggage. Kurt, dodging
excited Frenchmen, saw him waving an enthusiastic farewell to a
dapper officer in the door of a compartment. He turned, in greet-
ing as enthusiastic, to Kurt, as the train pulled out unnoticed
amidst their shaking of hands and furious friendliness.

At last, "How do we get to Sauvergne, with all the impedi-
menta?"

There was the bus and the tram.

But the dazzling trunk? "I'm broke, you know."

Kurt, not yet familiar with Tony's extravagances, verbal and
financial, looked at the expensive luggage and tried to imagine the
cost of traveling in a first-class *wagon-lit* on the Train Bleu.

"How about a taxi? How far is it?"

"About twelve miles. It'd cost a fortune!"

But a taxi it was, and the bill of more than a hundred red francs, which to Kurt seemed enormous — more than a week's rent — Tony paid without question, and his tip to the driver was munificent.

It was dark before Tony was finally installed in two unused, hastily cleaned rooms under Rubin's house across the garden. Rubin had consented, with his usual gruff reluctance, to Tony's occupying these quarters. He muttered in his thick throat and growled his unwillingness; though all the while Kurt knew he was eager to rent, and he did his best to make Tony bargain. But Tony agreed to Rubin's first tentative suggestion, and only asked innocently, when the painter had stomped away, "Did he gyp me, d'you think?"

Unpacking was for Kurt a diversion and a privilege. The shining baggage was as correct within as without, a dream of sartorial perfection, and its disgorgement was accompanied by Tony's staccato recital of his trip from London. Prince Henry had been in the next compartment — Prince Henry come down to Cap Ferrat to visit the Duke of Connaught. The Prince's equerry had been most friendly — it was he Tony had waved at in Nice — and Tony was full of hilarious anecdotes concerning the royal family. Kurt sat in a window embrasure, grinning and silent, and for the time, forgetful of his trouble.

They went for dinner to le Chameau d'Or, the small *pension* near the chateau where Kurt sometimes took his evening meals. The gutters still gurgled with water, and the dampness of the cobbles rose, vaporous, in the early dusk, broken by the light of a ripely yellow moon through torn, uncertain clouds. As Tony had been in the boat, so he was in the dining room of the *pension* — the immediate center of the whole strange group, from the plump rusty-haired lady from Dublin, who painted watercolors, to the old and somewhat worn Comte de Breze, who, it was reported, had distinguished himself by keeping the harbor at Brest swept free of mines during the war. They were all talking together before dinner was over and the more recent events of Tony's life were known to them all. By the time the inevitable apricots arrived, it was hard to get away.

They managed to at last, however, and the fire in Kurt's damp small room was pleasant. A wind, heavy with wet, flowed blackly down the street. Kurt and Tony sat, their feet propped against the tiny stove. Tony talked — of himself, of the Barry play, of the foibles of a particularly blonde and vapid heroine in English pictures, of a friend's sudden departure for New York and the consequent offer of his house in Chelsea, of the house itself, next to the Sitwells, of the Scotch cook, of the "talkie" he might make, and then—

"You may just as well tell me what's eating you, Kurt."

Kurt's eyes lifted in surprise.

"What do you mean?"

"Oh, come on! You know you've been — well, if you'll excuse my saying it, you've been on the verge of bursting into tears ever since I came."

"Rats."

"No rats at all. You can't fool me, Kurt, me boy; I'm a smart little feller who's been about. You're either in love or out of it. Which is it?"

"You're all wrong—" and Kurt hugged his secret yet more tightly within him. It shouldn't be told. It must burn itself out, bitterly, smoldering, hidden.

"You can't fool me, you know. I'm here to stay for a while, and if you don't tell me tonight, I'll find it out tomorrow, or the day after that, or I'm not the man I think me!"

Kurt smiled, halfheartedly.

"An analysis, free of charge, my specialty. You're an introvert extraordinary — and I'm an extrovert in-inordinately. How's that for a start?"

"Swell," said Kurt, grinning, "but how about it? I thought this was to be an analysis of me?"

"Oh, you'll find me mixed up in it, don't worry. I'm mixed up in everything."

"Good Lord, Tony!" It was no good even pretending at seriousness, and yet the dull pain of the morning had not lessened. Chloe's words, "I like you too well to see you deluded," were a persistent minor accompaniment to the inconsequential cadenzas of Tony's chatter.

"See here!" Tony's voice was insistent. "I'm really serious now. You feel rotten, and I know your kind. You'll let things eat you and gnaw you until you wear yourself out, and you come to some sort of a melancholy solution in the end, maybe. But it's such a rotten way, such an unsatisfactory way out. If you'd only get it off your chest it would be over and done with. Right?"

"There's nothing wrong with me, Tony!" Kurt insisted.

"Oh hell! If you're going to be stubborn!"

They were silent. Kurt feared, and could not tell why he feared, Tony's "Good night," and yet he waited yearningly to be alone in the darkness — and yet — and yet—

"I — I had a letter this morning, Tony, that was upsetting. That's all, really. I'm sorry it's made me disagreeable."

"You're not disagreeable, you're unhappy. Was it from home?"

"No — no."

"Not money?"

"No."

"Then it's what I said at first."

Kurt kicked open the door of the stove, and the red flicker of firelight pervaded the room. He felt Tony's eyes, searching, quizzical, amused, upon him.

"Isn't it?" he insisted.

"I suppose so. Oh, shan't we call it a day? I'm tired. The sun will be out tomorrow, maybe, and we can walk. I think it's the rain as much as anything."

"All right. We'll do it — but don't think for a moment that you're shaking me off. I'll be hot on your trail tomorrow, and I'm a great little detective. And a great little comforter, too, you'll discover."

He rose and knocked the ashes from his pipe.

"Good night. Now for heaven's sake go to bed, don't sit here and watch the fire go out. It's a romantic and insidious occupation."

The next two days were inexplicable to Kurt. He had grown used to being alone, and Tony's presence was a novelty he could not at once adjust himself to. He had a suspicion that Tony was purposely being insistent in his companionship. Certainly he was ever-present. Kurt would hear his shout in the morning, with a sleepy start, and rise to let him in. Clad in silk pajamas and a crimson dressing gown, he would be standing in the garden with a flower or two to decorate the breakfast table. He would launch immediately, and with no reticence whatever, into the narration of more tales of his own life. They were unfailingly amusing, and Kurt marveled at his frankness. He himself could hardly conceive of such shameless disrobing of the past. It made, somehow, his own secretiveness seem miserly; yet he could not fancy himself divulging these prized, these cherished experiences to anyone. He was a miser of his emotions.

Tony's talk was principally of one Joda, and their mutual esca-pades. She was a New Yorker to the tips of her trim and efficient fingers; not beautiful, not even pretty, but smart, and with a body slim and fine and sweet and desirable and ready, apparently, for Tony whenever he should desire it. Kurt watched Tony curiously during these recitals, aware that his own silence must make him seem either very inexperienced or very shy. At the conclusion of each anecdote Tony would press him for confidences, but Kurt would put him off; whereupon Tony, with a shrug of his shoulders, would start another tale.

"I'm a regular Scheherazade and you will be too, you devil, before I get through with you. You've probably got a whole harem back in Manhattan and sit there scoffing inwardly at my shabby loves. Isn't it true?"

Kurt was embarrassed, annoyed, and angry at himself for his annoyance. He liked Tony — one couldn't help liking him — and these stories, so theatrical, so prolix, seemed singularly at variance with the personality that featured so glowingly in them. Tony was vital to an unusual degree, Kurt realized, but his head was that of a dreamer; and the fineness of his nostrils, the sensitiveness of his lips and hands belied the animal gusto of the escapades he related. At last, with a bravado sired by desperation, Kurt made the plunge.

"Tony — I've never had an affair with a girl."

"What!"

"I mean it. I never have; so if you think you're going to lure me into confidences by all these stories of yours, you're mistaken."

"But Kurt! You're — you're twenty-three — two years older than I, and—"

"Oh, come on. You're not half so surprised as you're pretending."

"But you must have some outlet — it's not human—"

"Why isn't it human? We're not animals."

"But we are animals! That's just it. When a boy is old enough to want a girl it's normal that he should have her. It's animal and normal. If he doesn't, he's abnormal."

"Yes?" Kurt was vaguely angry. "That's for me, I suppose. The animal ideal is the right one, of course!"

"Of course it is. You think you are an idealist, Kurt Gray, and you're just damned scared, that's all. I know what life is like in towns like the one you come from — prudish and petty and religious in the wrong way. I'm a pagan. My parents were always queer, always out of the rut of the ordinary. They died before I was twelve, both of them. There've been no anchors tied to me."

Kurt was silent. There was truth in what Tony said, and yet he felt a tantalizing certainty that somewhere there was a flaw in the argument, and it irritated him that he could not find it. He could think of nothing to reply, and Tony sat regarding him quizzically. After a time he spoke.

"Kurt — would you like to hear about my first love affair?"

"I suppose you think I should, for my own enlightenment. Really, though, I've read the usual novels, you know—"

"Don't be sarcastic. I'm not reprimanding you, God knows."

"Just what are you doing?"

"I'm trying to find out what's wrong with you."

"You mean wrong with me at the moment, or wrong with me generally and permanently?" He smiled.

"Both, and I've a hunch there's one answer. See here" — he was suddenly serious and leaned forward — "it's not what you think. My life has been so different from yours. I'm years older than you in experience. After my mother died there was plenty of money, for a while. I had a guardian, and I was sent to Kent School when I was fourteen. I was shy too, except when I was acting, and I acted most of the time, I guess. I was fifteen when they chose me to be 'leading lady' in the school play. I loved it, and I was convincing, I think. The chap who played the hero was sixteen, and big for his age. He was on all the teams, and I admired him. I'd never dared really try to know him — he wasn't in my class. But there we were, in the play. He was very bashful. The fellows kidded him unmercifully, and he wouldn't rehearse kissing me in the last act. We were both ashamed. The coach did his best, but it wasn't until the last rehearsal that he really did kiss me. You'll think me sentimental, Kurt, but that kiss was something I remember.

"Neither of us said a word after rehearsal, I remember. We dressed, and because we had so much to do with the play, we were the last to leave. We went out together, I remember. We'd rehearsed in the gym, and old Pop shouted at us when we went out to latch the door and snap out the lights. Dick snapped off the lights, and we stood in the darkness, with just a square of light through the screened glass of the door. He came to me. I couldn't see his face, but his voice was thick and strange — 'Tony,' he said, 'Tony — shouldn't we rehearse that again?' And then he grabbed me and kissed me over and over again. 'Oh — I love you,' he said — and then he shoved me away and ran through the door. He left school at the end of the term, and I never saw him again. That was my first love affair."

He settled back, watching Kurt narrowly.

The daring! How had he the courage to tell of this!

"You're shocked?"

"No."

"Do I know why you're not shocked?"

"I don't know. Do you?" Kurt, though fascinated, kept his eyes on the floor.

Tony was like a diver probing the depth of an unfamiliar pool. He leaned forward again in his chair.

"Of course I do. You're homosexual."

Kurt sprang to his feet and strode to the door, his hand on the latch, his mind pounding with confusion. Tony said nothing. The little stove cracked furiously. At last Kurt turned again, and leaning against the door, fixed his eyes on Tony, who was smiling strangely.

"I don't like that word."

"It's highly scientific."

"Oh, I know that, but it makes me sound like a biological freak of some sort — to be classed with morons and cretins and paranoiacs."

"And that's probably just what the jolly little scientists would think about it. No, Kurt, it's not the word that hurts you, it's having your little secret dragged out into the light. I was right, wasn't I?"

Kurt's silence was affirmative.

"I'm always right — it's intuitive. We queer ones can spot our kind anywhere, anytime. Be honest. On board the boat, wasn't there something between us before we ever met? I knew it; didn't you?"

"Yes, I knew it."

"You've been over here — how long? — four, nearly five months, and you haven't misbehaved once?"

Kurt shook his head. He felt will-less before this barrage of questioning.

"All right. I've diagnosed your case. Shall I prescribe?"

"Prescribe."

"Very well, Mr. Gray, I'll do so. You need two things, like most patients: an immediate relief and a permanent cure; so be docile. Your immediate relief is easy — I'll fix that myself. The permanent cure is another thing. For that you'll need a mistress."

Kurt felt himself pale, and a slow anger rose in him. What right had this debonair, this disconcerting youth to unmask him and criticize him and correct him?

"You think I'm pretty much of a mess, I take it." His tone was stiff and hurt.

"Oh, come, don't be uppish. I'm only trying to tell you why you are so damned unhappy — and I'm right."

"Oh, of course you are right!"

"Cut the sarcasm. I *am* right. I know your secret, don't I?"

"Tony, I'm sorry I was angry — but I can't help it. You've got my secret, all right, but only such a skeleton of it. I—"

"I know all about that too. Well, such being the case, don't you think it's up to you to do a bit of narrating?"

Kurt was quiet, thinking confusedly. Why not tell, and yet why — and yet why not? And at last, with an effort, he did; but it was the fire he watched, and one of Tony's slender hands — not Tony's lips, which he feared might curl, or his eyes which might shine with amused derision. That he did not want to see.

So the story came out: his home, his boyhood, his college days; his almost accidental initiation into this strange world of strange young men; Derry; his groping for a faith to justify his desiring flesh; David; Chloe; the ironic triangle that had shattered itself on a bench in Central Park; his ideal, always his ideal; Plato, and Havelock Ellis and David's liturgical symbolism, all fused into a high credo by Kurt's own burning need for such a credo.

Tony listened quietly to the stumbling end. Then he leaned forward and put his bands on Kurt's knees.

"Look at me, Kurt."

Kurt turned his head and lifted his eyes, half-afraid of what the face might reveal. He was reassured.

"Listen to me — boy. I've heard I don't know how many stories from I don't know how many different fellows about this sort of thing, and how it came to be with them — they're all alike in ways, and all different too. There's something in your story, though, that's stronger than most, because there's something in you that's stronger. You were lucky, you and Derry, to drift into the thing as you did. We're not all so fortunate." He smiled, bitterness twisting his lips. "Your story is different there. It's different, too, in having a girl in it at all, and it's different most of all because it's cleaner than most — and it's awfully much less promiscuous. Kurt, please don't think I've just wormed these things out of you for curiosity or to satisfy my own perversity. It's not that, truly it's not. I do think my prescription is right. What about Chloe?"

This sudden intrusion of the specific again sent Kurt's resistance rising like an icy flood. "Girls are out of it, Tony. I've told you that."

"And I'm telling you you don't know. You think I'm an enigma because I know both things. I had to make myself be normal, Kurt — drive myself to, and it was hard as hell. But I did it, and I learned to like it. A woman's body, boy, is a sweet thing."

"But I couldn't," Kurt protested. "I'm just not made that way."

"What do you mean, you're not 'made that way'? You're not deformed, are you? Your organs are normal, aren't they? It's mental, Kurt, all mental."

Here was the old, old argument again, the one he had fought over so often, so futilely, and at last, he thought, to a successful finish — begun all over again. He rebelled at it, and at this disturbing creature whose mind was jousting at his own sad certainty and threatening to topple it once more to the ground.

He burst forth:

"Oh, you know! You know! You don't know! You don't know me, you don't realize what you are saying."

"Oh, yes, I do." Tony's voice was distressingly calm. "I know what your ideal is. It's rather fine, but it won't work."

"You mean a man can't love a man? You mean I don't love Derry, or David, or they me? You mean you didn't love the boy in the school play?"

"I don't mean that at all. I thought, until I met you, I was disillusioned for good and all. I don't think you've changed me much, but you've surprised me, chiefly. I didn't know anyone of our kind could be so — so pure, so abnormally innocent, so late in life." He laughed.

"You say 'our kind.' That means something, doesn't it?"

"Of course it does. I don't say we're like the run of men. We're not, obviously. The run of men are disgusted with our sort of thing with a disgust we can never fathom. But on the other hand, we can go them one better. We can have their kind of love and ours too. We can love and be loved. We can make love and receive love. We can be man and woman both."

> *"And I, Teresias, have foresuffered all*
> *Enacted on this same divan or bed—"*

"What's that?" asked Tony.

"It's a poem. But never mind. There's another line I don't care so much for. Oh, Tony, it all sounds well as you say it. But mine sounds well, too, though not quite so glib."

"The trouble with you is this love business. I know what it is. It's exalting and fine for a while, and then it's a torture machine that eats the heart out of you — it's suspicion and jealousy and unhappiness. It's the bunk, and I'm through with it."

"How can you get through with it? Love might get through with you, I should think, but how can you get through with love? You can't."

"You're a deep one, Kurt, and I've a notion that this letter of yours from Chloe is the first real blow your love has had, isn't it?"

"I suppose it is."

"Well, there will be more, take my word for it. I might even deliver a few myself."

"What do you mean?"

"Never mind, just now."

They fell into an uneasy silence. It was as if an invisible veil had drifted between them, making the harmony each desired a nebulous impossibility. Kurt accepted it glumly. Tony writhed and tried to tear it apart.

"Look here, Kurt. Our problems are so different. I've told you of my amours with various girls. There've been many more fellows than girls. I've been shockingly promiscuous. I've slept about rather indiscriminately, and—"

"You wouldn't let me say that of you, Tony," Kurt interrupted.

Tony smiled. "Probably not. But I have, really, and—"

"You've — you've slept with people you didn't love?"

"Good God, yes!"

"That seems — ugly to me."

"Ugly? Not at all. That's where we're so different. You imagine you must have love, whatever that may be — mooning and sighing and mental elation and despair, to justify, to consecrate the animal part of your lovemaking. That's the bunk. Lovemaking is just a jolly good game, that's all, like tennis. If I see someone I want to sleep with, for whatever reason, for what he says, or how he looks, or what he is, I do my very damnedest to arrange it. And when it's done it doesn't mean a bit more than a game of tennis would mean. That's the way to take your love, Kurt. Take it for the moment, drop it, and forget it."

"Do you always forget it?"

"Always."

"You're lying, Tony, and you know it."

"Well, perhaps. I make a pretty good job of forgetting, at any rate, and that's better than what you are doing this minute — half-sick with worry and fear for what someone three thousand miles away may be doing or saying or being."

"What about Joda?"

"Oh, Joda — Love's all alike, Kurt. People don't think so. You know that, and I know it — we have to be on our guard every minute. It's damned funny these people who call themselves normal can't see that. I've known men who loved their dogs and their horses more than their wives, and nobody ever accused them of being 'queer.' Oh no! They are normal — he-men. But we're perverted. And there's no difference, none at all. You love a boy just as you love a girl. It's less satisfying, but that's physical, and has nothing to do with the emotion. The emotion's the same."

Kurt was silent, confused, buffeted about by this strange and perverse discourse as by a playful wind, now in agreement, now in smoldering, inexplicable rebellion. He did not know what he thought, where he stood. He waited dumbly for this dismaying conversation to end. Chloe's letter — "I don't want to see you deluded" — seemed confirmation enough of the rightness of Tony's hedonism. Yet something dark and deep cried out against it, cried out for the perfection of love — for the unfolding and consummate love that makes of each lover both slave and master, both lover and mistress — for the complete reciprocation of love that poets dream of — for the complete, full, inundating resolution of the dissonances of two personalities. "Love is not love that alters when it alteration finds," came singing to his mind. But Tony, in exasperating tangent, started reciting, with the persuasive skill of the actor, the subtly poisonous lines of Swinburne:

> *"For the crown of our life as it closes*
> *Is ashes, the fruit thereof dust.*
> *No thorns go as deep as the roses,*
> *And love is more cruel than lust.*
> *Time turns the old days to derision,*
> *Our loves into corpses, or wives,*

And marriage and death and division
Make barren our lives.

"Come here," he said. "You're going to take the cure."

He took Kurt's hand and pulled him, bemused and uncertain, into the bedroom.

II

BREAKFAST was difficult for Kurt. The feeling of lazy well-being that had lulled him a few hours before was gone. He was self-conscious, seeing himself only as having fallen neatly into Tony's trap. He fussed about with the kettle and toast, avoiding Tony's eyes. When at last they sat opposite each other at the yellow table, he forced himself to look Tony squarely in the face. He saw there what he had feared to see — a gentle derision.

"I know you're laughing at me," he said sulkily.

Tony laughed in earnest. "Oh, Kurt! How funny you good people are — one little slip and you're all upset."

"One little slip's all that's needed, isn't it? You'd have me think so, anyway. I've proved to you now, I suppose, by last night, that my — my ideal, as you call it, was just a sorry illusion."

"You liked it, didn't you?" Tony countered.

"Yes, I liked it — which weakens my case the more." He waited seriously for Tony's reply.

"Then what more can you ask? The moment's enough. Look — the sun on this yellow table and these blue cups, this steam rising through it. It's rather nice — a moment I may remember, unexpectedly, twenty years from now — a moment that may come floating up out of unconsciousness like a wooden rosary from a drowned man's hand. You see? The whole problem of life is to get enough moments crowded into it so the spaces between won't be so deadly."

"But the moments — if they came too close they'd soon be as common and as dull as the spaces between them, wouldn't they?"

Tony said nothing for a moment. Then he countered with a question.

"What would Derry think about this — or David?"

"Derry wouldn't mind, I'm afraid. He would think he had made a conquest and be pleased as Punch. David would mind, terribly—"

"You're sure David would? Well, he might at that."

"Why do you say that?"

"Because I know your David, or at least I think I do."

"You — you know him?" Kurt was aghast.

"He's from Philadelphia?"

"Yes. Yes, he is."

"And does he — you might not know this — does he ever mention a friend named Brosken — Ozzy Brosken?"

"Oh — Ozzy. Yes. Ozzy is his guardian."

Tony looked at him for a moment in amused surprise, and then threw back his head and shouted with laughter. "His guardian!"

Kurt, puzzled, steeled himself for some new sally.

"Kurt Gray! How can you be so goddamned innocent!"

What did he mean?

"Why, say! Ozzy Brosken is notorious. He's an American Oscar Wilde, belated and much less clever, but the same type — too heavy, too soft, too old. He's got a place in Philadelphia that is like nothing else on earth. I went there to a party once when I was playing at Shubert's. And what a party! It was there I met your David."

"Yes?" Kurt's breath seemed constricted. Tony did not, or pretended not to, notice his extreme agitation.

"He has an enormous studio — why a studio, I don't know — he certainly doesn't do anything — hung in a sort of saffron-yellow Venetian velvet — no furniture but divans and cushions and low tables — so many cushions you almost walk on them. You don't walk really, you crawl. It's a sort of glorified mattress. I came after the show and there was a room full of 'the boys' lying about in heaps. Some were in evening clothes, some quite arty, and a good many in the most elegant gowns. A black boy, dressed in a gold turban and sandals, passed cigarettes and served champagne. Somebody played somewhere; it got more and more amorous, and there were — diversions. Brosken had got, from somewhere, two kid acrobats — contortionists, really — Japs — and he had used their contortioning to his own ends. He brought 'em out dusted with lavender powder, and they gave a performance that was nobody's business."

"And — and David was there?"

"Oh, very much there. He was Ozzy's special prize at the time, so he was in high regard. Kurt! What's the matter!"

Kurt had risen and walked to the door. Tony rose to follow him.

"You're white as a ghost."

"Nothing — nothing," Kurt murmured. "I — I'll walk a little," and opening the door, he went out.

He drew his hand across his eyes at the sudden brightness of the morning sun and stumbled over the cobblestones to the path leading up the hill behind the town. His mind was a torrent of confusion. Chloe was right, then. He'd been most awfully duped. David — Derry — Chloe — Tony — David's eyes, Tony's curling lips, Derry's easy enthusiasms, Chloe's pain, always Chloe's pain. He could not understand. And what was become, then, of this love he had plighted with David that last night in New York, that fine high ideal? He saw again David's eyes, and his faith came back to him. And then it was all effaced by Chloe's scrawling handwriting, and Tony's so certain phrases, refuting it. The gravel rolled and crunched beneath his feet, and the brightness of the sky and the far-gleaming sea seemed gross impertinences. He flung himself at last into the grass, and sobbed with vexation and his own confusion.

David's eyes — David's eyes — David's eyes — candid and sure and kind and disturbing. There must be some beauty in all this crassness to cling to. He stopped crying as suddenly as he had begun, cursed himself for a fool, and started down the hill again. At the foot of the path he saw Tony, shading his eyes, searching for him. They waved almost simultaneously, and both broke into a run. When they met by an open stable door acrid with the smell of goats and burros, Tony seized him by both arms.

"I'm sorry — gosh — I'm sorry, Kurt. I was jealous of your David, that's all. He's probably a good sort, away from Ozzy, and for that he's probably not to be blamed. All of us — except maybe you — have things we're not happy about, and don't talk about—"

"Except maybe you, you mean?" queried Kurt, smiling at him.

"Go ahead, I deserve it. Why do I make acquaintances everywhere I go, and so few real friends?"

They fell into step, walking back toward the house.

"I don't think you really want to know, do you?"

"Probably I'll be offended — and won't believe you — but tell me anyway. I've told you enough, Kurt!"

"You give yourself away too freely, that's all. Ten minutes with you, and they know everything about you, except this one thing — and I wonder sometimes how you manage to except that. You certainly skirted the edge yesterday at the Rubins'! When Mrs. Rubin waxed sociological, you remember?"

"I know. I was furious. It was so obvious they liked you better than me. I talked foolishly."

"Well, try my prescription. I've taken the first dose of yours, and it wasn't bad," and taking Tony's arm, he continued beside him down the hill.

Once more between them there was the perfect harmony that comes into being, sometimes, between old friends — a harmony so finely attuned that Kurt anticipated Tony's sudden veer in conversation by the subtle telepathy all friends know.

"You see, Kurt, in all this you've been fortunate and I've been unfortunate. You've liked, I think, the right people, and so far they've not disappointed you. But they have me, so many times, and I've rushed to the far extreme. You don't know what some of these creatures are, that's all, so you can't understand my bitterness."

They turned once more into their own street.

"O Lord!" sighed Kurt.

"What's the matter?"

"The Rubins are at it again — swinging on our garden gate."

They stood there, apparently in heated conversation.

Kurt waved and shouted, "Hello." Mrs. Rubin turned and waved, though somewhat dubiously. Rubin turned heavily and stalked off across the garden and out of sight.

The arches of Tony's eyebrows went suddenly Gothic. "Something's up!"

"Oh, something's always up with those two. They used to keep me awake nights screaming at each other. Watch your step, Tony, for heaven's sake."

When they opened the blue door that led into the garden they found Mrs. Rubin sitting on the steps of the low terrace, moodily poking with a twig at a snail which clung to the damp coping beside her. She was young — twenty-six, perhaps, fully twenty years younger than her husband, small and dark, with a thin face, thin lips and nose, and enormous black eyes, half-concealed behind heavy-rimmed glasses.

Kurt disliked her, had from the first. She always reminded him of a rat, pushing its way into places from which one tried to exclude it. She had been a social worker of some sort in New York, had met Rubin there and married him — why, Kurt could never conceive, for they were glaringly unsuited to each other in age and in temperament. Rubin, gruff, selfish, crude, grossly conceited, yet possessing a real talent for paint; Georgia, moody, introspective, prying, as selfish as her husband, and utterly inefficient as cook or housekeeper, constantly at loose ends with her husband's personality, and yet passionately proud of his achievements, and reveling, as a gourmand might in a choice store of food, in his celebrated friends. "We were up at the Harrises', at Cimiez, last night, and Frank was telling Leo—" or, "We're half expecting Sherwood Anderson down next week from Paris—" or, "Norman Douglas is up at Mentone again and we may drive down to see him one of these days" — these were typical of her most frequent conversational overtures.

This morning she was gloomily silent.

"Cheerio, fair lady! How's tricks?" said Tony.

"Oh, shut up. You make me sick, all you men make me sick — especially if you're artists."

"Well, that let's us out at least," put in Kurt.

"It doesn't let you out. You're artistic, and that's worse. My God! I thought when I was in Henry Street that I ran up against queer people, but this has me beat."

Her rage seemed too great to empty itself exclusively upon its real object, her husband, and spilled over onto these two as well.

"Somebody's done wrong by our Nell," Tony contributed.

"Because I can't cook a steak the way he likes it, and because I won't wash out his goddamned brushes three times a day, he calls me a slut and nearly has a stroke. He will someday."

"Oh, snap out of it, Georgia. Your lot's not so bad."

"No?" Her voice was brittle with vindictiveness. She rose and started to the upper house, her face tense with emotion. Then, half turning, she threw out, "Some of us can have wives to our taste, apparently!" and disappeared through the door.

Kurt and Tony stared at each other, amazed.

"That dirty wench!" exclaimed Tony.

"What's she driving at?" asked Kurt.

"It's clear enough what she's driving at. At you and me. She's been prying, apparently. I think we're going to move."

"Oh — she couldn't! How could she? Anyway, it's Rubin she's sore at. When she gets over that she'll forget this other too."

"Don't you think it, Kurt. She's a vindictive, mean little rat" — Kurt approved the epithet — "and she's out to do me no good, and if in the doing she slashes you a bit, it's all right with her. I know these people. They praise themselves for being broad-minded, but they're really intolerant as hell — and they can make us damned uncomfortable. Let's not give them a chance."

That afternoon they walked by the valley road to St. Paul — St. Paul-du-Var, growing up out of the green valley in a surprising ridge of compact stone. Smaller than Sauvergne, its charm was different. The old Roman wall was damaged so little that they found they could walk almost the whole circuit of the town on its crumbling top. The one long street that ran through the town along the spine of the hill was flanked closely on either side by the heavy stone façades of old houses, with grated windows and enormous studded doors, forbidding and secret. Here and there, however, one of them would stand open, giving a glimpse through long

tiled hallways to open arches looking westward over the steeply
dropping hillside, with the vivid tops of orange trees in small walled
gardens; a pitcher of freshly drawn water from the central fountain;
or the crablike back of some old woman scrubbing a doorstep, as if
to show that life for her was frugal, clean, and sufficient.

Tony was frankly excited at these few accidental glimpses of an
intimate and different world.

"Who'd ever think it!" he exclaimed, seizing Kurt's arm. "It's
here we should live, not among those splotchers and dabblers in
Sauvergne. It's like us — at least it's like you, Kurt, hiding your real
and important life behind a wall as noncommittal as this."

Kurt smiled. "You're talking now exactly as I talked the other
night, Tony. You're not being very consistent or logical."

"Logical? Of course I'm not logical. Who could be, with all this
about you?" — he swept his free hand in an inclusive gesture. "I'm
not saying you were wrong, all wrong. It's things like this damned
Rubin nastiness that make your ideas seem right, really." He
stopped and planted his back against a convenient wall. "They
think we're nasty. But it's they, always, who are nasty — nasty and
sneaking and suspicious, and even jealous. That's it! She's jealous.
It's the idea of Rubin, bull-necked old Rubin, not really satisfying
her; and two young men she'd like to have falling over themselves
to seduce her, not caring a damn about her."

Kurt was surprised at the depth of Tony's feeling on the subject.
He would have expected him to be scornful, perhaps, humorously
and lightly malicious; but this fragile head pressed back against the
old wall, this tense throat, these nervous hands, displayed a new
and unfamiliar seriousness.

"Come along," said Kurt, tugging at his jacket, "come along!"

They turned a slight bend in the street and came upon the
square, which was really little more than an angular widening of
the street to accommodate a low circular fountain, and beyond it a
stone arcade beneath which, sunken slightly below the level of the
street, was a series of long troughs — the village laundry. On the
right was an *épicerie* displaying vegetables, wooden-soled shoes,
threads and needles, canned tomatoes and peppers — a display
which again brought to Kurt with a mild and pleasant nostalgia the

over-the-river grocery in Barton, where, as a little boy, he had sometimes been sent to buy soap and tea and clothesline and other household necessities. At the fountain the street divided into a thin "V," continuing on the right past the *épicerie* up a gradual rise of the hill to the heavy Romanesque church at its summit, and on the left descending slightly between rows of the same solid houses.

They took the left fork, and before they had passed the fountain, Tony stopped. "This is it!" he said.

"This is what?"

"This is where we're moving to."

There was, Kurt then observed, beside the tall carved doors that provided the only relief in the wall opposite the fountain, a small sign: *"Appartement meublé à louer."*

"Don't you feel that it's right? It is! I know it is!" and before Kurt could reply, he had lifted the iron knocker and sent its dull thunder echoing through the house.

Tony's premonition was right. That night they sat reviewing their find — its square dark living room with red-tiled floor, great oaken cupboard, and hooded fireplace; the bedrooms, high-ceilinged and looking down an olive-grown hillside and across a valley; its small kitchen with charcoal oven and copper kettles; its garden overlooking the same hillside and valley in three terraces, with pots of angular flaming geraniums and orange trees gold-globed with fruit; and most of all its Stephen Daedalus, the small mongrel puppy with floppy ears and sad eyes, that, whining at the door during their inspection, had so won them that Tony had at once adopted it and christened it for Joyce's strange hero. They were deep in their planning when Rubin came in with no more warning than a surly grunt. His face was red, and his peacock green tie, which he always affected on his trips to Nice or Cannes, was awry. He was drunk.

"See here, fellows" — his voice was thick, and he rubbed his knuckles through his coarse, almost negroid hair — "I'm sorry, but I gotta use this room, and I guess Georgia thinks she doesn't want anyone up at the house anymore" — this to Tony. He stared with a sort of oxlike and smoldering malice at Tony's bright head. Kurt started to speak, but a look, a something passing like a spark from

Tony's mind to his own, made him stop. "I'm sorry—" Rubin began again, a little disappointed that his victims did not seem more perturbed. But this time Tony interrupted airily:

"Oh, don't feel badly about it, Rubin. It's really quite a coincidence. You see Gray and I just rented a place this afternoon up the valley, and we were just wondering how we should break the news."

Rubin was too drunk to conceal his disgruntled surprise. "B-but's — but your rent's not up yet, an'—"

"Oh, that's all right," retorted Tony, "we won't ask you for a refund. We're going out tomorrow, as a matter of fact."

"Oh." Rubin grunted, rubbed his chin, and, turning unsteadily, went out.

Tony rose and flung the door completely open — "to air the place out," he explained. Kurt continued to stroke the soft ears of Stephen, who sprawled by his low chair.

"Well, I was right, wasn't I?" asked Tony, turning back into the room. "Let's take a walk. Stephen needs the air, I'm sure, and God knows I do!"

III

NEXT DAY they moved, and the simple action of transferring their belongings to a new place seemed to mark the opening of a new chapter for them both. Sauvergne, for Kurt, had been fallow. He had done no work. The rain, with its depressing monotony, the new surroundings, the natural laxity after a summer of hard work at Fontainebleau, and the sudden complication brought about by Chloe's letter and Tony's arrival — everything had worked against the mental peace that composition demanded. In St. Paul, things were different from the outset. There was none of the ravening loneliness that had made the early days of rain at Sauvergne a torment. Tony was good company, when company was wanted. Furthermore, Tony's vivacity, his scoffing intolerance of the sentimental, made introspective probings and questionings and self-pityings seem puerile, and strangely — for Kurt — out of place.

Their life together, without any haggling, fell at once into pleasant and congenial grooves. Tony made the keynote speech on their first evening in the new quarters. The fire crackled and spat, and the lamp Kurt had extinguished.

"See here," Tony began. "You want to work here, don't you? Well, so do I. I've got a jolly idea for a play. I don't want my play spoiled and you don't want your concerto or whatever it is spoiled. They both will be if we start this thing off wrong. We've misbehaved once — at my suggestion. That was part of your cure. Well, you know how I feel about that. I enjoyed it — and I hope you did. For me that's enough."

"And you're not quite so sure about me, is that it?"

"No, I'm not. Your experience with this thing has been — I don't suppose I can admit that it's been right, considering my philosophizings to you, but it's been pretty clean and fortunate. I expect the other night was the first time you ever slept with a person you didn't love, or fancy you loved. I'm afraid—"

"You're afraid," Kurt interrupted, "that being a simple country lass I'll fall in love with you." He was smiling in the flickering half-light.

"W-well — yes. That's what I'm afraid of."

"Why are you afraid of it?"

"Because I like you too well."

"That doesn't sound quite logical to me, but we'll have to let it go at that. You're arbiter in this matter — it's up to you."

"All right, then, I *am* arbiter, and it's all settled. We'll be" — here his voice became mock-dramatic — "we'll be, Lord Fortescue, as though nothing had ever passed between us."

And on that basis the month proceeded, day after perfect day. Kurt reveled in the house, the rugged picturesque town, the ordered simplicity of life; and Tony, too, was less restless than at Sauvergne. Elise, a stodgy girl the owner had recommended to them, came each morning, prepared their breakfast of strong tea, crusty bread, and preserves, did the necessary housework, got ready a simple lunch, and departed. After a forenoon of work — Kurt in the garden or in his room, Tony on the balcony of his — they would meet to eat what she had left for them.

They would walk, then, until teatime, along the twisting climbing road to Vence, or, more often, some inviting path through fields and wooded hills; or, descending to the valley, play like two ten-year-olds in the shallow water of the Var, making toy boats and ports to harbor them in, with bridges and docks and fortresses and lighthouses. Or they would take, sometimes, the jerking trolley to Villeneuve and thence towards Grasse, dismounting wherever they chose and walking the pleasant miles back to St. Paul, with Stephen lagging at their heels, for dinner at the inn and a quiet evening by their own fire.

Never, it seemed to Kurt, had he known such utter content. The past, by a willful forgetfulness, had faded to a dream — a background for the present, but, for the moment, impinging on it scarcely at all. Tony was in part, at least, right. To worry, to question, to submerge oneself in a sticky swamp of conjectures about things one couldn't hope to change, was stupid, undeniably. He thought of his mother, worrying always about him, worrying this very day, he knew, about his health and his safety — and he knew whence his own propensities came. David, Derry, Chloe — the strange triangle would intrude itself again in his life inevitably. But the moment was good, and the triangle should not be allowed to throw its wedging shadow across it.

His work was going well. After the weeks of morbid idleness, ideas were fertile, and they matured with surprising docility. Out of an old tune his mother had sung to him as a boy, the old New England ballad "On Greenfield Mountain," he was evolving a score that pleased him hugely. To himself, as he worked, he fancied the music patterned itself, loosely, after the quaintly sentimental tale of the young farmer who, as retribution for mowing on the Sabbath, was struck down by a blacksnake — and died at the side of his own true rural love, a perpetual warning to the ungodly. The melody, with its slowly dragging opening measures followed by the incongruously accelerated refrain, lent itself surprisingly well to adaptation; and he found himself working at it with an ease and a willingness that surprised him.

They had been a fortnight in St. Paul, when one evening Kurt played parts of his suite to an enthusiastic audience of two: Tony and Stephen. The latter's enthusiasm centered principally on the piano pedals, and manifested itself in clumsy attacks on Kurt's feet. Tony's, however, was genuine and sweeping. His temperament made him particularly susceptible to music that was gay and vivacious and a bit satirical in intent. And Kurt, basking in this unaccustomed adulation, was in high spirits.

"It's your turn now, Tony. I haven't heard your second act yet — and I'm all agog to know what Miss Beesely said to the Duchess."

Little persuasion was needed. The table was shoved aside, and the room became an impromptu stage where Tony, playing all the roles with equal verve, enacted his still unfinished play. It was, it seemed to Kurt, a brilliant thing in its way, brittle, sophisticated; a comedy of manners bordering perilously on burlesque, yet skirting the edge with such agility that this feat alone added delight to the performance.

"I'd like to try my hand at music to a libretto like that sometime," he said when Tony had concluded the Duchess's last crisp retort, and, with a regal gesture of an imaginary lorgnette, collapsed on the divan. Tony was silent a moment. Then he leaned forward into the glow of the fire, eager with the idea.

"Well, why don't you?"

"Do you mean it?" queried Kurt.

"Why not? Why didn't I think of it before? It's a corking idea, Kurt. The spirit of the thing's right, isn't it? Make it an operetta, not just a musical comedy. Go Gilbert and Sullivan. We'll be McGauran and Gray. Will you? You could do it in swell shape. When'll we start? I know enough producers in New York to give us a hearing, and who knows, the novelty of a musical show with a plot and music might make a hit with them — if the shock wasn't too severe just at first!"

Tony's enthusiasm was contagious, and they both went to their beds that night much later than usual, full of the new idea.

It prospered amazingly during the remaining weeks of their tenancy. Kurt, when he set himself to it, worked rapidly. His head buzzed with tunes, and his fingers were hardly able to keep pace with the pen. The libretto was finished in three days, and both Kurt and Tony set themselves to writing lyrics with a joyous zest that was the best possible background for the emerging operetta. An unexpected mordant sense of humor in Kurt, whose existence he had hardly suspected, and a certain gift for pertinent rhyming, made him an able contributor; and between them, *The Duchess Decides* took form with a speed that surprised them both. The tunes, Tony insisted, were corking — gay, light, lilting — and the lyrics, thought Kurt, were quite above the average. The air of the old house was frivolous with music — harmonizing voices that made up in ardor what they lacked in skill, tapping toes, shouted suggestions that echoed through the old walls with, often, startling incongruity. The blue warm air outside, however, the gold-globed orange trees, the teeming scarlet geraniums, were an understanding company. The staid dark citizens, seeing these mad young men, one dark, one fair, marching down the cobbled street arm in arm to the tune of some outrageously shouted and quite unfamiliar song, were surprised, but tolerant. *"Ces américains — ces artistes — ils sont vraiment fous, fous, tous sont fous!"*

Blue day fled after blue day, and gold day after gold. They had been a month in St. Paul, a month Kurt was to look back upon often and regretfully as a sort of golden interlude — a perfection of living never again to be captured. Tony's work on *The Duchess Decides* was done, and he was restless. For Kurt there loomed the not too pleasant task of preparing acceptable piano scores to the various numbers he had so glibly concocted. The sheer physical and mental strain of writing down so many black dots and flags and signatures and bars and rests he dreaded, but he set himself to the task and got along well enough so long as Tony left him alone. But Tony was restless. The manuscript of the play was like a gift of money begging to be spent, a bottle of champagne begging to be drunk, an adventure begging to be lived — and he was impatient at the methodical scoring and the slowness with which it seemed to move.

Kurt was too busy to regret the passing of that perfect sympathy he had so much enjoyed, but he sensed the tension of Tony's uneasiness, and worked the harder to set it at rest.

On a day that seemed the climax of all these perfect days, a day like old Tokay, Kurt and Tony met as usual at breakfast over their steaming bowls of tea; and for the first time, it seemed necessary to talk of plans. Previously it had been tacitly understood by each that the forenoon was to be for work; any discussion that might occur over the direction of the afternoon's walk came at lunchtime. But this morning Tony was ill at ease.

"What's your program this morning, Kurt?" he asked, testing with a tentative and careful fingertip the heat of the bowl.

"That second-act chorus — the hussars. It's tricky, and if it doesn't get a good harmonic background, it'll be a total loss."

"Oh, damn the harmonic background!" said Tony petulantly. "It's a grand day — why not forget it for once and go for a walk with me and Stephen?"

"Yes? You know you'd be blaming me in your mind every step of the way for not being at work on your — on our opus. What's the trouble, anyway?"

"Oh, you know well enough. I'm bored, and I'm raring to get our *Duchess* to the producers. There isn't another thing I can do on it — it's all up to you — and I can't sit around here and listen to you thumping out those damned chords on the piano all day — they seem so senseless, all by themselves like that — don't seem to be getting anywhere. Come on along — it'll do you good."

But Kurt was not to be persuaded. He left Tony morosely crumbing a crust of bread on the checked tablecloth for Elise, grumblingly, to pick up, and went to his own room. He stood for a few minutes at the long window swallowing deep lungfuls of the almost liquid sweetness of the morning. On the top of the low hill opposite, and beneath him, a barelegged girl tugged at the tether of a laden burro, as loath, apparently, to be at its rightful task this glamorous morning as he was himself.

He turned to his chorus of the hussars with a reluctant but determined mind. Overhead he could hear Tony's slippers thrown down and Stephen's silly scramblings across the tiled floor, and then the heavier steps and the slamming door that told him they were out of the house and that he must work in earnest.

He sighed as he fumbled with his pages. There was no swift and illuminating stroke of inspiration in this. It was drudgery — no more. The writing down of what was singing in the mind so clearly, so self-evident — this was simply a matter of knowing how, and it always made him impatient. He could fancy himself so much more entertainingly, and, with some conceit, he thought valuably, occupied. So he was not polite when Elise, perpetually puzzled by the vagaries of her two strange employers, fumbled at the door and made it apparent that she was anxious to make the bed. *"Non, non, non! Laissez-moi, je vous implore! Je suis très occupé!"* And a few minutes later he threw down his pen in exasperation when the latch again rattled and the door was partly shoved open.

This time, however, it was not Elise, but Tony. Kurt sat back in surprise.

"You back so soon?" he said.

Tony kicked at his walking stick and looked out of the window. Then he turned.

"It's awfully foolish of me to stay on here, Kurt, without a thing to do." He spoke hurriedly. "I haven't too much money, and I can't get a part in New York this season if I'm not back soon. Then too, I'd like to see what can be done with *The Duchess."* He looked at Kurt, for the first time since he had come into the room, straight in the eyes.

"Would you mind awfully?" he asked. "You could stay on here as long as you liked, and—"

"Stay on here alone? I guess not! Or do you think I might have an affair with Elise just to complete your cure?"

He grinned derisively. Then he rose and put his hands on Tony's shoulders.

"See here, kid. If you feel you've got to go, that's all there is to it, and you mustn't consider me. I wouldn't stay on here without you, on a bet — it wouldn't be right at all. But I can go on down into Italy as I planned at first, and finish the score in about two weeks of steady work. Then I'll have to be about this scholarship business again."

"How long does that keep you here?"

"Until June. That gives me plenty of time for Rome and Munich and maybe my last month in Paris."

"Yes. Well, now that I've decided, I'm not going to put it off. See here — knock off work, get on some respectable clothes, and come to Nice with me. We can find out about a boat for me, and the trains, and I'll treat you to a farewell dinner. What say?"

It seemed an occasion for some special celebration, and in an hour they were off by way of the jerking trolley to Sauvergne and the careening motor bus to Nice. Here, their errands done, and an *apéritif* sipped at one of the cafés fronting the square — where Tony took an especial delight in pointing out three distinct young men at three distinct tables who were distinctly on the lookout for male companionship, and whom Kurt, in his innocence, would not have looked at a second time, or a first — they strolled along the shore to Reynaud's. The dusk was just descending, a lavender veil; bringing with it, up and down the shallow curve of the bay, erratic rosy lights. A cool breeze from the Mediterranean decided them to sit inside. They chose a table against the far wall of the café and turned their attention to the menu.

"Who's your girlfriend?" Tony asked suddenly. Kurt, looking up, discovered a plump lady across the room smiling at him and waving a glove. Kurt waved back.

"You remember her — at the *pension* in Sauvergne? Kathleen Horan. She's Irish, and she paints — guess what?"

"Watercolors!" said Tony.

"Right. She's really a good sport. Has enough money, apparently, to do as she likes, and she likes to live the genteel bohemian life wherever the fancy strikes her. She was at Sauvergne before I went there, and left soon after you came. I think she's in Villefranche now."

Tony ordered champagne and the dinner was proceeding pleasantly when Kurt felt Tony's hand clutch his knee under the table.

"Look what's arriving!" he whispered.

With considerable gaiety a party of four had come in and taken a long table against the wall next to that of Miss Horan, who was viewing their somewhat alcoholic joviality with beaming tolerance. Leo Rubin, red of face, talking loudly through his flat nose, was host. Mrs. Rubin, in a tweed suit — looking ready, as Tony whispered to Kurt, to psychoanalyze the universe — chattering volubly to the other couple. Frank Harris, Kurt overheard, might be down to spend the next weekend with them.

Kurt listened intently.

"Harris interests you a good deal, doesn't he?" Tony said, amused at Kurt's attentiveness.

"Of course. Doesn't he you?"

Tony shrugged his shoulders and countered with a question.

"You've read his life of Wilde?"

"Yes."

"Like it?"

"W-well — I thought it was a biography of Harris as much as Wilde. I liked parts of it; parts of it annoyed me."

"How?"

"His attitude. It's the typical attitude of the he-man, making a great show of his tolerance for Wilde's perversion, and wanting all his readers to know exactly his own position."

"Well, why not?" asked Tony, with a light laugh. "It wouldn't do him any good to be classed as one of Oscar's boyfriends."

"Oh, don't! Of course, he's excusable. But how can he be expected to write a really sympathetic biography when he has no understanding of the thing that underlay all Wilde's troubles?"

"But—" Tony interrupted.

Kurt paid no heed. He spoke with an animation that Tony found new and amusing.

"Before you came, Mrs. Rubin gave me his autobiography — *My Life and Loves.* Have you seen it?"

Tony shook his head.

"It's — it's appalling."

"It shocked you?" asked Tony, smiling quizzically. "I've heard it was pretty raw."

"Yes, it shocked me — but not the way you think. It wasn't the moral thing in the puritanical sense that shocked me, it was the bad taste — such an obvious pandering to dirty minds. He tells in nauseating detail about his affairs with women; and here — this is what I'm getting at — he describes his lovemaking with great gusto. Lust, there's no better word, strange caresses — tongue, teeth, hair — things surely as perverse as what he deplores in Wilde. But because it's a man and a woman, it's all right. The real object of 'this thing called love,' normal love, is creation, isn't it? Babies — new humans. Really, then, any part of lovemaking that hasn't that immediate object is perverse."

Tony started once more to interrupt.

"No — wait. I'm not saying that I approve of that idea — and you certainly don't; it destroys your game of love. What I objected to all through the book was Harris's opacity, his inability to see how little difference there really is between his sort of dallying and — and ours. Almost at the end of the book he seems to see the light — but he doesn't see it graciously, and I hated that. Hated it!"

Kurt's face was flushed. The champagne had taken effect, and Tony was surprised at his vehemence.

But Kurt had not finished. "You remember the night you gave me the lecture? You said then that love was all alike. You were right about that. So is lust. Each kind of passion — man-and-woman passion, man-and-man passion — has all degrees of love; from love that is pure and high and fine, down the scale to lust that is ugly and despicable and beastly. Each kind has its prostitutes, its procurers and pimps and 'houses,' and each kind has its ideal lovers. It's Paola and Francesca, and Dante and Beatrice, on the one hand; and it's David and Jonathan, and it's Shakespeare and Willy, on the other. The only difference is — the only damned difference is that for us there's no way of getting social sanction — so we go around the world like a lot of sorry ghosts, being forever ashamed of a thing we've no reason to be ashamed of."

He put his chin heavily into his cupped hands, and the glasses tinkled with the impact.

"Oh, see here!" Tony admonished. "Forget it, for now, at least. The Rubins have discovered us."

It was apparently true. Rubin himself was grimacing at them maliciously, and the whole party was eyeing them with some amusement. It was obvious that they were being discussed.

"He shouldn't do that!" Kurt whispered, and then, abruptly: "Where's the bill? Let's get out of here. Let's get out."

His hand shook as he rose. Tony, with a quick perception of
how difficult it would be to cross the café directly into these
contemptuous politely sneering faces, and past them to the door,
went first, and achieved the exit grandly, as an actor might be
expected to. He turned for a reassuring word to Kurt, and Kurt was
not behind him. Damn! He had forgotten Miss Horan. As Kurt
passed her table, his chin high, his face flushed and defiant,
without a glance at the Rubins' table, she had caught at his sleeve
and simpered, "Oh, Mr. Gray!" Kurt's willfully assumed nonchalance was totally upset by this unexpected salutation. He swayed a
moment, his hands moving helplessly at his sides.

"You seem to be in a great hurry, you two! You're not going back
to St. Paul so early in the evening, are you?"

"Yes. Yes, we are," Kurt stammered, his face burning, conscious only of the peering faces just at his elbow. Stephen,
floppy-eared Stephen, illogically flashed into his brain. "Stephen,"
he said nervously. "Stephen — our child — we have to see that
he's all right."

There was a snort from Rubin and a hoarsely whispered "My
God, they've got a child!"; a "Shhh!" from Georgia; and a madden-
ing assortment of snickers from the rest of the party. Kurt turned
and ran to the door, his eyes blinded with hot tears of mortification.
He started up the *quai* at such a mad pace that Tony had to skip
and half run to keep up with him. "Oh, what a fool! What a
goddamned fool thing to say! How could they laugh like that!"

He was half laughing and half sobbing, and Tony, with difficulty, drew him down on a bench by the waterfront and quieted
him. His own worldliness, his arduously acquired indifference and
superiority, were strangely shaken by the whole episode, and particularly by the storm of passion this quiet young man had sum-
moned up. It was partly the champagne, without doubt, but there
was a depth of feeling, a flaming intensity hidden away here that
he had not suspected. A quiet, soul-consuming bitterness, he could
have comprehended — the sort of thing he had encountered in
Kurt when he first came to Sauvergne; but this, this made him look
curiously at his docile companion of the past weeks and wonder
how wise his glib prescribings had been.

"Oh, come on, Kurt!" he said, tenderly. "What does it matter! What do they amount to, the whole lot of them! Come on, forget it!"

To Kurt this low-voiced sympathy might have been his mother's, and he a little boy again, white with hatred of the school bullies. Tony's arm across his shoulders was, somehow, his mother's arm; and, crying silently, he dropped his head into this consoling lap.

IV

KURT SURRENDERED his package, picked up his change, and sauntered out of the Bureau des Postes with a feeling that was partly relief and partly regret. The last pages of the piano score of *The Duchess* were off to Tony in New York. He had worked so steadily at it since coming back to Paris that it seemed strange not to have it hanging over him. He wondered vaguely whether he would hear from Tony at all anymore, now that the manuscript was completed; his letters had been so brief and so impatient for the rest of the score. He realized too, with a quick tightening of his throat and the old familiar heaviness in his chest, that the loneliness that had been hovering over him, kept away only by the steady routine of copying — the pedestrian setting down of notes and bars and signs, the armor of drudgery — was now descending with the pervasiveness of fog, and was to be dissipated about as easily.

He might have gone to his room. He had secured a small one on a third floor in the rue de Tournon, near Foyot's and the Luxembourg Gardens. But while it had seemed acceptable enough for a copy room, he now had for it a distinct aversion. February was barely over, but there was already in the air an intangible sense of spring. Kurt turned his back resolutely on the rue de Tournon and walked quickly into the Gardens. There were grayish green buds on the chestnut trees, and in their lacy shadowings spring seemed more than ever a new certainty. A number of old men played at *boules*, the balls clicking sharply together; the benches were dotted with students, alone, reading, in angular unconscious poses, or in twos, conversing earnestly, and with nursemaids, ribboned and starched, while children, screaming shrilly, rolled hoops as tall as themselves along the sun-flecked paths.

"—with ever-returning spring—" The half-line — from where he could not say — ran, a persistent refrain, through his head. Spring — spring — recurrent and recurrent — and always the same. Spring in Barton, with maple leaves like green small hands; with marbles in the schoolyard; with rubbish burning in backyards; with heavy-footed horses turning and turning in small garden plots as the plows turned up the moist earth — furrowing it patiently for seeds again, for growth again. Spring in Ann Arbor, with students strolling through the early evenings in couples, or alone — Derry and Kurt, together on a spring night on a moon-whitened hillside. Spring — spring — loneliness tugging at the heart, tears in the night, joy in the morning.

He swallowed. What the hell. He turned down the boulevard Raspail, looking now and then in the windows of the scattered, strangely assorted shops. The Dome. The Rontonde. Each crowded and noisy with chatter. He found a vacant table at the Dome and ordered a café au lait. It was pleasant here, in this babble of English and American voices, with only occasionally a phrase of French like a struggling crosscurrent. Young men in knickers and gay ties, some with beards, some with too-long hair; girls in smocks or smart gowns from the boulevards, sipping green Pernods. It might almost be, Kurt thought with a chuckle, some art school in New York — there was even a battered Ford at the curb.

He was startled by a bustling feminine voice just at his elbow — "Why, Mr. Gray!" It was Miss Horan. He jumped to his feet, embarrassed.

"Won't you — won't you sit down?"

"Thanks. Thanks. I've been hunting a studio, and I'm dead." She dropped into the chair, which, to Kurt's surprise, barely shivered. The waiter was beside them. *"Apportez mademoiselle du —* What'll you have, Miss Horan? Good. *Bière, garçon."*

"O-oh!" she exhaled relievedly, taking off her velvet tam. "I'm glad to see you. Last time I saw you you were in a great hurry."

Kurt blushed and stammered. "Y-yes. I — I — well, I made a very stupid remark, and your neighbors took it the — the worst possible way. I was quite embarrassed."

"You were? Oh, well, it's nice to be able to be embarrassed, you know. I can't anymore."

The beer arrived, and Kurt found himself curiously glad to be chatting with this large frowsy woman. It was a weapon, this casual meeting, against the encroaching loneliness, and for the moment he was happy. They talked at random until Miss Horan declared she must, positively, be off. Kurt walked with her to her room, which was just off the boulevard Montparnasse in a narrow court; bade her good-bye, and made for the nearest Métro. He was soon at the Opéra, and making for the American Express. There were several letters, and he thrust them all into his pocket jealously. He threaded through the afternoon crowds of the boulevard to the Madeleine, and thence into the Champs Élysées.

The great parkway, in this late afternoon, was kaleidoscopic with moving figures against the pale green background of spring. Kurt passed one of the Guignol theaters. The barelegged children were all gone, and the low benches empty till another day. A man was fumbling at the tiny stage door, his arms full of gangling puppets, in a strenuous attempt to fasten it. His wife stood by, chattering at him like an angry squirrel. Kurt, smiling, thought, "Poor puppeteer! She thinks he's a puppet too."

He found a deserted bench at last, and took out his letters. There was always, so far from home, an unaccountable reluctance to open letters, a wanton struggling against the very real impatience to know their contents. He sat holding them for several minutes, sorting them over, studying their casings, and arranging them in the order in which they should be opened. The two business letters from the Conservatory, the letter from Tony, the one from home, and last of all David's; for it was David, in this sudden softness of spring — David's eyes, David's promises — that recurred over and over again.

Tony's was the briefest note. He had secured a part and was in rehearsal. He was anxious for the complete score. "He'll soon have it and be satisfied," Kurt muttered.

From his mother — "The church supper was well attended — the snow is nearly gone — we've had to have the dining room repapered — your father is reading the seed catalogues — love — Mother"; and, scrawled at the bottom, "The same goes for — Dad."

David's envelope bulged. There were pages written in the flourishing excited hand he knew, perhaps, better than he knew the person who had set it down. Yet here was a love letter — a spring letter — bursting with promises and assurances, and begging for promises and assurances in return. This was the letter for such a day — ecstatic, and willful, and turbulent, and ridiculous, and wise. Surely, surely, David's high ideal was his forever. Not Tony's, not Chloe's, not the world's, but David's.

"M'sieu'—" A thin soft voice insinuated itself into his tumbling dream. "M'sieu' — you buy nice rug? Good rug — cheap?" A small Arab, a pile of rugs over his shoulder, held the edges of them out appealingly.

"No, no," said Kurt. "No rugs."

"Good rugs, cheap!" the vendor insisted. Kurt shook his head emphatically. The Arab drew closer, and shoved under his nose, from some recess of his loose garment, a card. In the glance he gave it, Kurt saw a tangle of white limbs, an obscene octopus of human flesh. "Peectures? Nice peectures?" the man whined. "Naked ladies — naked m'sieu's — two, t'ree, four, all together naked—"

"No!"

Kurt sprang to his feet in a rage, and was away before the astonished vendor could collect himself and follow. His heels bit angrily into the gravel path. Why must such vile things thrust themselves in, over and over? The lascivious picture, fight against it as he would, called up Tony's tale of the Philadelphia party — the amorous heaps of young men on saffron cushions, and David there, smiling and superior. What should he believe?

It was spring — spring. Love was in the restlessness of his soul. David's eyes said, "Wait — wait — wait—"; Tony's curling lips said, "You're in Paris, boy — find a *cocotte* and see what love is really like"; Chloe's smooth dark hair whispered, "Forget, forget, and come to me — to the Chloe you've never known — my lips — my breasts — my body."

He turned back into the boulevards, uncertain where to go. He realized that he was hungry; and, stopping at a small café near the Opéra, ordered dinner. He sat long over his wine and cigarettes, questioning himself futilely. Was he a fool? He was young; he had never known a woman; it was spring; this was Paris. Would it hurt? Dared he? Could he? David — David's eyes. Wanting only David, how could he?

He paid his bill and walked on in the dusk. The lights, lavender, yellow, were springing out of the half-dark like stiff, exotic, strangely phosphorescent fruits. He hesitated before crossing the place de l'Opéra. A cringing figure was at his side. "Got plans for tonight, buddy?" He moved away, impatiently; but the figure, little more than a voice in the gathering darkness, followed. "I'll show you the sights. Swell house — nice clean girls — seventeen, eighteen years old. Hot stuff, kid — you won't do wrong. I know Paris, boy!"

"Oh, so do I! Leave me alone!"

He dashed in front of a careening taxi, and his escape was signalized by the screech of brakes, an explosion of Gallic oaths from the driver, and a bedlam of protesting horns. He dove again into the Métro, boarded a train, and got off at the place Pigalle. He came out again into the garish night of Montmartre. The streets and cafés swarmed with noisy amusement-seekers — Americans, seemingly, predominating. It was a seething contrast of light and shadow. Faces, upturned, catching the shifting multicolored lights of the signs, were curious unhealthy flowers moving through a Walpurgis night, lustful and secretive, vulgar and perverse. He swung into the crowd. Le Moulin Rouge, le Chat Qui Fume, le Rat Mort, each drawing its quota of satiated, but ever-hungering humans. "Oh, why not!" he thought, and avoiding a half-dozen scalpers, he secured himself a cheap seat for a revue — *Paris Tout Nu.*

It was a nauseating performance, too obviously exhibitionistic to be remotely funny. The women were pasty and too fat, and moved through their "art poses" like dilapidated automatons. The men at either side of Kurt watched eagerly; nudging their neighbors when, as the climax of each number, one girl — slightly less fat than her sisters — undressed in some perfect masterpiece of bad taste, and took her seductive pose in the white pencil of the spotlight for the curtain. Kurt looked about him at these men — young, old, fat-jowled, thin, staring with amorous and bovine satisfaction at these successive tableaux — and shuddered.

The secret small triangle beneath this bit of sequin that each man lusted for. *Paris Tout Nu* — *tout le monde tout nu.* This it was to be normal — the Arab rug vendor, the pimp at the Opéra, the place Pigalle — a stud stable lacking the dignity that nobler and less self-conscious animals might give it. He fumbled his way out. The whole vile world seemed bent to thwart love, natural or unnatural, that was pure and worthy of the name.

This knowledge Tony was so anxious for him to achieve, this mystery that hides between a woman's thighs, might, conceivably, have been a mystery — Delphic, lovely, approached with fear and reverence; but now, in this fevered night, it was a dirty secret behind a bit of sequin that any man with a few francs in his pocket might buy. No, this was not for him.

From dark doorways as he passed, whispers came sifting into his consciousness — *"Cheri — cheri—" "Une cigarette, m'sieu'—" "M'sieu' — avec moi — m'sieu' — je vous donnerai beaucoup de plaisir—" "Cheri—" "M'sieu'—"* A rouged hand with cheap rings on it caught at his sleeve, a warm body pressed against him — *"Vous voulez m'acheter une absinthe, n'est-ce pas, m'sieu'"* — and he shook her off roughly. He walked rapidly, through light streets and dark, across the boulevards, through the Tuileries Gardens, along the Seine and across it, and along it again, calmer now, but abysmally unhappy.

Ahead of him, loitering, was a thin girl. Kurt stopped abruptly. Did he want this knowledge which the man-world thought so vital? Was all the raging of the last few hours nothing more than a noisy mechanism to defend him from his own fear? Was he afraid? Christ in heaven! Was he, under all this fine philosophizing, a beast like all the rest? The girl had stopped under a streetlamp, and was looking back at him curiously, her face masklike in its lilac flickering. No. Whatever it was in him, hungering, aching, unsatisfied, it was not for this, he knew; not for something to be bought, whatever it was. He felt in his pocket, hastened his step, thrust into the hand of the astonished girl a twenty-franc note, and hurried off towards the boulevard St. Michel.

There were still people in the cafés. He rounded the corner by the Odéon. The evening's crowd was just coming out. The night was warm and soft. He turned into his own street, stumbled up the dark stairs to his room, and lay facedown across his bed in the darkness. Spring was like running fire in his bones. He could — now, he thought, almost — No. No, eternally. He rose and switched on the light. The mirror across the room reflected the garish wallpaper. He crossed to it and stared at his face reflected there, intently, abstractedly, as a stranger might.

"You!" he said at last. "You! You should have bought the Arab's pictures, the whole dirty lot of them, and taken them to bed with you!"

He retired then, but he did not sleep for a long time.

PART FOUR

I

IT WAS ONLY going away, reversed; the film turned backward, the emotions too, like some topsy-turvy cinematic sunset — rising now from dim to bright, as, a year ago, they had faded from bright to deadly dim. As the great boat swung clumsily about in the river, the same crowd, apparently, stood like a swarm of puppets on the same pier, with the same mazy motion of the mass. And through the seething thicket of arms floated a red scarf. "Chloe!" he sighed, like one surprised that his expectation had been so perfectly realized. And under this serpentine of red were, he knew — yes, he could see them now — Derry and David. Derry and David and Chloe. Nothing had changed. The boat had swung into the river, he had fallen asleep, and now the boat was swinging back. Time was a ghost. It was all some little plotted trickery of fate.

They were, before long, shuttling away from the pier, crowded and laughing in a taxi, and deposited at a Village restaurant for lunch. "One of David's haunts," Derry explained. Kurt sat, his elbows on the table, staring avidly at first one and then another, and expostulating needlessly at intervals in the barrage of questioning, "Gee, it's good to see you all again!" It was cool and dim and there were few other customers. David's hand gripped his knee under the table, and David's eyes — David's eyes—

"I dug this out especially for you, Kurt, remembering last June." Chloe indicated the red scarf.

"It never seemed like you, that color," he replied, "but I'm glad you had it."

"I don't wear it anymore. I leave the flamboyant colors to the kid brother. I suppose you've noticed the necktie?"

"Very dada," Kurt approved.

"Derry's getting worldly. I only see him when our mutual friends arrive from Europe."

David sat frowning darkly at this badinage, but said nothing. There were silences during the luncheon, when each of the four felt the imposition of the presence of the others.

Luncheon over, Chloe twisted her cigarette in the brass tray and rose. "Back to the box factory for me! I'll see you again soon?" There was the wistful, wishful look in her face, as she turned to him, that Kurt knew and dreaded.

"Why, sure! Of course. Derry at least knows where to find you, doesn't he?"

"Oh, I suppose he's still got my number somewhere among his addresses. So long, all!" and she went out.

"How's she making out, really?" Kurt asked Derry. "She never said a word about it in her letters."

"Pretty well now, I guess," Derry answered. "The job at Columbia didn't last long. She's so darned independent, and she's very uppish. Doesn't approve of us, I guess."

David was obviously unwilling to talk now.

Derry continued. "She got this job doing decorating of some kind — toys, boxes, trays, candlesticks, and things like that. It pays fairly well and keeps her mind occupied, which is a good thing."

"Very," put in David.

Derry laughed. "Chloe and David don't hit it off so well."

"Oh, shut up, Derry. You're always putting your foot in it. And don't forget that you're a working man too, old bean. This whole forenoon," he explained, turning to Kurt, "has been a sort of *fête champêtre* in your honor, you see."

"Lord yes!"

Derry looked at his wristwatch, rose, and sauntered off with a theatrical nonchalance, waving a "See you later" as he went through the door.

Kurt watched all this unfamiliar posturing with an amazed smile. "What the devil's got into Derry?" he asked.

"Oh — it's a long story, Kurt. Here, let's go. It's only a couple of blocks to our rooms. I'll help you with the bags, and we'll walk it."

The room to which Kurt was led was on a third floor in MacDougal Street. It was almost a replica of David's room in Ann Arbor. Kurt sank back on the black divan, smiling. "Come here," he said, holding out his arms.

Later, quietness having enveloped them in the dark room like a soft cocoon, holding the two of them there together in the calm complete happiness that comes so seldom and becomes so cherished and so rare a memory, words, explanations, seemed inconsequential and petty. Kurt thought, and whispered his thought to David:

"What if life for both of us should end now — with this moment? Would you much care?"

"I shouldn't care at all," David answered softly. "I shouldn't care at all. Oh, Kurt, all this time you've been gone I've wondered so if it could really be — if I could really care for anyone as lastingly, as awfully, as I seemed to be caring for you — wanting you. I couldn't credit it, quite, knowing myself so well. But now — now that you're here, I'm sure, sure, sure. It's you and me now, Kurt — it's got to be."

David went to the delicatessen for food for supper; which, since Derry would be out, they decided to have in the room. Kurt, languid, happy, unpacked his bag. "It's you and me now, it's got to be." Tony's exhortations, Chloe's fears and desires, melted dimly into the past. The moment was too anesthetic for them to prick through into his consciousness; yet he knew they would have to be answered. "It's you and me now, it's got to be."

Supper was pleasant, and the evening that followed it, as they lay in the dimly lighted room — talking, carefully, slowly, with long intervals of silence; David trying so painstakingly to come to the complete sympathy and understanding that both desired. How very unlike, thought Kurt, those evenings with Tony in St. Paul it was — those evenings full of absurd endless discussions of absurd endless topics; Tony arguing heatedly for some far-fetched theory, not for the sake of the theory, but solely to bask in his own skill; his mind, hard, brilliant, veering off like a polished ball from the slightest hint of sentiment. Here all was soft and yielding and persuasive and lethargic.

David told of the winter with Derry, hesitantly, stumblingly. There was in him now none of the glib superiority Kurt had shrunk from when they first met. "All David has to offer you is a spineless idealism" — the phrase of Chloe's letter came back to him.

"Something happened to me, Kurt," David was saying, "when you left. None of the old — diversions — seemed to matter. But, how hard it is to get away from those diversions, Kurt. They fly up when you least are looking for them or wanting them. Derry and I took this place. Derry, I thought, would be good for me. I liked him very much. Oh—" he hastened, "not as I like you, Kurt, please believe me — but — well, you know Derry. I didn't very well, I guess. He's so damned sure of things, so solid, so little introspective, so little caring for the theories and reasons of things so long as he has the things. I thought he'd be good for me, but I'm afraid I've only been bad for him. You see I've — I've" — he took Kurt's hand and held it closely — "I've never felt so afraid before of — of telling things—"

"You needn't," said Kurt, reassuringly. "Maybe I know more about it than you think."

David, not noticing, went on.

"I started this sort of thing when I was such a kid, Kurt, and I'm so sorry for so many things since then. I ran away from school because I was bullied. A man picked me up in a restaurant, and was very kind to me. He seemed to offer the things I was wanting — a sort of *vie bohemien*, with money and clothes and an idle and beautifully sinful life. The physical thing was so new and so glamorous in Ozzy's establishment. There were always some of 'the boys' about. You don't know them much, do you, Kurt?"

"Not much."

"They're a strange sad lot, finding a feverish and hysterical kind of happiness in new associates — always new boys, new men. You're carried away with it when it's new, and sometimes even when you're older. There's a circle that's always getting wider. You get known, and sought after or avoided, but you get known. It's like some great and terribly secret society, with its own life, its own passwords and signs; and once you're in it, it's the very devil to break out. You get older, and you try to look younger. Your taste gets more and more jaded and you demand more and more per-verse diversions, and what happens to you at last — God knows. But the terrible part of it is, you're known, and marked, wherever you go. There's a circle here in New York, there's one in Philadel-phia, and Boston, and Detroit, and Chicago, and Hollywood — and anywhere at all you go, and there's always someone who knows you.

"Well" — he shrugged his shoulders slightly — "that's how it was here. I still don't know how it happened. I thought, anchoring myself to you and to Derry, I was safe, but one by one they'd find me out and come. I was out of it, truly I was — that's what you did for me, Kurt. I saw in you, you see, someone outside the circle, someone strong enough to stay outside and to hold me there — a way of escape. But they came, and Derry was swept off his feet. It was all new to him. He's in it now, and he shouldn't be, Kurt, for he's not the type, you know he's not. He's only in it for the thrill — not because he can't help himself, or because there's nothing else. He's so damned normal, really, that it's worried me like the devil. And there's nothing I can say. He knows too much about me, Kurt, and he can't see how different we are underneath."

For a long time they were silent. David, supporting his body on his elbows, played absently with Kurt's fingers.

"How do you manage, you two?"

"It's been a problem. Derry has had work most of the time. I've done some drafting for one of Ozzy's friends" — he made a wry face — "and, Kurt — believe it or not, I've sold three stories."

"No! I didn't know you—"

"I didn't know it myself. I've always wanted to, I guess. And when you came along, promising such fine accomplishments, it made me hate myself. The stories were pretty bad, I'm afraid — but I did them to sell, and they sold. I want to write a book."

"And you've already written some of it," Kurt hazarded.

"Yes, bits. But it's hard — and I've got to do it well — and I hate work."

"What's the book about, David?"

"It's — it's about us, Kurt — and this." David's eyes were darkly serious. "So you see it has to be done carefully, for it's got to be —

Oh, it sounds high-hat, but it's got to be a sort of vindication of our kind of loving, you see. A vindication to the world. Nobody's ever done it, really. Shakespeare's sonnets are, gloriously, but nobody seems to dare admit it. The professors, the fools, get all tangled up in explaining what's as obvious as two plus two. Shakespeare loved the boy actor, and he celebrated his love in the finest, cleanest, highest poetry of his whole career, and did it without shame. And now they manufacture all sorts of shifts and silly dodges to avoid calling Shakespeare an invert. O hell! All I want is to show people we're not monsters any more than Shakespeare was, that's all. Oh, I know the continentals have had a hand in it — Proust, and Mann, and Gide, and Wedekind; but it's America I want in my book — New York and Philadelphia and Hollywood and St. Louis and New Haven and all the rest. I don't know if I can ever do it."

"You can do it, David. I know you can — and you'll have to."

"Yes," he said slowly. "Yes, I guess I'll have to. It keeps me awake nights."

Again they were silent, until David asked, "What about Tony McGauran?"

"Tony? Nothing about him at all, David, more than I told you in the letters. He's a good friend, and that's all. He pulled me out of a frightful case of funk, and he was good company. We worked together on the show I told you about, and that's all."

"You're sure that's all?"

"All, absolutely all."

"All right, Kurt. I'm jealous as hell, and you may as well know it now as later. I think I'd knife anybody that wanted you. And you're so damned wantable, Kurt, though you don't know it. I'll worry every time you step out for fear you'll find someone you like better than me. I'll probably be bothering the life out of you if you so much as look at anyone. And if your show does go through, God help me!"

"Why?"

"Why! Kurt! You innocent! Don't you know that there'll be musicians, and dancing masters, and singers, and chorus men, and rehearsals galore? I'll be chewing my nails off here at home."

Kurt laughed. "There's no immediate danger, I guess. At least I daren't count on it. I'll have to see Tony tomorrow and find out what's doing."

David considered the prospect glumly, while Kurt watched him, amused.

They went to bed early, and Kurt lay awake for a long time in the unfamiliar room trying to adjust himself to this new order. At the pier that morning all had seemed unchanged. Now he knew that nothing was quite the same. He had left with a regard for Derry that seemed unshakable; and now, a year later, he lay bare with David, regarding Derry's clumsy amours with a detachment that was hard to understand. He had left with an affection for David so meshed about with David's symbolism and David's ideal that all his feeling was nebulous and uncertain — a spiritual ecstasy rather than a physical love — and now David's head lay close against his throat, and he knew that he loved David as he never could have loved Derry, loved him more deeply because his love was requited and understood.

And Chloe? What of Chloe? The relationship there was certainly unchanged? But no. In her that morning he had felt a growing hardness, something unyielding and shell-like that the year had built up around her, an accretion of bitterness that was a new barrier between them. Was he wrong? Would he, could he be happier with Chloe than he was now with David? As if sensing Kurt's wakeful questioning, David stirred in his sleep and laid his arm across Kurt's breast. No, no, no! What was there more than this? And finding David's lips, he kissed him again into wakefulness.

II

NEXT MORNING he left the apartment before either David or Derry, who had come in late, were up. There were three things to be done, and then he knew he must go home — home for the summer with his father and mother in Barton. Save for leaving David, the prospect was not unpleasant. They wanted him there, and it was only fair that he should go. But first he must see Tony, and have lunch with Chloe, and visit Korlov at the Conservatory to discuss prospects for the fall. He dared not count too much on *The Duchess.*

He breakfasted in Times Square, more raw and blatant than he had remembered it, and walked on into the Fifties. Tony wasn't up, but he finally came to the door looking tousled and theatrical in orchid crêpe pajamas.

"Good God, Kurt! Don't you know we professional people are never at our best at this hour? Come in and park yourself on the bed. How are you? And how are your sexual problems?"

Kurt grinned and tossed a blanket at him.

"I'm interested in *The Duchess,*" he said.

"And not in me? Ah well!" and he sighed dramatically. "Our damned *Duchess* is still with Breinig. He won't say yes and he won't say no, but he hangs on to the script as if it was the last button on his braces."

"And in the meantime what is the most vital juvenile of the American stage doing?"

"He is living on charity. You'll take me to lunch, of course?"

"I will not!" said Kurt. "I'm dining with a lady."

"And I can't go along?"

"No, you can't. You remember your instructions, don't you? You don't want to queer my cure, do you?"

"No. Oh no, of course not. In which case, I'm going back to bed. Let me know where you're to be and I'll wire you the fate of *The Duchess.* I'm glad we didn't leave her *enceinte* in the last act — she'd have had a family by now." And he crawled back into bed. Kurt, laughing, started to leave, when Tony called after him.

"O Kurt! See here! Is there anything really — uh — potential — in this luncheon date of yours? Come with me, if there isn't. I'd like to have you meet my Joda. She'd do you good."

"You still have your Joda, do you?"

"Oh my, yes!" He was exaggeratedly emphatic. "We still have our Joda, all of us. We call her the Little Mother of Yale.

She'd be very friendly, Kurt. I don't think she's had a composer."

"We'll let Joda go till later," Kurt said, laughing over his shoulder, and went out, looking at his watch. There was still plenty of time to visit the Conservatory before lunch. He hailed a taxi, and found Korlov engaged with a student. He sat in the corridor with the familiar, insanely mingling and dissonant sounds beating and snarling about him. At last Korlov's door opened and the departing student came out, looking very warm and tired, and Kurt saw the broad back of Korlov arranging sheets of music on the piano top. He knocked and went in. Korlov turned and, recognizing him, greeted him enthusiastically.

"Koort Gra-ee!" he exclaimed, and put his hands on Kurt's shoulders. "Ach, how glad I am to see you. Yust back from Paris, eh? I trust you haf not been bitten by the Antheil bug? Ach, that poseur! Auric, Casella! Madmen, that's what they are, madmen!"

Kurt smiled as Korlov fumed.

"You are laughing at old Korlov, eh? Ah well—" He shrugged his heavy shoulders with mock resignation. He fingered the music on the piano while Kurt told him of Paris and Fontainebleau and concerts and Phillipe.

"And what did Monsieur Phillipe say about your playing?"

"Just what you said, sir. That I'd never be a great performer — too impatient of routine."

"And you were sad then?"

Kurt smiled at the old man's quaint phrasing. "No, I was not sad."

"Good!" said Korlov. "You should not be. You can be a good composer, and God knows we have enough piano players already. What are you going to do?"

"I'm going home for a while, to Michigan. I'll have to find something in the fall."

"How would you like to teach?"

"What — and where?" asked Kurt.

"We haf a request—" said Korlov confidentially, as if there might be spies at every window, "we haf a request for a teacher at Brookway School. You know that school?"

"Yes, I've heard of it. New, isn't it, and in Connecticut, and disgustingly wealthy?"

"*Ja.* Oh, so wealthy!" He lifted up his eyes, and his hands expressed his incredulity at such lavishness. "A Mr. Brook gave how many millions I do not know, two years ago. The buildings haf been all finished now, and they will be open in September with about fifty students."

"Boys?"

"*Ja,* boys — up to college age. You would have there charge of all the music, teach harmony, and do, so they tell me anyway, about what you like. No discipline. One of these modern schools — not like my old Gymnasium — *ach nein.*"

"It doesn't sound so bad," said Kurt.

"No. For you it sounds good, to me, good. You would be free much of the time, and quiet for your writing, eh?"

"It's not a highly academic sort of place, I take it?"

"No." Korlov stroked his jowl thoughtfully with the backs of his fingers. "When do you go home?" he asked.

"I was going tomorrow, but — should I do anything definite about the place? Now?"

"Stay over one day, and tomorrow after lunch I take my car and we drive to this Brookway School, and you can see for yourself, *hein?*"

Kurt agreed, and departed, hurrying to the nearest subway station to take a train downtown. He arrived at the shop just about noon. As he climbed the dark flight of stairs, two girls, descending, eyed him curiously. He found Chloe scrubbing a recalcitrant spot of paint from her finger.

"Take a look in the shop while I get organized, Kurt," she said. He went through the door to which her dripping hand pointed. It was a large high-ceilinged room, light in spite of the grime that encrusted the windows. At the far end was a small but well-equipped carpenter shop. The rest of the room was filled with tables piled with wooden novelties; some ready to be assembled, some complete and ready for paint, others drying, some piled on shelves ready to be wrapped and boxed. The whole place smelled of shavings and paint and oil and turpentine.

"Why don't you wash your windows?" Kurt called.

"We did try it" — Chloe's voice came to him punctuated with gurglings of the drain, splashings, and blowings — "but it was so ugly outside we were glad when they got dirty again. Come on, I'm ready."

She took Kurt's arm and they were on their way.

"If you don't mind, let's go to a Chinese place near here. It's not much to look at, but the food's good, and it's cheap, and I daren't take more than an hour. Getting off to see you arrive yesterday forenoon was just about all I dare attempt for a while."

"And about all I'm worth too?"

Chloe laughed and squeezed his arm. When had he walked like this with a girl? Not since, a year ago, the two of them in so strange a tangle of moods had plodded the paths of Central Park, in a darkness more than physical. But this was not the same girl. He told her so.

"Of course I'm changed," she said. "You think I'm harder. Well, perhaps I am. One has to be, living here."

"The year has been happy?"

"It's been hell."

They turned into the restaurant and ordered lunch.

"One can't be happy when the thing she wants most she knows she can't have, can she?"

Kurt, embarrassed, avoided her eyes. Still the same, then, underneath. Still wanting his love. He was irritated and flattered at the same time. The situation, to the average fellow, would have seemed so simple; yet to him it was complex and impossible of solution. She wanted him. There would be no scruples, no evasions, yet the thought of physical union with her, with any woman, was a devastating fear.

"You don't like David much, do you?" he asked, not knowing why he asked — sorry as soon as the question was out.

"I despise David. He's ineffectual and weak" — the very words of her letter, Kurt remembered — "but it's not that alone. It's something deeper — a thing I can't explain. I dislike him as I dislike worms and spiders. O Kurt!" She leaned across the table toward him. "I've been so frightened at all this, so frightened.

Derry's made such a fool of himself. Don't you! Don't let yourself!
It's all wrong, this thing you're caught in, you three, and you can't
see it. You're not different, you just think you are, and you mix
everything all up and make the normal thing so difficult."

Kurt was flushed and silent. How could he argue this thing with
a girl, like Chloe? Didn't she suppose he had gone over it all a
hundred bitter times? Couldn't she see the difference between
perversion as a pose, a languid espousement of perfumed decadence, and perversion (how he loathed the word) that was deep in
the core of you, flooding your veins and arteries, making normality
unnatural and the natural abnormal?

"Kurt, I'm sorry. I don't know whether you're right or whether
you're wrong. But I know this: if you ever want — Oh, what's the
use..."

She hid her head in the crook of her arm, her hand clenching
her shoulder, and Kurt feared for a moment that she was crying.
Then she raised it and smiled wanly.

"The tea's good, don't you think?"

He was sorry for her. Pity swept him, and sent his hand
impulsively across the table to lie for an instant on her own.

"See here, Chloe. Don't let it all upset you. I don't know, maybe,
but just believe I'm trying to find out. It's all so uncertain, so at odds
with the everyday—"

"Kurt. Kurt dear!" Her voice was soft but insistent. "Let's say no
more about it. I'll help, if I can, and that's all the right I have to mix
in it at all. Now! Let's have some rice cakes, with fortunes in 'em
— and then I'll have to be back to the paint pots."

III   ·

F‍ROM THE TIME their car entered the Gothic arch and rounded the curve of elms that let through a glimpse of its truncated
Gothic tower, Kurt liked Brookway School. It was an amazing
place to find set down here in the rolling hills of Connecticut. Less

than a year old, the buildings had been so carefully designed and so skillfully aged that they seemed, like buildings he had seen in England, to have grown from the soil with the elms and oaks and maples. The headmaster, Dr. Leffington, was an Oxonian who had been chosen because his ideas were sympathetic with those of the founder of the school.

"The idea of the donor, you see, gentlemen," he explained, "was to provide a school where boys might develop their originality, their individuality. I am an Etonian myself, but I recognize the evils possible in that sort of school. Our aim here, then, will be to get men of the highest possible caliber — scholars rather than peda-gogues — and give them the greatest possible freedom with their charges; the method, that is to say, is inspirational."

"The place alone is inspiring," said Kurt.

"Quite a success, don't you think?"

The classrooms were large, heavily beamed rooms with individ-ual table-desks, rugs, prints; and, in each, a great-mouthed fire-place with benches built in on either side — "for discussions," Dr. Leffington explained, smiling. The commons, the dormitories, and all their furnishings were surprisingly beautiful and comfort-able. In his own study, Dr. Leffington turned to Kurt.

"Mr. Korlov tells me you're the sort of man we want on our staff here. Now I must tell you that I know very little about music. I have the average man's distrust of the usual temperamental performer, with no background and an enormous conceit. On the other hand I want to avoid the merely pedestrian music teacher."

"Ja! Ja!" put in Korlov. "These artists — they are sometimes — my God, how angry they make me. But they can play usually. This boy," and he laid his hand affectionately on Kurt's shoulder, "is not like that, no."

Both Leffington and Kurt laughed at the maestro's clumsy compliment.

"Your job here, as I see it, would be to teach harmony to those who are inclined, and to encourage all amateur creative talent, whether for composition or performing. The usual horrors — glee clubs and such things — we'll have to leave to the will of the boys, and to you. My idea, too, would be to inaugurate an informal course in music history and appreciation which would be interesting enough to draw in most of the school. I'm going to be successful, I think, in getting five thousand dollars this year for a concert fund, in which case you would act as impresario. Your salary would be two thousand plus your living. The masters will eat in commons with the boys, but you would have your own digs — study and shower — and I'll see that there's a piano in yours if you come. What do you say?"

"I say yes, emphatically. It sounds — interesting — more than interesting," he hastened to add. "I'm sure I shall be happy here."

"Good!" said the doctor. "We'll go to the secretary's office and settle it."

Kurt left Korlov at Washington Square. He turned into Mac-Dougal Street and ran up the stairs to David, eager to tell him of the new job. He tapped on the door a tattoo rapid and broken as a Gershwin rhythm, the words of his story rising in his throat, ready to burst forth as soon as David appeared. The door opened, and David stood in the dim light.

"David!" he began excitedly. "I've got a—"

"Kurt," David interrupted him. "I've — I've done a dreadful thing." He shut the door and leaned against it. Kurt saw then the whiteness of his face and noted the strained nervousness in his voice. He was in evening clothes, and his face was white as his shirtfront. Kurt's own excitement was forgotten in his concern for David.

"What is it?"

"Come here." His voice was high-pitched, hysterical. He drew Kurt to the bed and seated him, and then, lying down, put his head in Kurt's lap, his arm flung across his eyes. "I've broken with Ozzy."

"You've — David! Why! That's nothing to worry about! It's the best news I've had since I landed! I'm so awfully glad, kid. I hoped you'd do it of your own accord, and soon."

"Oh, but I didn't do it bravely, Kurt — there was a scene, and I acted like a fool. I only just got back in the house, and I'm — I'm not quite myself yet."

"What happened — do you want to tell me?"

"Yes. Yes, let me. He sent me a wire this afternoon saying he was in town for the night and asking me to meet him for dinner. I didn't know what to do. I'd been worrying about it, anyway — more, since you came." His hand sought Kurt's and held it fiercely. "I love you so — I knew there would have to be an end with Ozzy — but didn't know how — how to do it. Oh, this must sound strange to you, Kurt. But I'm an awful coward. Ozzy's been good to me in his way; he's given me clothes and money — he's kept me. He's fond of me, I guess — at least he's never stuck to any of the others like this. I didn't know what to say to him. You were always in the background, watching, and I was self-conscious and strange, I suppose, when I met him. He's so damned suave and can be so superior and so sneering."

David turned his body about so he could look more squarely into Kurt's face leaning above him.

"It kept up all through dinner. 'I suppose you've got a new lover,' he said. 'I suppose he's innocent and fine and all the rest of it. I suppose you're going to go Platonic again,' and then he began reminding me of all the thousand things I've tried so hard to forget. Kurt," he said solemnly, "I've got the worst temper a person ever had."

Kurt laughed incredulously.

"You don't believe it, but it's so. Don't ever, ever get me into such a state. I'm like a lunatic, Kurt — really I am. Something floods up in me like a hot red mist — and if I were stronger I suppose I'd be dangerous. Once, when I was just a little kid, traveling with my mother, the train stopped somewhere — Lucca, I think it was. I got angry at something and lay on the track and screamed and tore my clothes. They had to pry me loose before the train could go on. I've always had 'em," he said.

"Well, what happened?"

"Ozzy should have known better, but he teased me until I was blind with anger. Oh — I don't know what I said. I told him I was through, told him I did have another lover. I — I tipped the table over and ran out, and took a taxi here." He hid his face in Kurt's lap, and Kurt could feel his whole body taut and trembling like a violin string stretched to the point of breaking.

"Why couldn't I have done it decently! I always feel so — so strong, so swept along when I have a tantrum like that — and then when it's all over I see that I've been so weak and childish that I hate myself."

"Don't do that!" urged Kurt. "Maybe it wasn't done just as you'd like, but it's done, and I'm glad," and he held David's tense body close to him.

The minutes passed slowly. A thin streak of light from somewhere outside penetrated the curtain and fell obliquely across the small statuette, touching it to a weird lightness in the dark room.

"Don't leave me this summer, Kurt," whispered David. "I — I don't know what to do without you. Must you go?" — and then — "What — what if you shouldn't come back?"

Kurt held him closer and told him of the afternoon's interview.

"A boy's school, you say?"

"Yes, a prep school."

"I don't know whether I like that or not."

Kurt laughed. "Don't worry," he said. "I'm not interested in seducing adolescents, or adept. I'm interested in you. Remember what you said? 'It's you and me now, it's got to be!' And it has got to be, David. That's all there is to say — all that needs saying. You've no need to worry. I'm older than you, by two years, and my slate's pretty clean, isn't it?"

"Yes, Kurt. I wish mine were as clean. It's pretty well chalked up," he said ruefully.

"It doesn't matter. One break in the armor is as sure a sign it's not spear-proof as twenty. I thought until you came along that I was a — how shall we say it — a strict monogamist. You caused me a great deal of grief, David, then, when I felt Derry slipping away from me, to you. I never thought, then, that this could happen to me. But it has, so I've had to find a new justification for myself."

"What justification is there but love?"

"None, dear, none. Only the old one that so long as love is requited, the lover must ask nothing more. When it's not, he may go seeking. So it's up to us both."

Again they were quiet. David, again, spoke first.

"I don't know what I shall do this summer. I'll have to get a job of some sort—" Kurt knew he was thinking of Ozzy's checks.

"You won't go back to Ozzy?"

"Kurt! No! He'll hate me, after this. I — I want him to. It must have been a pretty scene!" He laughed bitterly.

"You care?"

"No, only I'm ashamed it couldn't have been done more decently. I'm glad, so long as I have you."

"Well, that's that, then. Summer's not long. In the fall, something will turn up. I'll have money. Maybe you can live near Brookway, and work at your book. Something's got to happen, dear. Don't worry, no, please don't. I'll have to leave tomorrow. Let's not think of anything unpleasant tonight. It's you and me now," he whispered, "it's got to be."

IV

A<small>T HOME</small> in Barton the summer days passed by quietly; a little monotonously, as he had known they would, yet pleasantly too. Things were not much changed. His mother was older, and his father, he thought, much older. Their obvious delight in having him back and their pride in his accomplishments, negative as they were, were at least partial payment for the things he missed; and the things he missed synthesized themselves into David. David's devotion, David's desirability, only seemed to make the gulf that yawned between him and his parents deeper and more difficult to bridge. It could never be bridged, he knew, and he wondered often if they felt it as strongly as he. He thought not. It made no outward difference. He had always lived inside himself, hugging to himself with miserly ardor his most real treasures of mind and spirit.

He found, one day, in a trunk in the attic, a box of old photographs; among them, a daguerreotype of his mother at seventeen. Here was a prim sweet-faced girl in a costume stiffly quaint, gazing at him with barely familiar eyes from the darkened tin — a pleasant picture, but not his mother. She had been young, she had had young men who loved her, she had had a love affair with his father, and he had been its fruit. Yet all this seemed more remote and unreal than it might have seemed in a well-written novel. He recalled the day he had had the rendezvous with Roy in the railway station in Grand Rapids; and, when he had come back distraught and frightened, his mother's confession to relieve him of his bewilderment — of the love that had been offered her before he existed. For the veriest moment, then, in his own chaos, this similar moment in his mother's life had pulsed with reality. She, the aging woman with lined wrists — his mother — was, for a moment, the startled girl confronting something unforeseen and appalling. But the moment, with its exquisitely attuned sympathy, had passed, and she was only his mother, the aging woman with lined wrists, sitting in a world outside his own trying to comfort him.

The barrier — the barrier. It was that that caused all the trouble. Ironical that a few years could erect so impregnable a wall. There was no way to penetrate it, no door, no crevice, no ladder over, no tunnel under, no path around, save only its dissolution by some miracle high and tender and brief as breath. And such a moment might come but once in their whole lives. There it was — three decades, and a world. He knew he could never tell them, never hurt them, never even explain to them this wall that shut them apart. He must go on with the evasions, the hypocrisy, the compromises that he despised.

And so, through the last slow weeks, his life seemed to him a thing divided. Here was the instinctive life, the life of eating and sleeping and breathing, the life of "drives after supper," of an occasional picnic at the lake, of torrid nights in the small familiar room over the porch roof. It seemed now so much smaller and shabbier than he had remembered it; and there was the nightly surprise of finding the heavy arms of the maple on the corner — whose leaves, as a boy, he could never have touched from his window — scraping the shingled roof and thrusting their darkness against the screen, to make more solid the curtain of wavering pale light the streetlamp cast against his wall. And here, too, secret and apart, the imagined life, so vital and precious, with David its core and its will and its passion.

He read, finding new delights in the sonnets of Shakespeare, in Shelley and in the patterned brilliance of Proust. The Baron de Charlus and Ozzy, Robert de Saint-Loup and Tony — and yet in all that flayed and slightly nauseous society of *"les hommes-femmes"* no figure, he knew, comparable to David or himself, or Derry, blundering through an unavoidable and uncharted fate. Somewhere, somewhere there must be an honest picture of it all — Plato and Michelangelo and Shakespeare as well as de Charlus and Jupien and the wry and sorry streets of Sodom.

David's frequent letters, as the days went by, became increasingly tormenting. Looking only to the day of their reunion, they were so crowded with his yearning that it was hard to forget their tumbling phrases, and in all quiet moments — during the day, at night before sleep — David was with him, but teasingly out of reach. David's eyes, his voice, his body in this posture or that, were with him — a profane and sacred pillar of cloud by day and of fire by night. Sometimes, his reticence breaking down before the vigor of his desire, he would send a poem, a fragment, a page of jottings ecstatic or sad, but always pregnant with promise of future joy.

"Love tears my ribs apart," he wrote,

> *and cracks my thighs,*
> *Love's irons are scorching out my too-sharp eyes.*
> *Love gnaws, a black jaguar, at my red heart,*
> *Love snaps the pieces of my brain apart.*
> *Love is a dove? Love is a petal-boy?*
> *Love is a rural song? A pale, calm joy?*
> *All you who say so lie. Love is a beast*
> *Stretching his claws from West to bloody East.*
> *If you should hear him snarl, and be afraid,*
> *Hide like the mole, be circumspect and staid;*
> *He'll pass you by — and you will breathe as well,*
> *But you will have foregone the joys of hell.*
> *You will grow old respectably and shriven,*
> *But you will have forsworn the pangs of heaven.*

Such exhortations were not conducive to work, and yet a new incentive was given him before he had been long in Barton. He had left with Korlov the piano score of his "Greenfield Mountain Suite," knowing that Korlov, in spite of his voluble derision of the modern, would send him a valuable criticism of it. Korlov's letter was better than he had hoped. Kurt could see the heavy old man writing the letter, as he had so often seen him in his studio, laboriously, with frequent consultations of a dictionary.

"Your suite," he wrote, "is good. It is really American, indigenous and yet sophisticated in treatment. Its cleverness is its worst fault, I feel. But it is a skillful piece of work, and you are a young man." He then advised Kurt to score the work for a small orchestra. "It is ideal chamber music. I think its charm will be best expressed by simple orchestration. You can rely for your much coveted modernity on the line of the composition itself, and its general conformation. Score it this summer, and I shall let the Chamber Music Society of the Little Symphony have it this winter."

The work, prodded on by this assurance of Korlov's, progressed slowly, and the summer passed. Often, after a letter from David, it gave him a singular satisfaction to walk alone, at night, as he had done so often before. He trod the same dusty straggling roads at the edge of town. Nothing here, either, seemed changed — elms, stars, the soft insect toccatas of the night — yet in his heart, what a change! Now there was at least some periphery of peace around his chaos; a happiness which promised, it seemed to him, more and more certainty as the years went by. It had been tested; the few days with David were, perhaps, a hardly secure basis for such optimism — but in the seething ocean of his uncertainty, this love, so perfectly requited, he fastened upon avidly.

When a lonely person grows older, because he is lonely (for whatever reason) there grows up in him, perhaps unconsciously, an ideal toward which he bends — an ideal of perfect self-reliance. Consequently when his loneliness is broken in upon by love, if that love is not recognized by its object, and requited, his whole nature rebels at his captivity. If he is introspective, as he probably is, the struggle is all the fiercer. He hates himself, his groveling will, and he cannot completely understand. For love in him, in anyone, has always in it an element that is beyond reason; and reason, for the lonely man, has become necessarily his arbiter. Why do I love you? Why do you love someone else? The eyes, the hair, the mind, the talents, the attitude, you say. But there is something beyond and behind, hidden and ineluctable. Others have finer eyes, and hair, and mind. Others are finer artists, and have more admirable philosophies, and yet we do not love them, you and I.

It had been thus with Derry; and now, that flame dead for lack of fuel, this other — in every respect so fostered and fed — seemed a miracle, no less. The basic problem, that which made any love of his furtive and secret, was unchanged. But that, too, he found, one could gradually adapt oneself to, as small animals of the wilderness adapt themselves by wile and stealth and subterfuge to an encroaching humanity. It raised barriers, tangles of barriers; but if only some open plot remained where two who loved could be free and happy, that freedom and that happiness could, he felt, overreach all bounds and fill all the empty crannies of his life, and David's, to such fullness that the barriers would matter not at all.

And so, through the slow quiet summer, this duality of life went on — the life in Barton and the life that proceeded curious and aloof in his own mind with David — apart, and yet more real, more constantly mixed in his thoughts and emotions than the familiar ways of home. To see David again, to be with David, became an obsession, by night, by day. Yet his eagerness to be off, for his mother's sake, and his father's, he valiantly concealed.

Kurt went east late in August as a lover to a fervidly anticipated rendezvous, feverishly eager. David. Grand Central. Must not kiss — must not. The taxi. The words saying nothing, filling the silence only. The stairs. The key in the door while his heart seemed ready to choke him with its pounding. The dark, and David. Oh, it was sweet, this, and certain. There was nothing to say, no need for words in this complete acceptance of each by the other, this fusion whose language was all endearments as old as love.

The week between his arrival in New York and his departure for Brookway was David's. He was working afternoons in a drafting room. Kurt would meet him for dinner. From then until lunchtime the next day they were together. Derry's evenings were occupied, as they had been in the spring. Chloe he saw but once. The old question was on her lips, the old longing was in her eyes, and his new happiness with David only made her question and her longing the more poignant. Nothing to do now. Did she sense it? He could not tell. Tony was playing in a summer stock company on Long Island, and was not yet back in town.

It was, both Kurt and David knew, a test, and at its conclusion they both knew that, unless the test had been too short, it was successful; for their parting was as difficult as their meeting had been eager. For the moment, nothing could change. Kurt had hoped, and told David of his hope, that there would be some way in which they could be together — work for David in Hartford or New Haven, within driving distance of Brookway. But after much discussion they gave up the idea as too uncertain for the present.

"Something's bound to happen, David," Kurt repeated again and again. "I can see you weekends, often — and something's bound to happen."

V

BROOKWAY WAS ALL he could have wished. As the door closed behind the porter and he dropped into the wing chair by the fireplace, it seemed so, at least. The quarters they had given him were on the top floor of a squat Norman tower which served as a bridge between the dormitory and the commons. Directly under him was the boys' lounge and library, and below that, the broad-groined arch that opened from the inner quadrangle to the athletic field beyond. The room was almost square, large and high-ceil-inged, with leaded casement windows on three sides. The bed, like some he had seen in Provence, was built into an alcove on the fourth side, and adjoining it was a shower. Everything, he sensed, had been prepared for his comfort — broad chairs, bookshelves, a small piano, soft rugs. It was all as he would have wished it, and he knew that here he would be happy. If only David — if only David—

Life very soon settled into a pleasant and not too oppressive routine. His own duties were so dimly defined that he could decide them for himself. The boys, for the most part, were well behaved and to Kurt invariably amusing. Money meant so little to them, wealth was so much a matter of course, and yet they were not snobbish about it.

He compared his own school at Barton with this — the girls mingling with the boys; the torn sweaters; the young and poorly prepared normal-school teachers; the riotous games of pull-away, on the school ground worn bare by running feet; the "shower," a trickling spray from a perforated pipe set into the dingy brick of the boys' toilet, for whose uncertain and miserly coolness the football team (Kurt never among them) had raced noisily through the dusty backstreets of Barton from the athletic field, and waited in naked and unruly turn — their gear hung confusedly on hooks in a long dark closet close by, along with the janitor's brooms and dustpans; the athletic field itself — two erratically leaning goalposts in a meadow; the recitation rooms with their scratched yellow seats and cracked blackboards. Here, the cool Gothic buildings set in the hills, now yellowing with early frosts; the quadrangle, green and quiet; the gym, the gleaming showers and lockers, the field, with its tennis courts, its open pool, its running track, and its trim equipment; the study rooms, inviting and pleasant, with book-lined walls; the masters, from Oxford and Edinburgh, and Amherst, and Princeton. What would this have done to him, he wondered, during those worried, unhappy, adolescent years? What was it doing to these boys?

As he came to know them, he found two or three that were as he had been — a little lonely, a little afraid of their companions; and he understood, and tried to make his understanding a bulwark against their loneliness. There were walks to take over the flaming hills, his feet scuffing through a surf of yellow and scarlet maple leaves, his body thrust through waves of burning sumac and laurel; there were long evenings alone in his great, square room with books and the piano; there were impromptu tea parties in his own room or those of some of the other masters, in waning afternoons, with quiet scattering talk of many things. With none of the masters was he intimate, though all were agreeable enough company. One, Scott, a thin swarthy Englishman, enormously tall, came often in the late afternoon for a few minutes before dinner — begging Kurt to play Brahms, for whose music he had an intense passion. He would lounge by the fire, his briar pipe seeming so much a part of his dark thin face that the slow ribbon of smoke issuing from it seemed an emanation of the man himself, a visual proof of an inner satisfaction. Scott taught algebra and geometry, rather grumpily, and in his spare time read Russell and Whitehead, and translated Descartes.

"Ruskin, wasn't it," he said one time, "who called architecture frozen music? Well, I call Brahms's music incandescent mathematics," and he sucked moodily at his pipe, with soft popping noises of his lips, like the repeated uncorking of a tiny bottle.

"I'll put in a request for Brahms on some of the programs this winter," Kurt promised him. "They're being arranged now. We'll have either the Flonzaleys or the Chamber Music Society for our opening concert."

"Get me a Brahms quartet," said Scott eagerly, "and I'll resign myself willingly to a year of pounding solid geometry into the heads of these young American plutocrats."

Kurt found ample excuse for frequent weekend visits to New York in arranging these concerts, so it was not until late November that David first visited him in Brookway. He was, as Kurt had so eagerly anticipated, delighted with the physical aspect of the place. The woods were brown now, with only here and there a touch of russet or copper that marked an oak, or green the sombre cone of a pine. And Kurt's room seemed to him, and to Kurt, coming into it from the chilly gold of that November afternoon, the most perfect place imaginable. A fire was blazing on the grate; and the peace of it, the quiet of it, was to them both supremely satisfying.

"We needn't go out tonight, need we?" asked David.

"Not unless you like. We'll have dinner in commons with the boys, and then we can do as we like." He held David to him. "Oh — it's nice to have you here, in this room, I've wanted it so long. Here — sit by the fire. I've some mail to look at."

"I'd like to look at it too."

Kurt laughed. "Still uncertain of me?"

"Can't help it. Let me see!"

Kurt dropped the few letters into David's lap, and he examined them one by one with mock thoroughness, lifting them to the light, pinching them between his fingers, holding them to his nose.

"Not a flutter in the lot. And lucky for you, too!"

"Don't worry, David. There never is — except those from you."

Kurt scanned them hastily, and tossed them, one by one, unopened, to the desk. "They can wait — except this," he said, tearing open the one remaining envelope. "It's from the concert bureau, and I'm still green enough as an impresario to feel important whenever they write to me." He mumbled phrases of the letter as he read it — "we submit tentative program ... trust ... satisfaction." He scanned the typewritten enclosure. Scarlatti. Bach. Mozart. Intermission. Brahms — for Scott, he thought, and smiled. Debussy, Georges Hue. Goosens. Kurt Gray.

"What!" he exclaimed. He read it again — "'On Greenfield Mountain,' an American Suite — Kurt Gray."

He rose instinctively. Something in his heart was like a beating of wings, a sudden fright commingled with a sudden joy.

"What's wrong?" David asked, anxiously.

"Nothing. Look! Look!" He put the program into David's reaching hands; and, sitting down at the piano, began playing scales as fast as his fingers could be driven.

"Kurt!"

Kurt stopped with a jangled dissonance and turned to David.

"Kurt! How — how perfectly swell! You never told me a thing about it!"

"I didn't know. Truly I didn't. It's Korlov's doing — must be. He's plotted to have its first performance here. I'll be scared to death!"

"Rats!" David said, seizing him by the arms. "Gee! I'm proud of you! Why do you even bother with me, Kurt? You're so — so damned talented — and I've never done a thing in my whole life to be proud of."

"Hush!" Kurt freed his arms and clamped his hand over David's lips. "Hush! You have! You will! You'll finish your book one of these days." David shook his head and struggled vainly to free his mouth, making muffled sounds of protest. "No," went on Kurt, "I've got you, and you'll listen. You'll finish your book if I have to kidnap you and lock you up to do it. And it'll be good. And if no one ever likes it but me it'll still be good — and I won't care a damn." He took his fingers away.

"You're a fool, Kurt, but such a precious fool."

Dinner in the commons over, and the necessary introductions made, Kurt and David walked briskly across the quad to Kurt's tower room. The stars were cold and brilliant, and their heels clattered sharply on the frozen path. "'Childe Roland to the dark tower came,'" quoted David.

"Was dinner an ordeal?" Kurt asked. "You were very quiet."

"They looked so young — so innocent. It made me seem terribly old and worldly."

They climbed the dark echoing stairs, and Kurt fumbled at the door a moment before it opened into the warm glow cast by the embers in the fireplace.

"I'll build up the fire a bit. We won't need a light, will we?"

"No. No." David drew the wing chair closer to the fire, and drawing a package of cigarettes from his pocket, put one absently between his lips. He made a wry face.

"What's the matter?"

"Scented. It's a box of Derry's I picked up — his latest brainstorm. They don't fit here. Haven't you something less — less decadent?"

"Sure. Here!" Kurt sat on the low stool by David's feet and rested his arm across David's knees.

"So they make you feel old and worldly," he mused. "I hope that meal dissipated any worries you've had about my — my conduct here?"

"Oh — Kurt, of course. How silly. It's — it's sacrilegious to think of it, almost, isn't it? I suppose there are some of our sort in the lot, but they're so awfully young. Most of them look awfully normal and athletic and all the rest when you get them all together."

"Don't they!" They smoked silently. Then Kurt went on.

"There's one youngster here — Clayton's his name — perhaps you noticed him — sat at the end of our table — that's interesting. He's got a remarkable talent for the piano; can be a really great performer if all goes well, within and without. He's sixteen, very precocious, very suave and sophisticated in his manner and conversation, but underneath, just an uncertain, unhappy kid. His roommate's a little younger, and a very handsome boy. Clayton got permission to use a practice room after hours from Dr. Leffington. I didn't know about it, and one evening I saw a faint light burning through the drawn curtains, and went up to investigate. When I put the key in the door I heard a great scrambling. It turned out that Clayton had been drilling young Green to dance, naked, to Debussy's 'Clair de Lune.' Green emerged from behind the screen, finally, very red and very much unbuttoned. David, I felt like a monster. I don't know, honestly, who was most embarrassed, the boys or I. I apologized, and tried my best to put them at ease. But Clayton seemed so sullenly sure that I didn't understand, and was laughing at him, that it was pretty hard. Thank the Lord I found them instead of Leffington or Scott or any of the rest. They might have been canned, I don't know. I had 'em both up to tea a week or so later, but it was pretty sad. I still don't know how they feel about it."

"That's rather a nice story, Kurt," said David quietly.

"It's so nearly a tragic story." Kurt laid his head against David's knee. "When I was just past Clayton's age, not so many years ago, I used to think about myself as I was at sixteen and swear that if ever I should come in contact with such a boy, I'd help him somehow to bridge that terrific loneliness and uncertainty. Now I wonder if I can, if anyone can. Those kids, they rebuff you, somehow. They wear an armor that I can't pierce, and it seems so wrong that they must just stumble through those years we've all known and could help them understand, so fumbling, so wretched, so afraid. Put that in your book, David. It belongs there."

He sat looking seriously into the fire. David too was silent, but it was he who first spoke.

"I'd like to get that in my book, because it's genuine and beautiful. A dark boy dancing naked to 'Clair de Lune.' It's Greece come to America. You've felt it, we've all felt it, the savage vindictiveness the normal man has toward our sort. We're all, to him, like the street-corner 'fairy' of Times Square — rouged, lisping, mincing. Those chaps too, once, had something in them too tender, and they went under. It's the army of us that doesn't quite go under that suffers, though. The streetwalker doesn't, in his heyday, at least, any more than the prostitute. He can be open in his tastes and obvious in his manner, and when the vaudeville comedian makes dirty cracks about him, he can laugh, somehow. It's we who can't laugh that matter." He paused. "Play something, Kurt."

Kurt played. The room, save for the irregular pulsing glow of the fire, was in darkness. He chose things he thought David would like, melodic and not too technical, for David's taste in music was untrained but positive in its preferences; and the evening slipped away with the familiar swiftness of time pleasant and enjoyed. In an interval between two Chopin preludes, Kurt turned.

"You like all this, don't you?" he asked.

"I love it," David replied simply, leaning back his head, and throwing his arms above it over the high chair back. The firelight, playing along his body, caught the fine curve of his throat and the underside of his chin. Kurt's eyes unaccountably filled with sudden tears as he turned again to the piano.

The telephone rang with a shrillness that shattered the mood of the room, of the evening, as thoroughly as an earthquake might have done. They both started involuntarily, and Kurt, muttering, "Damn!" went to answer.

"Hello. Yes. Yes, this is Kurt Gray. What? Who's calling? Oh yes, I'll wait." He held his hand over the mouthpiece. "That's funny; Bridgeport calling. Don't know a soul in Bridgeport."

David sprang to his feet. "Bridgeport? It's Derry!"

"Derry?" Kurt repeated, puzzled. "Whatever's Derry doing in Bridgeport?"

"His latest friend is from there. Derry says he's a Russian dancer, but why a Russian dancer should live in Bridgeport I can't—"

"Shhh!" Kurt warned, and turned again to the telephone. "Hello! Oh, hello, Derry. What's up? You're — you're what? Well, what happened — what's the—"

David was beside him whispering nervously. "Is he hurt, Kurt, is he hurt?"

Kurt silenced him with a shake of his head and a whispered "No." Then to the instrument, "Yes, yes. I don't know just how we can make it, but we will somehow. Yes. We'll be there sometime, as soon as we can. Don't worry." He hung up the receiver and turned to David, whose obvious anxiety, for some reason he could not take time to explain, piqued him slightly. He was more blunt than he should have been.

"Derry's in jail."

"Kurt! He's done something silly. I've been so hellishly afraid he would, and now, the first time I leave town, he gets arrested. How can we get there?" He was walking up and down, feverishly. Kurt stopped him in the middle of the room, grasped him by the shoulders, and shook him slightly.

"See here!" he said reprovingly. "It's probably nothing serious, snap out of it. You can't walk there. Let me think a minute. I know! I'll borrow the school station wagon. You wait here and I'll run to Dr. Leffington's — and for heaven's sake calm down!" There was a hint of irritation in his voice.

He ran across the dark quad, around the commons, to the headmaster's cottage. Dr. Leffington answered his ring. Kurt, a little breathless, explained. "I've a friend visiting me for the weekend. He's just had a message from Bridgeport — has to go there at once, and I was wondering whether I might borrow the school station wagon—"

"Why, of course, Gray. Wait; I'll get you the key." He started away, and then turned back abruptly. "I've a better idea," he said, reaching in his pocket and detaching a key from a ring. "Here. Take my roadster. I shan't be using it tomorrow, and you'll be much more comfortable."

He was insistent, and Kurt hurried back to David, whom he found pacing the floor like a caged animal.

Again he felt a mild irritability at David's inquietude.

"Come," he said. "I've got a car. Get into your coat and we'll go."

The car purred through the sharp night air, its lights picking out the road far ahead — a winding tape in the dark. David, tense, urged Kurt to greater speed, conjecturing, in a perfect ferment of nervousness, as to the possible causes of Derry's arrest. Kurt sat silent, driving as fast as he dared. His mind was divided between a very real anxiety for Derry and a steadily growing irritation that Derry should have been able so completely to supersede him in David's thought. The perfection, the quiet joy of their evening together was destroyed irrevocably, and his annoyance made him taciturn, unsympathetic and silent.

They reached the police station little more than an hour after Derry's call. David started at once to spring from the car, but Kurt, reaching his arm across, held the door shut, and spoke quickly.

"David. Listen to me. You're upset. Don't do anything that will make it worse for Derry."

"No. Let me out."

"Promise?"

"Oh — yes! For heaven's sake!" He wrenched the door open and was halfway up the steps before Kurt could disentangle himself from the robe and get out of the car.

"You're not very reassuring," he said, as the doors swung to behind them.

Once inside, David was quiet, his face white and set. Kurt was glad he might ask the necessary questions.

"We want to see Derry Grayling," he told the sergeant at the desk.

The sergeant, a heavy-jowled, florid man with a mouth that seemed much too small and childlike for his face, looked at them curiously.

"Yeah? Friends of his, hey?"

"Yes. He's here, I believe."

"Yeah, he's here all right."

Kurt watched David nervously, but David seemed frozen to icy silence.

"He's charged with what?" asked Kurt, disliking the man's insinuating smirk and his pursed lips.

"Accostin'. You know, makin' a date for immoral purposes."

Kurt controlled himself with an effort. From the way David's topcoat tightened across his shoulders, Kurt knew that his hands were clenched inside the pockets.

"It sounds — serious."

"It *is* serious." The man seemed to delight in the affirmation. He called an officer. "Get Grayling," he said; and then, turning to Kurt, "You two can wait in there. I'll give you five minutes."

Kurt took David's arm and showed him into the small bare room.

"If they do anything to Derry, I'll kill them. I swear I will!" David's voice shook. His eyes in his white face were abysmal, black with hate.

Derry came in with an officer who left at once, with the curt admonition to "make it snappy." Derry's habitual bravura pose had deserted him treacherously at the first sign of trouble, and he looked like a frightened child. David darted at him and flung his arms about his neck.

"Don't," said Derry. "Don't, please," and shook him off.

"What the devil have you been up to, Derry?" Kurt asked him seriously.

"I came out on the bus. I was to meet Ivan — that's my friend — at eleven o'clock. I got in about nine, walked around till I was tired, and then went into a fifteen-cent movie to kill time. Took the first seat I found, on the aisle. There was a man next to me, but I didn't pay any attention till he started shoving me with his knee, and whispering. I moved away as far as I could. He kept on whispering — the loud kind you can hear halfway across the theater, or seems so, anyway. I didn't see any place to move to. Wanted to know if I had a room, where I lived, and to shut him up, I answered. Then he wanted to make a date. I said no. He kept asking me, so loud I was scared. People were looking. He asked if I'd meet him somewhere next night at ten. He insisted, and finally to keep him still I said all right, I would. Then he flashed a light in my face, and said, 'I'm lookin' for pansies like you,' and took me out. It was awful. They put me in a big cell with twelve or fourteen men — tramps and bums and sneak thieves. One of 'em told me

I might get three years. I didn't know what to do, so I asked 'em to let me call you. O Jesus!"

Lowering his head, he cried, with only the twitching of his shoulders to indicate his emotion. David again had his arms tightly around Derry, and this time Derry did not object. "Oh—" breathed David. "How vile! How utterly goddamned rotten. I could kill that man, kill him—"

Kurt stood by, worried and sick, a little hurt too.

"Look here, Derry," he said as reassuringly as he could. "We can get you out, somehow. There's bail or something, and they can't punish you when they hear the truth of it. Buck up, and we'll see what we can do."

The door opened, the policeman's arm appeared, and a voice said, "Time's up."

"You shan't go!" David's voice was hysterical. "I won't let you go! The damned dirty bastards!" The officer looked around the jamb of the door in surprise. Kurt seized David tightly by the wrist. "Shut up! You're only making things worse," and to Derry, he only said, "Run along. We'll fix it as soon as we can. Just don't worry." David, as if surprised at Kurt's vehemence, stood dumbly gazing at the door as it closed on the prisoner. Kurt, over all his anxiety, was a little amused that he, the retiring one, should be giving orders to David, who in the old days had seemed so utterly self-sufficient in any emergency.

Through his connection with Brookway School, Kurt found he could cash a check, which, while it almost entirely depleted his small account, was sufficient to procure bail bonds; and sometime after midnight, Derry was released. They all had coffee, and Kurt took a room at a hotel, where the three of them sat until daylight, alternately gloomy and raging.

David's anger was personal and implicit. Derry had been insulted, and he should be revenged. Kurt's was more general and more philosophical. It was despicable that such a thing could be countenanced by the law; a trap, nothing less, and a vile and miserable trap at that. It was hard to conceive a man so degraded as to make such a traffic his nightly business. He yearned to spread abroad the injustice of it, as a zealot and a reformer. Derry, listening gratefully to their combined disapproval of the police and the society that empowered them, fell asleep.

The interval between this harrowing night and the hearing, which was set for the first week in December, was a trying one for them all. Kurt, back in Brookway, nursed a smoldering disgust for the whole thing, and such social philosophy as he possessed became misanthropic and bitter. And mixed with his vexation at the episode itself was the added vexation, that try as he would he could not put down, at the abruptness with which it had broken the quiet understanding between himself and David; an understanding that had seemed so perfect and invulnerable. He wrote of his disappointment to David, trying painstakingly to set down in words exactly what he was feeling. David's answers were only reiterated assurances of his love, his faithfulness, and his increasing affection.

"I'm afraid," Kurt wrote at last, "that underlying all this unhappiness in me, there is growing up a mean jealousy of Derry. It sounds appalling to say so, but I'm afraid it's true. I find myself wishing that the incident had happened to me, so that I might have been the one to profit by your solicitude and sympathy, which all proves, David dear, how much I care for you. And you're wrong," he continued, "to impute any responsibility for what has happened to Derry, to yourself, to your absence. It's silly. It might have happened to me, or to you, or to any young fellow at all who chanced to fall into the dirty trap. I don't want you to be Derry's guardian. In other words, I want you to be mine, and mine wholly—"

"Derry needs me," David's reply ran. "He's so blundering, and I can't help feeling he'd never have gone this way but for me."

"Oh hell!" was Kurt's muttered comment. "Didn't I know Derry first?" And yet he recognized that there was some truth in David's statement.

Derry was acquitted. It seemed unthinkable that he should not be, and yet the verdict was an unspeakable relief to them all. The lawyer Kurt had arranged for let Derry tell his own story; which he did, to Kurt's joy and considerable surprise, simply and directly. There were five women in the jury box, and it was easy to see from the first that their sympathies were with him. Kurt longed to leap

to his feet and denounce the officer responsible for Derry's arrest,
to denounce the whole rotten system of espionage that made such
things possible. He hoped the lawyer would, but he did so only by
implication, and so mildly that Kurt could have choked him. David
too sat through the brief hearing tense and white. The restraint of
regulation and courtroom etiquette seemed medieval and childish
when there were so many bitter-fine things to be shouted. Yet the
case was won; and it was better, perhaps, to accept the rule, to
compromise and win, than to defy the conventions and lose.

One of Kurt's own fears, and David's, had been the prolonga-
tion of the trial, a prying into Derry's life in New York, a dragging
into the case of their names, a scandal which would have been
tragic for either of them. But the lawyer was shrewd, and they had
secured an easy victory. The whole thing had cost them two weeks
of anxiety and Derry a debt of $500 to the lawyer and to Kurt.

This lack of funds which Derry's trial left in its wake, and his
own eagerness for a renewal of the bond with David, made the
decision of his parents to go to Florida for the winter a happy one
for Kurt. His father had been in poor health for over a year; and he
had at last yielded to Mrs. Gray's entreaties, and agreed to leave the
store in charge of Jeff for two or three months, and drive south. It
would be his first vacation in many years. Mrs. Gray was elated,
though she regretted the fact that they would not all be together
for the holidays in Barton as in former years. She suggested
tentatively that Kurt come to St. Petersburg instead, but he pleaded
the distance and the expense and promptly arranged with David to
spend his vacation with him in New York. Derry and Chloe had
decided to go to Michigan for Christmas, so he would have David
really to himself, a thing he coveted ardently.

With Derry a thousand miles away, the old footing between
them was resumed without embarrassment. Assurances and avow-
als, loving and being loved. After indulgence — indulgence craved
so fiercely, reveled in with such ecstatic and pagan joy — came,
sometimes, questionings. Tired, listless. Wanting only sodden
sleep and a cessation of all feeling in the dark anesthesia of slumber.
Was this his destiny? Was this his high bright goal? Work was
forgotten, unthinkable. His mind could not capture the fleeting

ideas that drifted into it, could not sustain them, could not, through sheer heavy inertia, weave them into a whole. He wondered at these two certainties which were, he knew, the most important in his life — the certainty of his joy in artistic accomplishment, and the certainty of this passion for David.

Was the one stifling the other? Could it? Was there no compromise? Was he, after all, so weak? Or was the thing itself at fault? Love. This love. Was it in essence different from the love that the world applauded, more ravenous, more insatiable? Artists married, and married happily, with no sacrifice of their art. And this relationship with David, what was it but marriage? How, save in one thing, did it differ? Yet that one thing, his logic told him, might be the cause of his unrest. He longed at such times, his limbs, his mind, dropping slowly into the well of sleep, for respite from this gnawing desire that would not be satisfied. Sleep — sleep. And yet, to thwart this love, to blanket it with resolves and prohibitions and remonstrances — was it wrong? Was it right? Beautiful? Ugly? The question, the ever-recurring question. Its freedom, slavery, its slavery, perhaps a key to new and free and unsuspected beauty. Why was he afraid of bonds — why were all young people, everywhere? Youth, finding restraint prudential, pedestrian, a little mean, shuns compromise as unworthy and uninspired. It flames and insists. And yet, is it not, this compromise, in its admission of the lovely and the vile, the pure and the sordid, achieving a synthesis, a sublimation into a new and pulsing reality — an end to be desired?

"Hush — hush dear!" It was David's voice in his ear, David's hand against his breast. "You jumped so — and you were mumbling in your sleep. You frightened me." And David's arm crept about him, an answer to all questions.

Two days before Christmas, with David gone to his afternoon work, Kurt called Tony. When he was recognized, Tony's voice came beating over the wire in his best Barrymore manner.

"Where the hell have you been! I've been trying to get you for four days! Wired your damned school, did everything but call out the state police!"

"What's the excitement?"

"*The Duchess* is sold."

"What!"

"Sure! That is, if you'll okay the deal. When can I see you? Where the devil are you? We can fix it up this afternoon still if you say so."

"I'm at — I'm in the Village," Kurt replied, remembering Philadelphia. "I can come uptown right away, if you like."

"Meet you in front of the library in half an hour. Okay?"

"Okay," agreed Kurt, and started to hang up when Tony added in a drawling affected voice, "I'll be wearing a blue shirt and reading a copy of the *New Yorker*. I'm blond and very handsome."

"Fool!" said Kurt, laughing, and letting the receiver fall. The whole thing was incredible, leaping out of forgetfulness this way, like an unpredictable golliwog from a box. He went to the rendezvous with a singing impatience that made the subway an encumbrance and the teeming sidewalks a plot to slacken him.

VI

WITH FIVE HUNDRED DOLLARS in the Brookway bank as his half of the advance royalties on *The Duchess Decides,* with his first orchestral suite in the repertory of the Chamber Music Society, with David more surely his than ever before, the postholiday weeks were redolent with a quiet satisfaction that was a new experience. The smoothness of life, the absence of any cause for worry, was lulling and pleasant.

The concert had been for him a local triumph. He sat in his room on the afternoon following the first performance of his suite, in the small concert hall of the school — smoking and looking out across the hills, gently salted with white, through a deepening amethyst air flecked with drifting snowflakes. He had been congratulated by everyone, it seemed, and the Leffingtons had given an informal reception for him and the ensemble at their own house at the end of the evening, when the concert was over.

His position at Brookway was sure, he knew; and in the quiet sweep of these hills, the strong dignity of these gray walls, and the calm beauty of the life around him, he sensed a deep and peaceful harmony to his own heart's tranquil singing. He let his mind go drifting down a dim vista of perfect days — days in which David could figure too, making the round complete and wholly good. There was a timid knock at the door. Kurt started and called "Come in." The door opened, but so dark had the room become that Kurt, his eyes still accustomed to the dimming but still faintly luminous window, could not tell who had entered.

"Who is it?" he asked, turning inquiringly in his chair.

"It's Clayton — Ford Clayton. May I come in a minute?"

"Why of course you may!"

Kurt rose and stepped toward him, feeling his way about the table. "Here, I'll make a light."

"No — please don't, sir. Just let me sit here on the floor by the window."

"All right, if you like."

Kurt wondered at this visit, for since the time he had blundered upon the boy and his friend in the practice room, weeks before, Clayton had been aloof and embarrassed in his presence. Kurt had tried his hardest to overcome the boy's diffidence, but he had met with only a polite but final reticence that was as effective as a wall between them. It had made Clayton's lessons difficult for him to teach, and was proving, he feared, a barrier to the boy's progress. Kurt knew instinctively now that Clayton desired this sea of dusk as a shield to cover his timidity.

"Maybe I shouldn't have come," said Clayton, sinking cross-legged to the floor. His face, thrust forward eagerly, was a study in shadows. The faint luminosity of the winter dusk, cutting across it strangely, gave it a look almost sculptural.

"Nonsense. Why not?" asked Kurt.

"But I wanted to tell you about your music last night," he hurried on. "It was — it was awfully — awfully beautiful," and he halted, lowering his head quickly, ashamed of the awkwardness of his praise.

"Thanks," said Kurt. "Thanks. I'm glad you liked it."

"Oh — I did like it. It was like — like these hills, somehow. I — I liked it," he ended lamely.

"He's about to run away," thought Kurt, and ventured suddenly to say what he had been thinking.

"I've hardly seen you, Ford, since the night I stumbled on you and young Green in the practice room."

The boy's arms, he knew, stiffened against the floor in protest against this uncovering of the past.

"I felt rotten about that, Ford," he went on quietly. "I knew I interrupted something that meant a great deal to you, and I regretted so strongly. I hope you've forgiven me?"

"—was all right," the boy mumbled.

"You're afraid I don't understand, but I do. You're like I was, a good deal," he went on, "set apart from the rest of the fellows here because of your — your taste. They are a healthy happy lot of young animals, but thoughtless, thoughtless. Ford" — he leaned forward, elbows on his knees, his hands gesturing palely in the almost dark room — "there's a thing in some of us that makes us lonely and unhappy, often. But there's always a compensation if we seek it out, in ourselves, maybe, or in one or two of our friendships. Yours and Donald's may be like that. Your music and your love of all beautiful things is another, maybe a more certain one — I don't know."

He fell silent. The boy said nothing. His face was barely visible now, but Kurt made no move to light the lamp at his side. This quiet, this darkness, might go on forever. There was nothing more to say. In a strong dark flood the sense of the destiny of this boy swept over him, the destiny of all such boys everywhere — their heritage of desire and shame, of uncertainty, of deception, of hypocrisy, and of tumultuous joy and burning regret, of friends without friendship, of concealing the truth and revealing the lie, and ultimately — what? Would such a one be better off never to know, never to recognize his inversion for what it was — but to live lonely and apart in an incomprehensible and unfriendly world? No. No. Whatever happened ultimately, whatever advancing years might bring, knowledge was necessary. There would be moments of flame which perhaps, in the end, would recompense one for the hours of dust and ashes and gaunt bitterness. "I will show you fear in a handful of dust—" Fear — fear—

He shook himself. It was as though these conjecturings were to be sloughed off like a snake's dry skin, yet he knew it was not so. "These fragments have I shored against my ruin—" He rose slowly and felt his way, hands extended, to the piano.

"Here's a thing I've been working on," he said to the motionless boy whom he could no longer see. "No one's heard it."

His fingers, seeking and finding in darkness as certainly as in light the smooth cool keys, in finding them and compelling them to sound forth his own design, the patterns of his own dream, seemed to touch a certainty that could never be questioned; and he played as though the piano were a suddenly revealed savior. Here — here, in these slight tinkling sounds, pulsing off into silence, was a language without equivocation or deceit. He finished, but his fingers clung to the keys as if loath to let them go. There was no sound from the boy by the window. Had he gone, then? Kurt turned, unwilling to break the spell of the moment, and turned on the light behind him. Clayton sat where he had first placed himself when he came into the room. His hand was across his eyes, shielding them from the intruding light. He rose awkwardly.

"I — I — liked—" he began.

"Oh, never mind," put in Kurt. "Tell me later. You'll have to be running now. It's nearly time for dinner. You'll come again, won't you — anytime you like?"

"Oh — yes, sir!" Clayton edged to the door. His hand was in his side coat pocket. As if the movement cost him a tremendous wrench of the will, he pulled out a small package and thrust it toward Kurt. "Here," he said. "I — I got this during the holidays, and I thought — I thought maybe you'd like it."

He put the package in Kurt's hand and was gone.

Kurt regarded it curiously as he undid the wrappings. He found within a small bronze figure, scarcely six inches high — the figure of a boy. He turned to the light and exclaimed softly. It was an exquisite replica of Donatello's *David*.

David! He set it in the pool of light on his desk, the pert sweet figure. It might be David, his own David, standing pleased and nonchalant, regarding him. He turned it round and round, a strange tightness in his throat, awed at the unaccountable working of things, at the curious pertinence of this gift. Life ached in him. Dressing for dinner, dinner too seemed too utterly mundane. His plans for a quiet weekend at Brookway were suddenly distasteful, and engulfed in a vast intense longing for David. The chimes across the quad shook out a deep preliminary clanging. Six o'clock. There was still a train for New York at 6:50. He could make it if he hurried.

Ten minutes later he was striding down the dark road to the station, his heels ringing on the frozen ground. His mind sang with the crisp stars; and through it, like a suddenly remembered, a suddenly emergent theme of music, ran an idea he had fondled secretly, tentatively, for weeks — never allowing it until now, in this sudden strange elation, to break through to the surface into the realm of practical conjecturing we call planning. But planning he was now, his mind leaping forward swiftly like a spring freshet newly released. To share the idea with David was now his whole thought. In the train the rumble of the wheels was a counterpoint to this new and whirling melody. It would be the test they had both wanted, and thanks to *The Duchess*, it now seemed within the realm of the possible.

There were, he knew, many places in the vicinity of Brookway, abandoned farms that could be bought cheaply. He would buy one. Together, when summer came, he and David would repair and restore the house, furnish it as they chose. With David's help it would be easy. Then, by fall, they could establish themselves there together for a year — perhaps forever. Kurt felt sufficiently secure in his position at the school to believe that no objection would be raised to his living outside the school precincts. Some of the other masters did. David could write his book. He could continue teaching and writing. There might even be a new collaboration. Into a hundred variations the theme evolved itself, and from it grew a hundred themes new and divergent. To share this fervid dream with David — this was all his thought.

It was nearly twelve before he reached David's door. He rapped, but there was no reply. He found the latchkey David had given him, inserted it in the lock, and went inside. It was dark and quiet.

"David!" he called. "David!" He fumbled along the wall to the lamp and lighted it. The room was in considerable confusion; David's clothing was flung about on the floor, bureau drawers were open. Disappointment and pique mingled in Kurt's mind. Why should David be away tonight of all nights? He peered into the half-open wardrobe. David's evening clothes were gone. Kurt moved about the room mechanically picking up the scattered clothing, and setting things to rights. On the table lay a small white envelope from which protruded a folded note. Kurt examined it, and a sudden wave of fear swept over him. He opened it nervously. "David:" it read. "Meet me at the Empire Theater at 8:30. After the show we shall go to my apartment. Important. I shall expect you, Ozzy."

Kurt swayed a moment, his eyes closed, his fingers pressing whitely against the tabletop, sickening at the irony of this thing. David! David! How could he have done this thing! His vows! His promises! He had deemed it all so perfect, so sure an augury of peace and happiness, and now it was smashed like a fragile wineglass. He paced the floor dry-eyed and miserable, catching at each turn, with a certain perverse satisfaction, a glimpse of his white face in the mirror. He sat on the bed, rigid and sick. The ideal so carefully rebuilt, so seemingly certain, was chaos. Who was right then?

He could see Tony smiling cynically, and hear his voice saying, "Don't be a fool, Kurt. Take your pleasure and then forget it, and there'll be no regrets." He could see Chloe, aggrieved, and hear her saying, "This proves me right, doesn't it, Kurt dear? There's nothing in your sort of love to build on. Come to me! Come to me!" David untrue — David with Ozzy — David in he knew not what disgusting mélange. It was sickening. And what was to be done, now? If he waited here, David would return eventually, and ill as he was from the shock of David's philandering, he knew in the heaviness of his heart that David returned, with even the most tenuous of explanations, could reduce him to tears and to an apologetic abeyance of all his suspicions and jealousy.

He did not want that. He wanted David to know himself found out and to suffer from that knowledge as he was suffering now. He was a fool. There might be a hundred explanations of David's absence besides this note from Ozzy; there might even be legitimate reasons for such a note — yet he knew, almost with nausea, that his excuses, excuses so pathetically sought for, were pallid and unlikely in the face of the circumstance. He envisioned himself doing heroic things as he sat in this quiet room. He framed braggart notes, reproachful notes, notes cynical, notes sad, notes nostalgic and tender, notes bitter and despairing, to be left for David's perusal. "I have gone to Tony." But he didn't want Tony. "I have gone to Chloe." But Chloe seemed less than ever desirable. The lover in him, the aggressor, was lost in passivity, in a flooding desire to be loved by David, by David. He lay facedown on the bed, David's dress shirt clutched to him, and sobbed hysterically.

For a long time he cried, his body shaken by sobs. Then, in a swift revulsion, he saw himself duped; saw David, swearing eternal faithfulness, reverting, behind his back, to the old wanton and forsworn ways. Hard as it would be, he should be punished. Kurt went to the littered table, seeking a blank piece of paper. There was none. Under a pile of notes and half-written pages lay a copy of *Le Cote de Guermantes*, its paper covers soiled and crumpled. It was flattened to a passage heavily underlined. *"Pour l'inverti,"* he read, *"le vice commence ... quand il prend son plaisir avec les femmes."* So? He would sin, then. *"Le vice commence—"*

He seized Ozzy's note, reversed it, and wrote hastily:

"I hoped to see you. If you have any explanation, write me at Brookway. Kurt."

VII

IT WAS NEARLY three o'clock, he noticed, as he crossed the quad Sunday afternoon. The stone tower stood staunch against a sky very blue and very cold. The sun came down on the snow-covered earth with a brilliance that belied its lack of heat, its hard whiteness seeming the very source of cold. False gold, false gold. The fire in his room was laid, and he shivered as he lighted it. A telegram was on the table. It would be from David, and it would explain, but perversely, he avoided it. He wanted, here in the privacy of his own room, to take the inventory of his emotions that had been impossible on the interminable trip back from New York. David's words, however reassuring, could only be a complicating wedge now. The other must be settled first. He drew a bench close to the fire, warming his hands and arranging the sticks to encourage the small licking flames.

That he had come off badly as Chloe's lover was primarily obvious to him; yet mingled with the chagrin this thought occasioned, in the part of his pride which was masculine and conventional, was a sense of relief — a sense of the sorry satisfaction one feels when his own predictions, unhappy as they may be, are perfectly fulfilled. For it had turned out precisely as he had known it would, from the time the possibility first occurred to him. He had gone to Chloe, not from desire, but solely in pique, in mortification at his wounded disappointment over David's defection.

His wave of bitterness had, he realized now, carried him through the first difficult stages of the brief liaison. What had taken him on to its consummation in the small hotel room when that first flare of hurt and anger had begun to subside, he did not know. In this quiet room the whole thing seemed a fiction; credible enough if it were an episode from a novel or a motion picture, but that he should have been one of the actors in it was unthinkable. And yet, somehow he had been swept through it by a strength not his own.

Like a motion picture the events of last night came to him now, in flickers as fitful as those of the eager fire there on the bricks of the hearth. The hotel register — F. Gray and wife, Columbus, Ohio. Yes, with bath, please. The mounting elevator, a tumbrel rolling him to his own particular guillotine. Chloe's face. The departure of the bellboy, leaving them alone together in the small room in the early hours of the morning — a severing of human contact which, meaning nothing in itself, seemed as significant as doom.

Nervous eyes and fingers. Bravado. Trembling, Chloe's breasts and curving body. Not David — not David. A willed and artificial passion that, to them both, was pathetic. Flames that for all his fanning, and hers, would not burn. Flames that Chloe, seizing upon avidly, pretended with a futile pretense were flames indeed, and not the tissue-paper wavings of a theatrical fireplace. Whose humiliation was greater, his or Chloe's, he could not say. She had stood her disappointment without a word of reproach or contempt. She had done her best to deceive him into the thought that he was the lover she had longed for him to be. But that he was not, that this was the end for them as well as the beginning, she could not help but recognize. Her pretense was a little wistful and at the same time a little self-conscious. There would be, at least, no more uncertainty of that sort. Chloe was wrong, and Tony. Who was left to be right—? Proust? No, David — David. The telegram would tell, maybe. He turned in his chair and reached for it.

His hand, fumbling for the envelope, upset something which clattered to the floor. He stooped and felt for it under his chair. It was the *David*. He held it upright in the palm of his hand, facing the window. Behind it the distilled yellow light of the winter afternoon, thin and fine and lucent, as honey, threw the tiny figure into tender silhouette. Kurt set it on the deep ledge of the window, and kneeling, turned it slowly about, smiling at the impertinent angle of the hat; the slim arm holding the broadsword as a boy might hold a baseball bat; the attenuated thigh; the round knee joints; the slight swell of the belly; the small round buttocks.

He turned, almost with reluctance, to the telegram. "PLEASE TRUST ME," it said, "CAN EXPLAIN EVERYTHING ARRIVING BROOK-WAY NINE FORTY SEVEN TONIGHT DAVID."

Kurt let the yellow square of paper slip to the floor, and a calmness flooded over him that he had never, he thought, known before. Kurt and David. You and I. It's got to be. Tonight David would be here with him, in this room, and the plan he had for the future, the house, the books, the music, the quiet, the whole precious dream, he would share with David. The certainty of his love for David, of David's love for him, was as absolute and as right and as restful as this pale and now fading light of the March afternoon. From the shelf nearby he took a book of poems he had bought in New York, opening it at random, leaned forward, and tilted the book to the dimming light. "Herakles and the Preliminary Fleece," he read.

And as he crashed through bush and chaining vine, damning them all, and shouting out for Hylas—

for Hylas. And suddenly, unaccountably, he was a little boy again, and back in the ugly oak chair beside the front window in the house at home, straining his eyes over the Tanglewood Tales, or Bullfinch, or Gayley.

Hylas, the pale Praxitilean boy,
Dropped slowly through a world of wavering green,
Like a slow-motion picture on a screen,
Unreal, white, haloed with the alloy
Water had made of his metallic hair,
A floating sea-frond, gold and verdigris,
To the cool dim and pendulous langour he
Had only seen in those perverse dreams where
Perfectest bodies by his narrow bed
Wove a white ravishment in his sleeping head.

Across the page fell the shadow of the *David*, reversed and distorted. He closed the book quietly and lay back in his chair, smiling and content, the years commingled and integrated in an enchantment he was unwilling to break. This poet, somewhere, understanding. Herakles and Hylas, David and his Jonathan, Kurt and his David, Clayton and his dancing disciple. Strange that so suddenly, from such a swirl and seething, life should smooth to the calm of a summer pool — a pool so pregnant with quiet strength that all the fears and distrusts sank into it and out of sight. Strength here against laughter and derision, strength here for the spectral years ahead, strength, and joy in strength.

A knock at the door.

"Come," said Kurt, and almost added, "Mother."

It was Herbert, the porter, with a bundle of firewood.

"Bless me, Mr. Gray! Didn't see you at all there in the dark, sir. Reading? In that light? You'll strain your eyes, sir. Better let me put on the lights."

Kurt smiled in the darkness.

"All right, Herbert. Put them on."

EPILOGUE

IMAGINE A VERY OLD GENTLEMAN entering a very modern bookshop and somewhat hesitantly asking the proprietor if by any chance he has a copy of a novel called *Better Angel* by one Richard Meeker. The proprietor replies, "Yes, indeed. It's quite popular, and I think you'll like it. It's a well-written book." "I'm sure I shall," said the old gentleman. "You see, I wrote it." And that is why this old gentleman, Forman Brown, is writing this epilogue for the new edition of the book.

In the early 1930s, when *Better Angel* was originally published, there were no gay bookshops, no gay press, and no acknowledged gay community. I was lucky, in fact, to find a publisher willing to take a chance on a book "on a very sensitive subject," as the blurb on the jacket said.

To my surprise, the book did rather well and to my delight, reached a good many of those who, as I hoped, would understand and appreciate it. Indeed, I received 30-some letters from men, young and old, who had found in it some hope and dignity and who thanked me for telling their own stories.

Was it cowardly for me to use a pseudonym? Perhaps and perhaps not, for in those days acknowledging one's homosexuality was not done. I was 32 when the book came out. My parents, whom I loved, would have been devastated by such a revelation. Then too, I was just beginning to acquire some small reputation as a writer in New York, having had two books of verse and a collection of puppet plays published, and I had just landed a job as a writer on the CBS radio network. It seemed to me then that suddenly throwing open the door of the closet could prove too damaging to my budding reputation. All things considered, and with the benefit of long hindsight, using the pseudonym seemed the prudent and the sensible solution.

But today I turned 94 years old, the door has been flung open, and I find being out of that closet very good indeed. That my book is being so much more widely understood and accepted than it was 60 years ago, I find especially gratifying. And so it is that, better late than never, I have asked to have my name firmly attached to *Better Angel,* for once and for all.

Mr. Kennedy, in his introduction, quotes a reviewer of the 1950s edition of this book who asked what had become of Kurt and his comrades, and who suggested hopefully (almost wistfully) that a sequel would be in order. I never did get around to penning a companion volume to *Better Angel,* but since, like so many other first novels, mine was largely autobiographical, the least I can do is to lift the curtain on its cast of characters and their lives before and after the time depicted in the book.

First, of course, comes Kurt, who is onstage from the beginning of the piece and there at the final curtain. His actual name is Forman Brown, and since he has treated himself, on the whole, with reasonable fairness, we consider the second name in the cast, Derry.

Derry, actually, was a distant cousin of Forman's, Harry Burnett, and he too, I believe, I have treated fairly, though to have done him justice was quite beyond me—his fun, his unpredictability, the charm that made a circle of friends inevitable. He survived to become known as the Dean of American Puppetry, a title that I'm sure both pleased and enormously amused him. In *Better Angel,* he more or less played himself.

And Harry's older sister, Mary Burnett, must not be forgotten since she appears in the story as Chloe, a girl who was bright enough, and brave enough, to face the facts of the situation, and to accept them.

Next comes David—actually Richard Brandon, called Roddy— the one great love of my life. He too in typical theatrical fashion, had been born in the Pittsburgh area as Brandon Rhodehamel, but

finding this name so often mispronounced had become Richard
Brandon and remained so for the rest of his life. When he died in
1987, I found among his belongings a fat sheaf of papers—cards I
had given him over the years and verses he had cherished. This
particular one I wrote and gave him in 1977 on his birthday, which
was also the 50th anniversary of our first meeting, in New Haven.
I quote it because—what more can I say about him?

> My love, I'd love to write a verse
> to warm your heart and fill your purse
> and show you that, in all this earth
> there's not one thing of any worth
> that hasn't you as part of it,
> as flesh and bone and heart of it,
> and if you ever have a doubt
> just take this scrap of paper out
> and know that what I write is true—
> You are my world, my world is You.
> Happy birthday,
> Forman

Finally, there was Tony, the fourth member in our cast. Tony
was actually Alexander Kirkland, a young actor of about my own
age who had made a name for himself in one of the early Theatre
Guild productions, *Men in White.* He was handsome, he was sophisticated, and something entirely new in my experience. He was
witty, amusing, and a wonderfully attractive traveling companion.
We were together, off and on, for the balance of my months in Europe. When we parted I came to Los Angeles and he went to New
York. We never met again, and I learned to my considerable surprise that shortly after he returned he married Gypsy Rose Lee.
I'm sure they made a witty and handsome couple.

As for the three of us—Harry, Roddy, and me—long known as the Yale Puppeteers, we toured extensively and established three theaters in Los Angeles, then in New York, and finally returned to Los Angeles, where in 1941 we set up the Turnabout Theater. This theater boasted two stages: one for marionettes and the other, at the other end of the theater, for live revues.

During 15 busy years there we managed to establish one of the most unusual and successful small theaters in the land. We seemed to have found the answer to our dreams: Harry created hundreds of marionettes, I wrote all the songs and sketches, and Roddy kept the whole thing running. I also wrote lyrics for several musicals and special materials for performers from Sophie Tucker to Bette Midler, including more than 50 songs for our star performer, Elsa Lanchester. The 15 years of the Turnabout Theater were the happiest of our careers, and happy I'm sure for our audiences.

The story of the Turnabout Theater has been recounted in a documentary by Harry's nephew—and my distant cousin—Dan Bessie. He is an independent filmmaker who as a child had enjoyed our puppetry. In *Turnabout: The Story of the Yale Puppeteers,* Dan has captured the songs, stories, and marionettes of the Turnabout Theater—and our memories of them. I have been very touched by the kind messages I have received from people who have seen the video on PBS and elsewhere.

In 1987 the Los Angeles Drama Critics gave an award to Harry and me for our contributions to the theater. The actual award, like the seats in the theater, was reversible. On one side it read:

To Harry Burnett and Forman Brown
They brought theater to our town.

On the other side:

To Forman Brown and Harry Burnett
We can hear the laughter yet.

Roddy, alas, and now Harry, are no longer here, but wherever they are, I hope it is where the long years of our work together are still remembered, and the laughter still echoes.

FORMAN BROWN
Hollywood, California
8 January 1995
94 years old today